Peregrine

KEEPER OF PLEAS
BOOK THREE

ANNELIE WENDEBERG

Paperback Edition

ISBN: 978-91-989587-5-1

Proofreading: Tom Welch

Cover Design: Nuno Moreira & Annelie Wendeberg

www.anneliewendeberg.com

Part One

*The real voyage of discovery
consists not in seeking new landscapes,
but in having new eyes.*

Marcel Proust

One

WHAT DO you say the morning after you've stuck a knife into a man's heart, and you and your wife watched him twitch his last in a puddle of his piss? *Good morning, dear. Pleasant night?*

No, Sévère wouldn't expect his wife to appreciate the humour. Not that he had a chance to utter these words in the first place. Alone, he sat staring over an expanse of white tablecloth. Silver platters held muffins, sausages, eggs, honey, jam, and butter. It was as if Cook and Netty expected an army, not a lone man in a wheeling chair.

He ran a palm over the atrophied muscles of his left thigh, trying to appreciate this weakness as one of the best alibis a murderer could ask for. It was what he'd planned, wasn't it? Though the charade drifting more and more into harsh reality was...not quite what he'd expected.

Sévère's gaze slid to the empty chair across from him.

Four weeks.

Four long weeks without a word from her.

The last time he'd seen her, he'd watched in horror as she

dug her thumb deep into the neat knife wound he'd inflicted on Chief Magistrate Linton Frost. One swift and deadly strike to the heart. The man hadn't even had the chance to cry out before he died.

The murder kept replaying on the back of his eyelids whenever he dared shut his eyes for more than three heartbeats. It mattered little whether it was day or night.

He wasn't troubled by remorse, not in the slightest. But the surprise that had seared through him upon discovering his wife had been watching was as fresh now as it had been four weeks before. She had been just as prepared to end Frost's life, just as hungry for it as Sévère himself.

The sight of his wife approving the deed still unsettled him.

Although "unsettled" seemed to be an inadequate description of what he'd felt that night. Yes, he'd been deeply shocked, perhaps even a touch horrified, and he still was. The intimacy of that moment robbed him of breath.

A faint cough yanked his gaze away from his wife's vacant seat. The new maid (what was her name again?) regarded him with a subtle nod towards the teapot.

'What is it?' he inquired sharply.

'I was wondering if you would like more tea, sir.'

'No, thank you. You may leave.'

With a demure curtsy, the maid retreated from the room, leaving Sévère to his ruminations.

His gaze slunk back to the empty chair where Olivia typically sat, his thoughts drifting to that morning when she had slipped away with Rose before the household stirred. No farewell, not even a hastily scribbled note, taking only two meagre bags that seemed scarcely sufficient for their journey to the Isle of Wight. Only Higgins, the coachman, had known of their predawn departure.

A flicker of resentment flared up. Did she truly hold him in such low regard that she could not entrust him with something as trifling as her travel plans? The question gnawed at him. He didn't even know if she intended to return at all. Was there anything that bound her to this place, to him? No, nothing. The divorce papers had been signed by both of them. And yet, there was the mysterious fact that Olivia refused to file the documents. He didn't know what to make of it.

One day she chose to stay, seemingly affronted by his assumption that she would be glad to leave. The next, she simply vanished.

What on earth transpired in the head of that woman?

Or any woman, for that matter.

Sévère let out a low groan as he raised his cup and sipped a lukewarm infusion of...was that herbal tea? He grimaced at the taste. Revolting! What the dickens was Netty playing at? He spat the tea back into his cup, slammed the offending vessel onto its saucer, and summoned the maid to remove the scarcely touched breakfast.

The maid flitted about without making so much as a sound. He requested black tea, emphasising the word black, ensuring she understood that if she dared deliver that hay-infused water ever again, she might as well trade her post for that of the scullery maid.

Sévère paused. Did he even employ a scullery maid? He'd have to address the matter with Netty. The financial situation wasn't looking too bright now that every Londoner and their mutt knew the former Coroner of Eastern Middlesex had been accused of a heinous murder and led to a trial (Who knows fer sure if he done it or no!), where it was revealed that his wife had a questionable past as a former — and a notoriously infamous

— prostitute (Who knows fer sure if she wasna still working horizonterly!). He'd been promptly stripped of his post as coroner, moved to the dismal pit that was Newgate's condemned ward, and so robbed of both his freedom and mobility.

The relentless gossip mill continued to grind feverishly. He'd stopped reading the newspapers three weeks ago.

A dainty silver platter sitting on the tablecloth held the morning mail, a precariously balanced stack of letters. The volume of correspondence in Sévère's office had grown to two sacks in four weeks. Roughly two dozen of these missives had come from extraordinarily daft knuckleheads who deemed their thoughts on his wife's past profession worthy of his attention.

For seven long years, Olivia had been a prostitute — a fact now known to all of London, thanks to his ill-fated trial for a murder he had not committed. Those opinionated dolts never cared that she'd been abducted at the age of nine and forced to sell her body to men who humiliated her every single night. None of it had been her choice. Yet, in their eyes, she was to shoulder the shame.

As if a man was incapable of self-control and couldn't be held accountable for his despicable actions. They also chose to overlook the crucial detail that it was Olivia who had apprehended the real murderer and saved Sévère's life.

Alas, such inconvenient facts did not align with the preferred narrative.

But strangest of all, it was London's seedy underbelly that had taken notice. Countless pleas for help from mothers who'd lost a daughter, girls who'd lost a sister, and prostitutes who'd lost a friend, addressed to Sévère & Sévère Private Detective Agency, were waiting to be read.

. . .

Sévère raked his fingers through his hair. His infirmity had been made abundantly clear; he had ensured as much when his coachman carried him down the front steps of the Old Bailey. The newspapermen had eagerly devoured the spectacle, peddling the tale to any who could spare a ha'penny. The city was well aware of his limitations, and yet they sought his aid.

He snorted. He knew well enough that all correspondence directed to their Private Detective Agency was intended for Olivia, not him. In his current condition, he'd be hard-pressed to catch a cab, let alone a criminal.

Should his wife ever choose to return, she would find a surplus of clientele awaiting her services. As it stood, the household would have to depend on her earnings. He had squandered a considerable portion of his inheritance on a grand townhouse ill-suited to a man of his current standing, purchasing it under the delusion that he was invincible — Solicitor Gavriel Sévère, Coroner of Eastern Middlesex, aspiring expert in forensic medicine.

Absurd!

Huffing, he tucked his chin against his chest and shut his eyes. Who would have guessed that a poisoned chemise and a serial killer would snatch away his career, his reputation, and the life of a dear friend?

Olivia, though, had risen like a phoenix from the ashes. She'd been his beacon of hope.

Sévère's hand lifted to his throat, to the tender skin where a noose would have squeezed the life out of him. The rhythm of his pulse throbbed beneath his touch. 'You'll be done for without her, chap,' he murmured.

'Enough of this.' He yanked back the wheels of his chair and pushed toward the door.

His wife was nothing but a miracle. She seemed to possess the uncanny ability to land on her feet, no matter the trials life threw at her. By now, she'd probably set up her apiary on the Isle of Wight, restored her grandfather's former home, and fulfilled the dream she'd had for years.

Likely, she'd not return.

Sévère reached for the doorknob as feet clattered down the corridor. The small, swift feet of a nine-year-old. Surprised, he swung the door open and called out, 'Rose? Olivia?' He chose to ignore the hopeful lift of his heartbeat.

'It's just me, Mr Sévère!' A voice clear as a bell. Rose came into view, wind in her hair and sunshine on her cheeks.

'Where's my wife?'

'Said she had to go see someone.' Rose flashed a smile. 'Dropped me and the luggage off. Left with Higgins.'

'He had the horses ready?'

Rose shrugged, giving him an 'isn't it obvious?' look.

Sévère exhaled a sigh. His gaze touched on the sparkle in Rose's eyes, her straight-backed posture, the energy that rolled off her. He couldn't help but say, 'You seem well.'

Her gaze cooled. She took a step back as if to say, 'Yes, but now I'm back here.'

'Where's Alf?' she asked.

'Down in the kitchen, perhaps? I haven't seen him today.'

She dipped her chin and turned to march off to Olivia's private quarters. The girl's hand hesitated over the doorknob. A small nod, as though to brace herself, then she stepped through the door and out of view.

Sévère cursed himself. He had no clue how to talk to a young girl who'd been violated. Slipping a blade between her assailant's ribs had been incomparably easier.

And facing Olivia... He couldn't think of what to say.

Sévère pushed himself to his private quarters, locked the door, and stripped down to his undergarments. He affixed his brace, tightened the buckles, and pushed himself to stand. He grabbed his cane, took a step and then another, reminding himself that only two more months remained. He had pledged to feign frailty, to maintain the illusion of confinement to a wheeling chair for at least three months following the murder of Chief Magistrate Frost.

The perfect alibi.

And yet, he couldn't suppress the creeping suspicion that his body was succumbing, that the disease was gaining the upper hand. His left leg was gradually losing strength. How much longer until the chair ceased to be a facade?

Angry, he struck the tip of his cane against the rug. 'Cease wallowing in self-pity!'

He reached up and grabbed the metal bar affixed to the doorway between his library and his bedroom. And then he hauled himself up. Again and again, until sweat ran freely down his spine and his muscles were on fire.

After Sévère had washed and donned his attire, he heard the familiar rhythm of Olivia's footsteps echoing down the corridor. Without pausing, she strode past his room. Her door shut with a resolute click.

Sévère's mood darkened. This simply would not suffice. He promptly vacated his quarters and proceeded down the corridor, rapping once upon her door and barging in without waiting for her invitation.

She stood by the window, her back to him, her silhouette strangely frail. 'I need to be alone.' Her voice was soft, almost begging. Small vibrations ran through her shoulder blades.

'You are back,' he said.

Silence.

Cold prickled down Sévère's spine. 'What the deuce happened?' He pushed his chair farther into the room.

The sound of creaking wheels snapped Olivia's spine straight. 'Sévère, leave. Please,' she growled in warning.

'Olivia, what happened to you?'

'I will not ask again.' She turned and lifted her arm.

At first, Sévère saw only her face, and how...desolate she looked. Her eyes were hollowed out, and her countenance bore an unfamiliar pallor.

His heart clenched.

Then his mind registered the straight line from her eye down along her arm to her hand, and finally, the mouth of a revolver.

SÉVÈRE'S GAZE shifted from the maw of the revolver to his wife's face. He couldn't quite decide which of the two looked more terrifying. Before words could form in his mind and leave his mouth, a violent shiver ran through Olivia's arm. She dropped her hand and deposited the gun on the windowsill.

'I've scarcely returned, and you already disregard my wishes,' she murmured.

Searching her gaze, he found only emptiness and exhaustion.

Sévère gave a curt, silent nod, and deftly manoeuvred his wheeling chair out of her room. As soon as the door snicked shut behind him, he barked, 'Netty!'

Grinding his teeth, he exhaled a growl. Willed his fists to unfurl. Flexed his fingers and pushed himself forward. 'Netty!' he called again, but the housekeeper was already hastening up the stairs and aiming for him.

As usual when his disgruntled voice reached her, Netty

wrung the lifeblood from her hands. 'Mr Sévère, sir, do you require assistance?'

'Go find Higgins and tell him to meet me in my library at once.'

'But he just—'

'Now!' He nearly clipped her shoes with the wheels of his chair as he rushed past her and into his private rooms. Sévère wanted to wrap his hands around a throat. He wanted to crush whoever hurt Olivia.

The knock at the door drew his gaze. Higgins stepped inside. Sévère wasted no time. 'What the bloody hell happened to my wife?'

Jaw ticking, the coachman pushed one hand into his trouser pocket. He took off his bowler and held it in front of his stomach, tapping his pinky against the rim. 'Have you spoken to her?' Higgins asked in a low voice. Upon Sévère's narrowing gaze he added, 'Sir.'

'I did. She answered by pointing a gun at me.'

'I will not betray my mistress' trust,' the coachman uttered with a nervous bob of his Adam's apple, his eyes darting around the room.

Sévère motioned for him to take a seat.

'I value your discretion,' Sévère began. 'I will try not to pry into any confidences she may have shared with you. But I want you to point me to the cowardly pig who did this to her so that I may kick his worthless life out of him.'

Higgins bowed his head, his hat seemingly holding all his attention. 'Mrs Sévère won't appreciate such a course of action.'

Sévère leaned back in his chair, eying his coachman. 'Ah, so it's someone familiar to her. Perhaps even someone she holds — or used to hold — in high regard?'

Higgins remained still, his voice barely above a whisper. 'There's nothing you can do.'

'Dammit, Higgins! You took her somewhere and put her in danger, for heaven's sake!'

Higgins's head snapped up, his gaze sharp as a razor. 'I would never put her at risk, as you very well know!'

A dangerous glint in the man's eyes told Sévère that he'd crossed a line. He didn't care one bit. 'So you say. What else could have such an effect on her but her past? What have you done, Higgins?'

Higgins straightened. 'Are you asking me to resign?'

Moments ticked by as the two men locked gazes. Higgins had nowhere else to turn, scarcely anyone would employ a man such as him. Sévère understood this and used it as leverage. 'I am considering it.' After a tense moment, he added, trying to soften his voice but with little success, 'I want to help her, goddammit!'

Higgins puffed out a breath and ran his fingers through his whiskers. 'She... She went to see her parents.'

Sévère's stomach dropped to his knees.

He watched Higgin's hands as they removed the lint from his bowler with mechanical precision. In the ensuing silence, he could hear the clock ticking on the mantelpiece, the breathing of his coachman, and the scraping of a fingernail against the rough fabric of the man's hat.

Higgins, his voice low and uncharacteristically subdued, spoke. 'They wouldn't even admit her, sir. I didn't eavesdrop, but their intentions were clear. They did not want her.'

Something roiled under Sévère's skin. A furious beast. He could feel the sharp edges of his words on his tongue as he replied. 'Her *parents* turned her away? The very ones who failed to protect her as a child?'

Higgins's gaze darkened. 'It appears so.'

Sévère nodded. 'Thank you, Higgins. You may leave.'

The coachman rose to his feet, his shoulders stiff. 'I don't appreciate being blackmailed, sir, but should you need help with Mrs Sévère's...issue, all you need do is point me to the person that needs a roughing up, and it will be done.' With that, he turned on his heels and left, closing the door with a bang.

In the silence, Sévère felt the weight of Olivia's sorrow bearing down on him.

'Blast it all!' His fingers clenched around the armrest of his wheeling chair until the polished wood creaked in protest. Abruptly, he went slack as panic rushed ice-cold across his skin. Olivia had her revolver loaded and ready, but those bullets were certainly not intended for him.

He wished he could fly. But his arms were as useless for that task as his legs were for running. He hurried his chair toward the door, flung it open, and rushed through. The resounding clatter of the doorknob hitting the wall and the sharp crash of a picture frame shattering barely registered in his mind.

Olivia's rooms seemed too far away, the number of pushes of his hands against wheels countless. With his heart in his mouth, Sévère kicked at the door with his good leg. It refused to budge, stoking his fear. With a growl of frustration, he grasped the stubborn doorknob and nearly twisted it from its screws.

Olivia didn't even turn her head, much less acknowledge him. She was framed by the dim light filtering through fog and drawn lace curtains.

'Give me your revolver.'

'Would that ease your mind?' Her voice was as crisp as frost.

'Yes. It would.'

'I'd rather keep it.'

Sévère risked a glance toward Rose's adjoining room. The door stood ajar. The girl sat on her bed, hairbrush clasped in both hands, her expression undecided about his presence.

'I won't leave without the gun.'

'You are not to contain me,' she growled.

'I am not containing you. You may go wherever you wish.' Catching the softness in his voice, he hardened himself and added, 'But I won't allow you to shoot your brains out while Rose is watching.'

Olivia tilted her head just enough to see him in the corner of her vision. 'I don't plan to kill myself.'

His wheeling chair creaked as he sagged against the backrest. 'I'd still prefer to hold on to the gun for a while.'

She turned fully then, her black eyes smouldering with fury. 'And take away the one illusion of control I have over my own life? And what will you have me do then, *husband?*'

He knew he was moving on precarious terrain, so he whispered a plea, 'Tell me what happened, Olivia.'

'I learned a lesson. That is all.' With that, she turned her back on him and continued gazing at the world outside the window.

She did not emerge from her rooms for three days. On the fourth day, Sévère had had enough. He placed a tray with coffee and biscuits on his lap, rapped his knuckles against her door, and waited.

Silence was the only answer.

He counted to twenty and turned the knob.

The room was draped in shadows, with only a sliver of light breaching the heavy velvet curtains. An armchair stood by the window, and it was from this spot that her voice emerged. 'Have my intentions not been sufficiently clear, Gavriel?' Fatigue and frustration coloured her words.

He was struck by a sense of intimacy as he heard her use his given name. She rarely addressed him thus.

'I have brought coffee.'

'You are not my servant.'

'No. But I am your friend.' At least he was hoping she would see a friend in him one day. If he were honest, he would have to admit that he harboured more profound intentions, ones he had no illusions she would ever accept. He pushed further into the room, halted by her side and poured coffee into two cups. She glanced at his offering for a moment before accepting it from his outstretched hand.

'Why are you here?' she asked.

'I grew tired of solitary coffee breaks.'

'It is hardly my obligation to provide you with company.'

'I thought we were past that,' he replied, his tone tinged with gentle reproach.

She lowered her cup onto her lap, her gaze fixed on the gap in the curtains.

In the dim light, he noticed the shadows under her eyes. 'Didn't you get any sleep?' he asked.

'Why should it concern you?' There was a terrifying lack of fight in her voice.

'Please talk to me, Olivia. I want to help.'

She inhaled deeply before meeting his gaze. 'For once in my life, I find myself unable to adapt.' Her eyes returned to the window, the timbre of her voice hollow. 'For once in my life, I regret all that I am.'

Sévère felt an unquenchable urge to reach for her hand and intertwine his fingers with hers. She was the most courageous woman he knew. No, not *woman*. Person. He told her so, and she snorted.

'Why did you return? I thought you were content on the Isle of Wight. Did news travel that far?' Sévère had hoped the distance to the Isle of Wight would shield her from the tales of the murderous coroner and his infamous wife, but perhaps such hopes were naïve. After all, nothing sold quite like stories of misfortune and shame.

'No one bothered Rose or me.' She drained her coffee and motioned toward the plate with biscuits. 'Must I eat those before you will grant me some peace?'

He moved his chair closer to the heavy curtains and slid his fingers down the midnight blue velvet. 'You wish to be alone in this dark place?'

'Yes,' she whispered.

'I cannot permit that.'

She scoffed. 'I couldn't care less about your notions of what you can or cannot permit me to do. I don't answer to you. Our marriage is a facade. If you require a reminder, I can show you our contract.'

With effort, he shifted his chair, its wheels catching on the rug and bunching it up. 'Do you truly believe that's what this is about? That you, as my wife, owe me anything? Obedience? Servitude?'

Her gaze flickered coldly. Good. At least there was anger. Better than the dark void staring out of her.

'As your friend, I cannot stand idly by and watch you suffer. Merely a month ago, you pulled me from the darkest pit I ever had the misfortune to find myself in. Did I mention that I contemplated taking my own life in that dreadful cell? It was you who stopped me.' After a pause, he added, 'You are in that same dark place now, and I want to lift you out of it. If you allow.'

In the soft light, her eyes took on a silver hue. She swallowed and set her chin, yet remained silent.

'I shall return later with supper.' With that, he manoeuvred his chair out of her quarters, closing the door softly behind him.

Three

SHOULD anyone have asked her how she felt, Olivia would have found no words.

Although the term 'drowning' might have matched her best moments, it was a word reserved for the living. She wasn't sure that applied to her anymore.

Throughout her years of servitude to this madam or another, this client or that one, she had clung to a single hope: To save up enough funds to establish an apiary on the Isle of Wight, to be entirely independent of the whims of others. The dream of freedom, wild and outrageous, had been her float amidst a sea of despair.

And now she was sinking.

She rubbed her right pinky over the smooth silk of her dress, feeling the persistent itch that served as a harsh reminder of her loss. A bee sting had shattered her dream of freedom and independence like fragile glass meeting unyielding stone.

Cut adrift from what had been the source of her willpower, she did not know who she was any more or what she desired.

A shudder went through her frame as she recalled the

harrowing moment when a bee had nearly ended her life. Beekeepers were all too aware of the potentially fatal consequences of bee stings for some people. Her pinky had swollen, the inflammation spreading up her arm, tightening her throat, stealing her breath for agonising hours. With Rose's help, she struggled to reach the shore, seeking respite in the chill water. When she lay in the surf, with the clouds pressing down on her and the sea tugging her skirts, she knew that a second sting would take her life.

A profound sense of insignificance settled in her bones then. If a small bee could shatter in a single moment what had been her lifeline for years, what was the meaning of anything she ever hoped for?

And if her dreams and hopes meant nothing at all, surely her very existence would weigh even less?

In a blunder of naivete she would forever despise, Olivia had made a solemn journey back to London to see her parents and her little brother for the first time since she'd been abducted from the safety of her childhood home.

Her mother's harsh words, delivered just before the door slammed in her face, had cut the last vestiges of willpower from Olivia's soul: 'Your memory deceives you. You were not taken. You went willingly.'

Numb, Olivia turned back to the window, tracing the patterns of the heavy brocade curtains. She avoided gazing out onto the streets, where the people and the world freely moved forward.

Life goes on, they kept telling her.

But inside of her, life did not go on. Inside, where, for years she had cultivated the fury to drive herself forward, there was now only a void.

~

Sévère moved to sit behind his desk, once graced by an armchair now deemed redundant. He hated that the thought made him maudlin. He had weightier issues to worry about.

He selected a cigar from an ornate box, struck a match and sucked fire through the compacted tobacco. Satisfied with the ribbons of smoke trailing toward the ceiling, he rested the cigar on a crystal ashtray and reclined. With an eye on the smouldering tobacco, he forbade himself any thoughts of Olivia while he charted a course through their financial quagmire.

A snort escaped him. Their economic predicament was uniquely his to bear. The household staff would easily secure new positions. Except for Higgins, of course. Olivia, he wagered, faced with the threat of financial ruin, would relinquish her self-imposed duties and retreat to her beekeeping idyll on the Isle of Wight.

And himself? Would he wallow in self-pity?

Another snort punctuated the silence.

There was a note tucked in his financial ledgers. He retrieved it and studied its contents. Before Johnston's murder, which had led to Sévère's infamous trial, his earnings surpassed his expenses by a substantial margin.

Following his release from Newgate prison, however, his income dwindled to a mere pittance. Only a few days prior he'd been paid one pound sterling for informing a widow that her deceased husband's will was indeed nonexistent and that the only living relative of her late husband — her brother-in-law — would inherit custody of her children unless she remarried promptly. Sévère omitted the brother-in-law's callous plans to rid himself of 'the brood' by banishing the seven-, nine-, and eleven-year-old children to an orphanage whenever some 'harebrained lawman should dump them at his doorstep.'

Sévère's solicitor practice had once been bustling with activity. While not quite enough to make him a wealthy man, it was sufficiently busy for him and his officers to occupy each day.

Then there was the coroner's office. He wavered between a sense of relief at its loss and a twinge of regret. The ceaseless clashes with the constabulary and justices had drained the joy out of unravelling the mysteries behind suspicious deaths. Still, he yearned for the intellectual challenges that came with investigating a case, debating it with Olivia and Johnston, and presenting the jurors with the evidence they had gathered.

'Damn, Johnston. You left too early,' Sévère murmured. He felt the presence of the chessboard on a side table behind him. Just by the window, next to a small ivory elephant, the chess board he still hadn't set aside. He and Johnston used to play while dissecting cases.

But there was no point in getting sentimental now, was there?

He forced his attention back to the note. The data were unambiguous: Revive his legal practice or sell his townhouse.

'Three months,' he said, nodding to himself. Three months to reinstate his standing and bolster his income, well before his finances dwindled, leaving him with no choice but to sell the house and start over somewhere else.

But where to find clients? Nowadays, it was rare that anyone sought counsel from Solicitor Gavriel Sévère, shunned for his ties to a scandalous woman and his trial for the murder of Dr Johnston.

The fact that he'd been acquitted following the true perpetrator's confession (occasioned by said scandalous woman) mattered little in the eyes of the public.

Sévère jotted a reminder in the note's margin: 'Advertise in all newspapers.'

Surely, someone must be desperate enough to seek legal counsel from a man with Sévère's reputation?

His focus returned to Olivia. He picked up a letter she'd penned when he'd been held at Newgate. Crafted as if discussing a witness rather than revealing her true identity, Olivia's careful wording aimed to obscure their meaning from the watchful gaze of the prison wardens.

On the other case, we recently discussed.

I talked to Miss M, the woman who was sold into prostitution as a young girl. I'm not sure if her statement is relevant to this particular case, but I believe you should know about it anyway.

Known as Miss Mary in her professional realm, first crossed paths with Sévère under somewhat dubious circumstances. He and Inspector Height had questioned her within the walls of Madame Rosseau's establishment, a high-end brothel catering to society's upper crust. The memories of that encounter now seemed distant, almost surreal.

Sévère braced himself for what came next. He would never be able to read the following paragraphs without fury welling up in his guts.

In her own words:

"Many men told me they loved me. And I hated it. I could predict with some accuracy when they would say those words. Their gaze, their expression would soften. They would look at me as if I were their princess, their saviour, the only woman who understood all their needs. Because it was always their needs they saw, their urges, their body, their wishes. They hid their egoism behind their countless mutterings of "I love you so, my sweet," because most weren't dumb or blind enough to completely ignore

that they were using a child — and later a young woman — for their pleasure, without ever asking what she needed or wished for herself. Or what she didn't want. When I saw that expression on my husband's face — that softening — everything inside me went dead. I felt like a tree that had suddenly lost all its leaves to an autumn gust. And then, everything revolted. Rarely have I been so angry at the wrong man.

It was Sévère who had ignited her anger. He'd peeled back her armour and she resented him for it.

He squeezed his eyes shut for a tense moment. His fingers quivered as he read the next lines.

I never wish to hear those words again, never wish to see that softening. Please understand that I am not sorry. I have been made to be this way. And I don't have more in me.

She truly believed she didn't have more in her. But Sévère would make it his mission to prove her wrong. He had always fancied himself cold-blooded. Maintaining aloofness was a principle he held dear. As a solicitor and coroner, he eschewed the concept of absolute truth, acknowledging only varying perspectives and narratives.

Who was a victim and who the perpetrators scarcely concerned him outside his profession. Nor did people in general.

But Olivia... Surprisingly enough, this warrior soul with a tongue as efficient as a guillotine and armour as prickly as a cactus, persistently eroded his exoskeleton of indifference.

Sévère had never encountered a soul with such ferocity in

her compassion, such unyielding protectiveness towards the vulnerable. Her actions spoke volumes. She had broken down the doors of Madame Rosseau's to rescue Rose, now her nine-year-old ward, from a grim future of relentless exploitation.

Or what some euphemistically described as 'work.'

Rose, a mere child, had been plied with opiates by Madame Rosseau — her own mother — bound to a bed, and subjected to the lechery of Chief Magistrate Linton Frost for a sum of twenty pounds sterling.

It goes without saying that Rose received no remuneration, then or later, nor did she ever acquiesce to the violation. Yet, that was the false narrative all brothel keepers spun to the authorities when a girl was foolish enough to report the offence. 'She insisted she was thirteen!' they would always claim, regardless of the girl's true age. And, invariably, they evaded justice.

Sévère's fist collided with the desk, sending the ashtray into a clatter. The smouldering cigar tumbled off its rim and scorched the finish of the mahogany.

'Enough!' he rumbled. Gathering the cold dinner and a random letter from the disarrayed pile on his desk, he exited his office and made his way towards Olivia's quarters.

Sévère entered his wife's rooms, bearing a platter of cold beef and bread. He cleared his throat and said, 'You have a client.'

Immediately, he regretted his choice of words, wishing he could take them back. He clumsily pressed on, 'In fact, there are more than two hundred. I selected one for you.'

Olivia's response was sharp, dripping with mistrust. 'What the dickens are you talking about?'

Did she think he was trying to prostitute her?

Of course, she did.

He calmly extended a letter towards her. 'You run a private detective agency, do you not?'

Olivia's jaw softened as she looked down at the letter in his hand.

'Each is addressed to Sévère & Sévère, so I took the liberty of opening them. A good number of intriguing cases but I doubt we can ask for more than a guinea each.'

'I'm not interested,' she replied, turning away, not even acknowledging the dinner he'd brought.

'Your interest is irrelevant. You signed a contract.' The reason he had asked her to become his wife was that he needed someone with wits to help him solve cases. His former Officer Stripling, competent in administrative tasks and exhumations given a prompt and a clear site, lacked the finesse for interrogations, let alone solving mysteries. Stripling had abandoned his post the day Sévère was arrested for murder. No great loss, as Olivia had all the skills he required in an assistant. The marriage existed on paper per her insistence, though she also surprisingly insisted on consummating it.

He would never forget that night.

Olivia straightened her spine and finally shifted her gaze to the letter Sévère proffered.

Shooting him another suspicious look, she unfurled the letter and began to read. With a disdainful huff, she dropped the missive back onto his lap. 'I can't help her. And you can't, either.' She turned away to stand by the window.

Sévère's eyes lingered on the parchment, the slanted handwriting of a distraught mother whose daughter had been taken by a seductress. The term 'seduction' in such a context baffled him. Yet, it was the word everyone used to make rape sound more palatable.

'They are asking for your help and you refuse?' he asked icily.

'What are they to you, anyway?' she spat.

Relief swept through him as he saw anger flash through her posture. He would take her wrath over her bleak hopelessness any day.

Uncertain how to proceed, he debated between softness and directness. Opting for the latter, he continued, 'Must they be my wife, daughter, friend, or sister for me to hear their plea? Isn't their desperation enough reason for us to intervene? I can't do this without you, Olivia. You urged me to amend the law to safeguard girls like her. And now you've resigned yourself to staring at the world through a glass pane. Why return to London at all if you have no intentions of helping these girls?'

Silence.

'Perhaps you should return to your apiary,' he added.

No response.

After a long pause, he asked cautiously, aware that she might shoot him with her gun or throw the heavy brass lamp at his head, 'What happened between you and your parents?'

Unspeaking, she shifted her hand to the revolver on the window ledge.

Sévère held his breath.

When she finally broke the silence, her voice held a dead emptiness that made his spine crawl. 'You are exhausting me. Leave me be. There's nothing I can do for those girls. Neither can you. Or anyone.'

Four

SÉVÈRE SAT AT HIS DESK, shoulders aching, fists balled, and his mind fresh out of ideas. Another pile of letters had arrived that morning. Seeking Olivia's counsel again had yielded a sharp and sudden response: a porcelain vase hurled at the wall mere inches from his head, her eyes ablaze with ferocity as she warned him that next time she wouldn't miss.

Dropping his gaze at the parchment before him, Sévère felt hopelessness slip beneath his skin. But surrender was not in his nature. Nor would he stand by and idly watch Olivia continue down that dark road for much longer. Alas, he felt clueless about how to extricate his wife from the depths of her melancholy.

'Curse it!' he snarled and summoned Netty.

He scribbled a few lines on a piece of paper and passed it to his housekeeper. 'Higgins is to deliver this message to the offices of Mr William Burroughs at Oxford Square. I'd prefer if he brought Mr Burroughs along right away.'

Burroughs was a behemoth of flesh and cunning, and precisely the shrewd barrister Sévère needed. The man had been instrumental in securing Sévère's release from prison. But beneath a layer of reluctant gratitude, Sévère felt an uncomfortable itch, one he wasn't sure he could stomach for very long: Burroughs had once counted as among Olivia's regulars.

He forced himself to swallow his bitter resentment. If Olivia could put up with Burroughs and even go so far as to seek his legal counsel, then Sévère could, at the very least, make an effort.

In the upcoming battle, pride was a luxury he could scarcely afford.

Sévère eyed the rotund man seated across from him, his gaze scrutinising the furry head that shook with a chuckle.

'I'm surprised you don't yet grasp it.' Burroughs' words carried a mocking lilt, grating against Sévère's sensibilities. 'You have to get it into that thick skull of yours that the law abets the exploitation of girls and women. Always has.'

A spread of tea, crumpets, clotted cream, and jam lay amidst the piles of paper that littered Sévère's desk. He sat back, jaw tightening as he regarded the barrister. It was evident they would face an arduous challenge, an uphill battle, but Burroughs' candid assessment served as a stark reminder of just how steep that mountain truly was.

William Burroughs' moustache had collected crumbs as he nibbled on one crumpet after another. 'The law, my dear Mr Sévère, offers no protection whatsoever. A girl of thirteen, coerced or frightened into a house of ill repute, and drugged into acquiescence, is deemed complicit in her own defilement. If she's younger still, the brothel keeper will feign ignorance, claiming she duped him with a false statement about her age. It's immaterial if she gave no consent, nor if her compliance was wrought through deceit or brutality. It's immaterial if she never grasped the nature of the situation until it was too late, or even cried foul through every moment of her violation. She's seen as a willing participant unless she can prove, beyond doubt, her opposition from the start and her innocence of age. But how could she ever prove that for goodness' sake? It invariably comes down to her word against that of her assailant and the brothel keeper. No one will believe her. She's tainted by lying with a man who is not her husband, and so her credibility as a witness is stained and her humanity discredited. In all my years as a barrister, I've yet to see the law shield the victim. Quite the contrary, it shields the assailant. It's hardly shocking, considering the law has been shaped by men, for men.'

Sévère's gaze lingered on his guest as he absorbed the bitter truth. He steepled his fingers, elbows resting on the desk, the chaos of papers beneath him a stark reminder of the task ahead. His mind told him they were fighting a losing battle.

A dull ache inched up Sévère's left leg, and he rubbed his thigh in a futile attempt to alleviate it. 'How do these brothel keepers manage to procure underage girls?'

William Burroughs blew air through his lips, scattering crumbs onto his burgundy silk waistcoat. The specks clung to the fabric, but he didn't bother to brush them off. Their presence seemed an inevitable part of his day. 'It's a well-oiled machine,' he explained, his tone matter-of-fact. 'The more affluent brothel keepers employ accredited agents to scour workhouses, sift through servants' registries, and linger by prison gates for girls who are in for their first offence and left adrift upon their release.'

And of course, Sévère mused, no one wasted a single thought on the harsh reality faced by girls and women who'd once been convicts. He hadn't wasted a single thought on them, either.

Not until he'd gotten a taste of a rotting prison cell and impending death by rope.

Sévère tilted his head towards the sacks by the door. 'Have you seen these? Hundreds of letters, all pleading for help to find missing daughters, sisters, and friends. And these are just the ones who reached out to us. There must be ten times, a hundred times more missing girls and women. Have you ever tallied those numbers? Has anyone? And have you ever considered the appalling disparity between the actual number of rapes and those officially reported?'

William rolled his eyes. 'It's a pitifully small figure that makes its way to the authorities. A mere handful each year.'

'Doesn't surprise me. And this here doesn't either. Take a look.' With a flick of his wrist, Sévère hurled an envelope towards William. It spun awkwardly through the air and landed with an undignified plop in the cream pot.

William quickly plucked it up, dabbing it dry before taking one long look at the sigil. Arching his bushy eyebrows, he said, 'House of Lords. You proposed changes to the Prevention of Crimes Act?'

Sévère scratched his neck and produced a gruff nod. 'Several times, in fact. Not that it made any difference.'

William dropped his gaze back to the letter to read the brief response. 'At least they refrained from overtly suggesting you shove your proposals up your arse.'

'"We are looking into it" has that implication.'

William's gaze flicked up, meeting Sévère's. 'Proposing to raise the age of consent to sixteen is a bold move. Especially when half the Lords benefit from the status quo.'

Half of them? Sévère's brow furrowed. He had mulled over that very point, but the figure gave him pause.

As if sensing Sévère's scepticism, William leaned forward, his scrutiny intensifying. 'What else do you imagine wealthy men pursue in the dark hours if not expensive liquor and young women?'

A fair question, Sévère conceded. The vices of the privileged were hardly a mystery.

'Perhaps you should propose limiting their liquor consumption,' William added, a wry edge to his voice.

The absurdity of the notion drew a derisive snort from Sévère.

William leaned forward and placed a fist on the desk, 'The crux of the matter is that you're suggesting they give up one of their favourite pastimes. And put in the work of amending the law. They won't budge if all you do is kindly ask. You have to force their hand.'

Sévère arched an eyebrow. The notion of demanding the upper crust relinquish an indulgence did indeed carry a certain audacity. 'Publicly, you are saying?'

William's moustache twitched, a glint shone in his eye. 'Absolutely. As loudly as decorum permits. Should you care about decorum, that is.'

For a fleeting moment, Sévère's mood soured, the memory of William's familiarity with Olivia surfacing unbidden. He swiftly banished the thought, recognising the futility of dwelling on the past. With a soft exhale, he leaned back, following the wisp of cigar smoke towards the ceiling.

He needed Willam Burroughs' advice, if not his help, and he had to come to terms with the man's past. It wasn't as though Burroughs was the only man in London who frequented brothels. Sévère had done that regularly and thoroughly until...

Well, until he was confined to a wheeling chair all day. Until Olivia had forced him to take a good long look at the harsh reality of prostitution. Until he could no longer ignore that purchasing a body meant violating a soul.

'You've encountered your fair share of women in this profession,' Sévère said, avoiding eye contact. 'What becomes of those who give up?'

'Give up what? Hope?'

'What else?'

Plucking a crumpet from the tray, William scrutinised it before setting it back down. 'There's not much to say. Without hope, one has nothing. Whether a whore or a queen, hope is what keeps you going.'

Sévère's gaze snapped to William. 'How does one offer them hope, then?'

William shrugged. 'By promising them what they desire most: change, protection, respect. Ah, but what am I saying? A revolution is what's needed! Gutting the old system and forging a new one that values them as human beings.'

A snort escaped Sévère. 'A utopian dream, and you well know it.'

With a twinkle in his eyes, William popped the last crumpet into his mouth. 'Perhaps. But the real question is: Can one fundamentally change the law without breaking it first?'

Sévère entered Olivia's private quarters holding up a pillow to shield his head from potential projectiles. Fortunately, the peculiar sight left Olivia too flustered to throw anything at him. With a sense of relief, he placed a platter with dinner on her bedside table and picked up one of the two glasses of brandy he had brought.

A flickering oil lamp cast dancing shadows across the walls, its light a warm glow reflecting off the whitewashed doorframe connecting Olivia's rooms to Rose's adjoining quarters. The child sat in a dimly lit corner, her watchful gaze fixed upon Sévère.

'I need your advice on these.' He lifted a stack of letters from his lap, then motioned at the food and drink. 'A peace offering.'

After taking a sip of the brandy, he rubbed his aching leg and began to read aloud.

My dear Mrs Sévère and Mr Sévère,

I am in a state of great distress as I pen this letter to you. My darling sister, Emily, has vanished...

And so the letters went on, one variation after another of desperation and heartbreak. Through it all, Olivia remained silent and seemingly disinterested.

She was last seen in the company of a mysterious woman.

...

Oh, how I fear that she has fallen prey to deceitful promises.

...

Please, I implore you to uncover the truth and bring my dear sister back to us.

...

My family's happiness depends on it, and my soul is consumed with anguish until she is returned to us.

...

My heart cries out for her.

...

Yours faithfully,

...

Yours in distress,

...

With deepest concern,

...

With trembling hands and a mother's love,

Almost every letter bore the signature of a woman, rarely that of a father or brother. What had become of this world?

'Five pounds,' Olivia whispered, interrupting a letter penned by a distressed woman pursuing her lost niece, who'd been sold by a desperate mother to a brothel keeper. 'A child bartered for less than the price of a funeral.' Tiredly, she eyed Sévère. 'You can't stem this tide.'

He dipped his chin. 'Perhaps not the tide but we may yet redirect a modest stream or two. For now.'

From the dusky corner of the room, Rose observed Olivia and Sévère with the keenness of an owl. There was a tension there, an unspoken expectation. Did the girl believe Sévère might charge into battle as easily as Olivia and Higgins had stormed the brothel room where she'd been held captive?

But perhaps it was that simple. Progress was often as elementary as placing one foot in front of the other.

Sévère reached for the next letter and began to read again. He sensed the kinship between Rose and Olivia, deeper with the ordeal the girl had endured. Theirs was a bond carved from darkness, a mutual understanding etched with wounds unseen.

'Stop,' Olivia said abruptly. Her breath hitched. The room seemed to constrict around her. 'The previous one. Read it again.'

He didn't like the paleness of her face, nor the set of her jaw. He cleared his throat and read, smoothing the young woman's stumbling grammar:

. . .

To the lady detective Olivia Sévère,

I pen these words to you with my heart consumed by fear for my beloved sister Alice. It all started when a seemingly kind lady invited us for sweetmeats and led us to a stranger's house. She claimed the woman was a midwife, but my mother's midwife was nothing like her. And then she made us undress, saying she needed to see if we were "nice girls." I protested that we were, but she ordered us to lie down anyway. My brave sister realised what the lady intended and helped me escape. I went to the police and they spoke to father but Alice is still not home.

Please, I beg of you with all my heart, please help me find my beloved sister.

Yours with faith,
Harriet Green

With his stomach in knots, Sévère regarded Olivia intently, unsure what emotion he'd seen flitting across her face. It was something other than the bleakness she'd worn for days.

A primal glint. A feral thing with claws.

But when Olivia turned toward the window, crushing disappointment swept over him. His shoulders drooped. He shut his eyes and tucked his chin to his chest.

Damn it all!

Clenching his fists, he decided he would do it alone. He'd change the law for Olivia's sake even if it would be his undoing.

But then came a voice that could have cut glass, 'I know that vile creature. The Midwife. I know where she lives and where she examines and stitches up girls. We're taking the case. Send for Harriet Green and her parents.'

Five

MORNING LIGHT TRICKLED through the lace curtains of Sévère & Sévère's Private Detective Agency's office. Ribbons of cigar smoke hung lazily overhead. Shadows clung to the corners of the ill-lit room.

Olivia watched Harriet Green take a seat across from Sévère and herself, her parents flanking the girl, all three fidgeting in their seats. The air was thick with the aroma of Sévère's cigar and the metallic tang of nerves.

Harriet, a girl of perhaps nine or ten, twin braids snaking down her shoulders, voice quivering, broke the silence. 'Did you find her?'

'We read your message only last night.' Olivia's words landed carefully, making no mention of the towers of unanswered letters or the slim odds of success.

The girl wilted, eyes downcast, fingers worrying at her braid. 'Oh.'

Sévère regarded the parents. 'What can you tell us about the woman who took your daughters?'

Olivia remained silent, her gaze fixed on the girl. Harriet

wore an expression Olivia had seen all too often — a look of mute anguish, of trust betrayed and innocence lost. She had seen that haunted look before. It stirred a familiar anger in her chest.

Before the Greens could muster a response, Harriet pulled in a breath. The dam burst and her tale tumbled forth in a torrent.

Sévère's focus sharpened as the girl recounted the seductress's charms, the lies cloaked in tender promises of shared prayers and sweetmeats.

As the details unfolded, Olivia threw a glance at Sévère. His jaw was tight — the only chink in his façade of detached scrutiny.

'Then she took us to a woman. Midwife she called her,' Harriet murmured as a shudder ran through her frame. 'She made us undress,' she whispered, eyes downcast, cheeks on fire. 'Said she needed to examine us, see if we were...good girls. We knew it weren't right, but Alice...she didn't wish to disobey.' Her throat bobbed.

Olivia's heartbeat picked up. She knew of such examinations first-hand. The Midwife was assessing if purity could be demonstrated so that the client could assure himself he had indeed purchased a genuine maiden — a prized commodity on the flesh market.

'After, Alice took me aside and pushed me to a backdoor, telling me to run and get father.' Harriet's voice was a trembling whisper. 'But I was too slow. I went to the police first.' She sniffed and blew her nose in a handkerchief.

Olivia felt a weight press hard on her shoulders. The dark recesses of mankind were familiar to her. Still, each new encounter with this trade in human misery stoked her fury. She shook herself and straightened up, wrestling with a tide of disgust that threatened to rise. Theatrics wouldn't get her anywhere.

Tears spilt down Harriet's cheeks. 'Please, you have to find her.'

Olivia watched the Greens' furtive exchange of glances, the lines of worry and fear on their brows, the restlessness. The father's fingers worked his hat, while the mother's hand kneaded a lace handkerchief.

Mr Green cleared his throat awkwardly. 'Mr Sévère, you must understand, our Alice...she is pure in heart, but if she has been...defiled, the stain upon our family would—'

'Your reputation? That's your concern?' Olivia spat.

The man's attention snapped to her. 'Of course, it is! After what she must have gone through already, I cannot in good conscience ask her to endure the whispers behind her back in the years to come. We shall leave London as soon as you have retrieved her.'

Sévère's eyes locked with Olivia's for a brief moment. Silent understanding flashed between them.

'Mr Green,' Sévère said calmly, 'let's focus on your daughter's safety. What progress have the police made? Any leads to follow?' Turning to Harriet, he added, 'Did you lead them to the Midwife?'

The Greens hesitated. Olivia fought the urge to lash out. How dare they call their daughter defiled?

The father's doubtful gaze drifted to Sévère's wheeling chair. Mrs Green nudged her husband, who cleared his throat once more and asked, 'Sir, with respect, how do you intend to pursue these criminals?'

Sévère's expression remained stoic. 'My mind and methods are intact, Mr Green. There is no need for your concern. My wife and I are more than capable of hunting down criminals and bringing them to justice.'

Mrs Green gestured towards Sévère's chair. 'Your assurances seem hollow, given...'

Olivia could no longer hold back her anger. She struck the mahogany desk with force. 'Only a month ago, this man and I caught a serial killer the police had been entirely unaware of. You will show my husband the respect he deserves or leave this house at once!'

'It's all right, Olivia,' Sévère murmured before turning to the Greens, 'You must have been aware of my condition before arriving here. It was widely reported in the newspapers. Arguing over my chair will not get you far, believe me. I have made several attempts, yet here I am still seated in it. If you are dissatisfied with our methods, seek assistance elsewhere and we will focus on another case. We have received numerous letters regarding missing girls and women, with more arriving daily.' He motioned towards the piles of letters stacked against a wall.

To Olivia, Sévère's increasing physical impairment was a surface flaw on the canvas of his capabilities. His mind was a blade. Besides, he was only feigning his inability to walk. Wasn't he?

She held her tongue, knowing that the prejudices of the Greens were a symptom of this blasted society. The same society that allowed beasts like the late Chief Magistrate Linton Frost to prosper, his activities unseen and unopposed.

She had never once felt remorse for having been involved in that man's demise. Her only regret was not being the one holding the knife that ended his existence.

The office was silent. Sunbeams touched leather-bound books. Smoke lazily wafted from Sévère's cigar. Olivia's gaze remained fixed on the Greens, her expression cold.

Mr Green shifted uncomfortably in his chair. 'Surely you understand—'

‘We do,’ Olivia interrupted, dismissing the Greens and their continued distaste with a brisk rise from her chair.

Harriet clutched her mother's hand. 'Please?' she pleaded in a hushed tone.

'There's still hope she's untouched, isn't there?' Mrs Green asked, her voice warbling.

Olivia scoffed, biting back a bitter response, all too ready to rip the illusion right off the parents’ eyes. There was no hope. All girls were raped several times over before the end of the day of their examination. But she stopped herself from saying it, brushed her palms down the front of her dress, and said calmly, ‘We can only promise to do our utmost. But you have to be prepared to find your daughter deeply traumatised. She will need your support. Not your judgment or condemnation.’

Mrs Green's lips quivered as she averted her gaze. 'How could you possibly know what our daughter—'

Eyes blazing, Olivia ground her teeth and slammed her knuckles against Sévère's desk. 'I know *exactly* what the Midwife does to girls. Your daughter won't return unharmed. If you keep bickering instead of acting, she might not come back at all.'

Mr Green stood, hand on his wife's shoulder. 'You are speaking out of turn, Mrs Sévère!'

Olivia leaned forward, voice dangerously low. 'Out of turn? No, Mr Green. This society is out of turn! Blaming victims, shaming abused children! What did they do wrong to deserve such treatment, such judgement? Are they truly the ones to blame when adults who should know better prey upon them? Tell me, Mr Green, if a vagrant clobbers you over the head and steals your clothes and your wallet, are you the one to bear the blame?’

'Your behaviour is unacc—'

Harriet cut across her father with a cry. 'Please!'

With effort, Olivia reigned in her anger and took her seat. 'The longer you hesitate, the more your daughter has to endure.'

Silence fell like an axe. Harriet's chin quivered.

Mrs Green whispered, 'Mrs Sévère, are you implying that you have...encountered the Midwife yourself?'

Olivia met her gaze squarely. 'On several occasions.'

'You... you were once... like our Alice?'

'Abducted as a child and sold into prostitution, yes. But my parents never bothered to look for me.'

Her confession struck like a thunderbolt. The shadows in the office seemed to close in as the Greens finally began to realise their daughter was presently living through a nightmare.

Olivia met Sévère's analytic gaze, memories of their prior conversations flooding back. For years, she had deluded herself, had clung to the belief her parents had searched for her frantically, hamstrung by the law from breaching brothel doors to rescue her. But she knew the truth now: Her mother and father had never cared enough to even try. They'd been more worried about what the neighbours might think than what was being done to their only daughter.

Sévère picked at his notebook's corner, brow furrowed. The Greens clung to the edge of their seats, paralysed with worry.

'Mrs Green,' Sévère said. 'The woman who lured Harriet away, she was entertained in your home, am I correct?'

Mrs Green hesitated, twisting her handkerchief. 'She took tea with us on four occasions. She spoke so kindly, offered help with our girls—'

Olivia's lip curled, her voice laced with venom. 'Help?'

Mr Green replied, 'Charity work. Helping families with young daughters. We were...deceived.'

Sévère asked, 'This woman, what name did she give?'

A flush of shame crept up Mrs Green's throat. 'Aurelia

Pembroke. She claimed to be a member of the Virtuous Maiden Society, protecting young girls from...from vices.'

A snarl built inside Olivia's chest.

Sévère asked, 'And where is this so-called society based?'

The Greens exchanged glances. 'The address she gave doesn't exist. That's what the police told us.'

'Back to my husband's earlier question,' Olivia said. 'Have the police raided the Midwife's home? Have they uncovered any leads to the seductress?'

Mr Green dug his fingers through his beard, rubbed them across his lips, and said in a dull tone, 'Unfortunately not. Harriet described where she and Alice were taken. The constables assured us of an immediate investigation, yet they delayed for two days before conducting the raid. They found nothing but a cobbler's shop and two apartments. The occupants professed ignorance of any midwife.'

'Was young Miss Harriet present to validate the location?' Sévère asked.

'Of course not! It is not a suitable environment for a young lady,' the mother interjected.

Stifling a groan, Olivia sat back. 'Give us the names of the coppers on this case. One of them is probably aiding the Midwife.' With resolve, she stood up. 'If you'll excuse us, we've got business to attend to. Our fee is a guinea a day. To start the search for your daughter, we'll take three guineas upfront, the rest on delivery.'

Mr Green jolted up, the chair screeching against the floor. 'Do you mean to say you'll need more than three days to find our Alice?'

Sévère's response was steady, 'How long have you been waiting for the police to find her?'

Mrs Green twisted her handkerchief between her fingers as Harriet said, eyes red and swollen, 'It's almost a week now.'

. . .

As the Greens departed, the morning sun dimmed behind clouds. The shadows in the corners of the office leaned closer.

'Olivia—' Sévère began.

She held up a hand to stop him. 'They trust we'll find their girl. Not wise, giving them false hope. The Midwife...' Olivia propped her hip against Sévère's desk and gazed down into his eyes, collecting her thoughts. 'I may have had a reputation, but the Midwife is in a different league. Several brothel owners and seductresses shield her. She's untouchable, with a waiting list months long for her dubious services.'

A corner of Sévère's mouth tipped up. 'And you knew that when I read the letter to you. How do you intend to handle her, my dear?'

'Don't call me that!' Olivia bristled at the endearment. She'd heard it often enough, muttered by sweaty clients.

Deep down, she lacked a plan. What she truly desired was to clutch that woman's throat tightly and watch the life draining from her vile body.

Disregarding Sévère's question, she strode to the window and peered down at the Greens as they entered a cab. 'You left willingly,' she whispered bitterly to herself. Those had been her mother's final words.

Would the Greens treat their daughter with the same disdain, once the neighbours discovered what had been done to her? Of course, girls like herself and the Green sisters went without protest when a charming woman offered kind words and sweets to a child who longed for affection and was entirely oblivious to how cruel the world could be.

But how did Olivia's mother know that she had indeed gone willingly? Had the police found Mrs Gretchen — her seductress — and believed the usual tale of 'she insisted she was of age and wanted to work for me'? Why would her parents have believed any of that? Why had they not demanded to see their daughter and ensure her well-being? It would have been so easy to confirm...

Unless.

Unless her parents had sold her.

The thought had not occurred to Olivia. With a sigh, she pressed her forehead against the cool windowpane as an endless darkness began to fill every crevice of her soul.

'Olivia?' Sévère asked.

She felt like a failure. Worthless. A waste of anyone's time and effort.

'Will you tell me what happened with your apiary?' A soft voice. One that had the power to peel back her armour.

In a rare moment of vulnerability, Olivia relented. 'A bee sting came close to killing me. I can't risk another. I sold the property. You'll have your money back in a fortnight.'

Each time she shared a private moment with Sévère, a chorus of warnings screamed in her mind: He will overstep. He will believe he owns you. He will demand more than you are willing to give. He will force himself on you. He will—

'I am so very sorry,' he murmured, his hand softly slipping over hers.

She pulled back, startled by his sudden closeness. 'Skip the pleasantries. I'll pay a visit to the Midwife tonight. Higgins will take me.'

Heading for the door, she heard Sévère's voice trailing behind, 'Am I supposed to twiddle my thumbs until you return? While you have all the fun? Thanks for coddling this old cripple, but I'd rather join you on this little escapade.'

She stopped in her tracks. Eyed him. 'It's a risk.'

'Probably worth taking, though.'

'You were going to give it three months.' Three months

until a "miraculous recovery" allowed him to regain the ability to walk gradually, ensuring no suspicion fell on him for the murder of Chief Magistrate Frost.

Sévère shrugged. 'I have until tonight to come up with a good plan. By the by, have you ever come across the Virtuous Maiden Society?'

Olivia gave him a terse shake of her head, left the office, and climbed the stairs to her private quarters.

The Virtuous Maiden Society. What a brilliant moniker for a fictitious charity that catered to seductresses.

In her room, she found Rose at the vanity reading a a book.

Silently, Olivia moved towards the girl. She looked delicate, vulnerable.

Olivia's fingers worked through Rose's untamed locks, seeking to calm her own nerves. Strands slipped like silk through her touch.

'Never fall in love, Rose,' she murmured. 'Never. Love is a yoke tying you to a man. You lose yourself, believing it's bliss. Believing it's all you ever wanted. Believing all of his sweet promises. But you're just a puppet dancing to his tune.'

From then on, silence reigned. It was their new code. Unspoken words lingered, filling the room with memories left unvoiced.

With each brush stroke, Olivia untangled not just the knots in Rose's hair but also the snarls of anger that writhed within herself. When she wasn't angry, she was indifferent. Numb. Most days, she could barely muster the energy to rise in the morning, wash, dress, and engage in conversation with Rose. Moving mechanically, a facade of normalcy to hide the void within.

And Sévère... The wretched man had a talent for digging his claws into her soul.

As Olivia began braiding Rose's hair, a notion took root in her mind. Their coachman, Higgins, seemed to be the only person aside from Olivia whom Rose trusted. Perhaps he could teach the child, guide her, impart wisdom on the ways of the streets, give her a sense of the freedom he found in mastering horses. A chance for Rose to grasp how independence might be claimed in a world intent on chaining her spirit.

Olivia would talk to him later. First, she needed a strategy for dealing with the Midwife.

The night she and Sévère had put an end to Linton Frost's existence, she'd felt a power surge up inside her, a beastly strength that she couldn't help but yearn for now.

It was the first time in her life she'd felt...although not unscathed, but certainly unbowed, unyielding, and prepared to face her innermost horrors.

She'd find that well of power again, she swore to herself.

Olivia pushed open the door of 'The Broken Bottle.' At once, her senses were assailed by the stink of cheap tobacco, stale gin, and vomit. The gambling den's dim gaslight cast long shadows across the room, the faces of its patrons obscured in a haze of smoke.

Olivia adopted a haughty posture as her eyes scanned the clientele and landed on a face she recognised.

She sauntered across the room, approaching a woman seated at a corner table and nursing a mug of ale. The woman's face bore the weathered lines of a hard life, but her eyes sparkled with recognition as Olivia drew near.

'Well, if it ain't little Miss Mary,' the woman drawled, her voice husky from years of smoke and drink. 'Didn't expect to see you in these parts again.'

Olivia slid into the seat opposite her. 'Betsy, you old tart. Still plying your trade in this cesspit?'

Betsy cackled, revealing a gap-toothed grin. 'Ain't got much choice, love. We can't all marry a rich toff and retire young.'

Olivia's laugh rang out, a perfect blend of amusement and derision. 'Oh, come now. You could've snagged yourself a gentleman if you'd put your mind to it.'

'Bah! Gentlemen don't want old biddies like me. They want fresh young things.' Betsy's eyes narrowed. 'Speaking of which, what brings you to this gay establishment? Surely not nostalgia?'

Olivia leaned forward, a smile on her face. 'Can't a girl visit an old friend without an ulterior motive?'

Betsy snorted. 'Not in our line of work, dearie. There's always an angle.'

Olivia reclined in her seat and gave a nod. 'Let's just say I've gained access to certain...resources.'

Betsy's eyebrows shot up. 'Oh? And what sort of resources?'

Olivia glanced around the room, ensuring all its patrons were too busy drinking, gambling, and engaging in other raucous activities to eavesdrop on their conversation. She leaned closer to her companion and said, 'You and I know there's good money in procuring certain...commodities for discerning gentlemen.'

'Commodities?'

'Fresh young things,' Olivia clarified, trying to put on a smile and keep her voice steady despite the bitter taste filling her mouth.

Betsy leaned in, her voice barely above the noise of the gambling den. 'Blimey, I never took you for that sort of beast.'

Olivia shrugged, feigning nonchalance. 'Times change. And

I've learned that morals are a luxury reserved for those who can afford them.'

'And how exactly did you come by them...commodities?'

'I've made some interesting acquaintances since we last met,' Olivia replied. 'The question is, how keen are you on coin?'

Betsy's gaze flitted about the establishment before returning to Olivia. 'What sort of daft question is that? What do you need from me, love?'

'I have the clientele, protection from the law, and can readily put my hands on fresh merchandise at a moment's notice. What I need is a trustworthy woman who can examine and verify the untainted nature of what I'm selling,' Olivia said.

Betsy drummed her fingers on the table, mulling it over. 'So you're coming to me for information?'

Olivia nodded.

Betsy's eyes narrowed. 'Fresh, you say? How fresh are we talking?'

'As green as spring grass,' Olivia replied, forcing a cruel smile. 'And twice as tender.'

A glint of interest sparked in Betsy's dull eyes. 'I might know someone. But information don't come cheap, love.'

Part Two

Normality is a paved road:
It's comfortable to walk,
but no flowers grow on it.

Vincent van Gogh

SÉVÈRE SAT AT HIS DESK, the afternoon light filtering through the window, casting a dull glow on the scattered missives before him.

Olivia's interest in the abduction of Alice Green had given him a glimmer of hope that his wife would find a way out of her melancholy. He wasn't even sure if that was possible, couldn't guess at the depths of her despair, or imagine what she felt after the thorough destruction of her dreams and having been cast aside by her parents.

They didn't even bother looking for me.

Had her parents been so callous as to tell her to her face they'd abandoned her as a child? Or had she deduced it from their lack of interest?

In any case, Sévère wanted to strangle them. However, there was the small problem of...logistics. While he was perfectly capable of strapping on his brace and asking Higgins to drive him up to Olivia's parents' house so he could meet them head-on, standing upright like a man, he could not jeopardise his alibi.

On the night of Chief Magistrate Frost's violent death, two vagrants had been seen leisurely strolling away from the crime scene. As long as Sévère could make everyone believe that his time in Newgate's condemned ward — that rathole of a prison — had worsened his illness to such a degree that he'd lost the use of his legs, he was safe from being suspected of Frost's murder.

Sévère had always considered himself cold-blooded. But his shell had gained plenty of cracks since Olivia fell into his life. A part of him yearned to confront her parents, to demand the truth and an apology for the injustice and cruelty they had inflicted upon her. But he knew better than to pour salt in Olivia's wide-open wounds.

And yet something needed to be done. He couldn't simply stand idle like the cripple he was.

His gaze drifted inward, revisiting memories of his childhood paralysis. Though his body had been a prison he couldn't escape, his mind had roamed free, devouring books and conjuring fanciful tales. When paper grew scarce, he inked illustrations upon his own skin — whimsical beasts and valorous heroes that defied the physicians' bleak predictions of a life forever bound to his goddamned bed.

And in his darkest hours, he traced secret messages of hope along his paralysed limbs, a tether against despair.

Two years later, he walked again.

A renewed sense of determination crept in. Olivia had waged battle upon battle throughout her life; yet now it seemed she had resigned herself to defeat. Anger flared in his bones. He would not stand by while she surrendered to anguish, any more than he had acquiesced to his own physical imprisonment all those years ago.

With resolve, he picked up a bottle of ink, dug through the drawers of his desk in search of a small brush, then made his way to Olivia's private quarters. Halfway there, he turned around and summoned a maid to bring tea. Better safe than sorry. Even though this was his own home.

Armed with refreshments, he entered Olivia's room after his knocks went unanswered.

She was seated by the window, her gaze distant as she stared out at the dreary London skyline, the weight of the world seeming to bear down on her slender shoulders. He'd grown to abhor the sight of her bleak stare, her self-imposed isolation, her dying fire.

As he shut the door noisily, she turned towards him. A flicker of annoyance crossed her features. 'Sévère. To what do I owe your repeated intrusions?'

He placed the tray on a nearby table, his gaze snagging briefly on a small chip in the fine china before turning to Olivia. 'We need to make detailed plans for this evening. I assume you have already made arrangements with Higgins?'

Olivia's response was curt, 'I have.'

He leaned back, expecting her to continue, but she remained silent, her attention drifting back towards the window. A fleeting sense of dejection washed over him, swiftly replaced by a flare of annoyance at her indifference. Suppressing a sigh, he said, 'I had something rather different in mind.'

Olivia's gaze drifted to the tray, her brow furrowing as she took in the ink bottle and brush. 'Are you turning to the arts now? Has it come to that?'

'A story,' he replied evenly, undeterred by her sharp edges. 'Though I would require your participation.'

She eyed him warily. 'What the deuce is this, Sévère?'

'Your hand, please,' he clarified, his challenging gaze holding hers. 'And your trust for a minute or two. If you can manage.'

Olivia glared at him but he sensed a hint of curiosity that

seemed to get the better of her. With a resigned shrug, she extended her hand. 'Very well. Two minutes.'

Sévère felt a spark of triumph as he settled beside her, and poured tea for them both. He took her proffered hand, noting the tension in her slender fingers as he cradled it in his own. Dipping the brush into the ink, he began tracing fine lines across her skin, each stroke deliberate and precise.

'When I was a boy,' he whispered, 'I would paint beasts upon my paralysed legs. Tigers, dragons, creatures of myth and legend. I imagined them giving me strength and magic. The ability to fly, to run, to escape this world that I had begun to hate.'

Olivia's gaze remained fixed ahead, pointedly ignoring the unfolding illustration on her hand. 'Is this tale meant to endear you to me? Poor little Sévère, confined to his feather bed, coddled by doting parents and a veritable army of servants and doctors. How trying it must have been, to endure such tedium for a few months.'

The arch of her brow and the bite of her words made it plain she was unimpressed if not annoyed. But he continued his ministrations, dancing the brush across her skin with deft strokes. He had weathered her barbs before. Her disdain was her armour, which he'd learned to navigate with patience. Well, until it ran out, that is. 'I don't require you to like me. I merely wish to distract you.'

'From what? My unreasonable moods? My hysteria?'

'From the drawing.'

As he blew dry the ink, she pulled her hand from his grasp and held it into the light. Paused. Ground her teeth and averted her gaze.

He remained silent. He didn't want to ask her if she was hurting because it was evident she was. He had drawn a delicate bee on the back of her hand. And on her palm, he had written, 'You are a warrior queen.'

He waited until she seemed to regain control of her breathing, then asked, 'Are we going to play married couple when we meet the Midwife? Or shall we be prostitute and client?'

She cleared her throat and turned to face him. 'No. I will be the procuress, Higgins my bodyguard and driver, and Rose the bait.'

He couldn't believe what he was hearing. 'What! Are you raving mad?'

'It was my idea,' Rose piped up from behind him.

He turned to eye the girl. 'You both seem to have taken leave of your senses!'

Rose crossed her bony arms over her chest and hiked up her chin. 'Pah!' Then she stomped back to her adjoining room and slammed the door.

Exasperated, Sévère turned to Olivia. 'Tell me you were jesting. Or simply amusing the girl for a moment.'

Unspeaking, she gazed at him.

'Bloody damn!' He groaned. 'Do I dare ask what role you assigned me?'

Her calm gaze held his.

'You can't be serious, Olivia.'

'I am. You will be the buyer.'

If he hadn't been sitting already, he would have needed a chair.

Seven

OLIVIA FELT as though her teeth might crack. Her jaw clenched tight until it ached alongside her tense neck and shoulders. She dug her fingers into the carriage's sturdy upholstery. She didn't want to ruin her dress, and the hide was far sturdier than silk.

They had a half-hour's drive ahead of them. Not much, by any standard, but time seemed to stretch endlessly. She could scarcely wait to reach their destination, yet she dreaded that her restraint would be sorely tested as soon as they arrived. To lay eyes on that wretched woman without making an attempt on her life would require every ounce of iron will.

She'd experienced the Midwife's 'services' first-hand when but a child. Or not a child anymore, as she'd been informed. Why was it believed that only a man could turn a girl into a woman? Who had handed them such power? For what purpose?

She couldn't help the fears drifting up from the murky depths of her memories. She'd buried so much of her childhood — or rather, her non-childhood. How helpless she'd felt.

The pain she'd endured. Hoping for mercy from men and women who had none, who saw her as nothing more than a commodity.

The Midwife knew that a tiny sip of laudanum would do little to dull the pain, knew that all girls cried and kicked when someone stuck needle and thread where they'd been brutalised only hours before. And they would be again the following night, and every night after until they'd had learned to accommodate a man.

That's what she'd been told. *Stop crying and learn to accommodate a man.* As though she were at fault.

The brougham careened over the cobbled streets, and with each turn of the wheels, Olivia's breathing grew increasingly shallow. It felt like someone was sitting on her chest. The walls of the coach closed in around her. Her heart hammered in her throat, cutting off all air. Her hands were clammy.

The rhythmic clatter of horseshoes striking cobblestones reverberated through the carriage, each impact like gunfire. Olivia flinched with every strike, the clatter growing more thunderous until drowned out by a high-pitched rushing noise.

A fist closed around her throat and her vision grew dark.

She
felt
like
dying
locked
in
a
cupboard
curled
up

terrified
the
next
client
would

An arm came around her, and then another, smaller one. She found herself wrapped up by Sévère and Rose. He whispered about bringing her home, encouraging her to breathe slowly, assuring her that everything would be all right. His thumb drew small circles onto her shoulder. His arms crushed her soul back into her body.

The carriage hit a particularly rough patch of road, jostling its occupants. Rose's forehead bounced off Olivia's chin. With a small, strangled sound, Olivia shook off Sévère's embrace and pressed her face into her hands, shoulders trembling.

Yet again, she had failed, couldn't even do this one small thing.

She had no worth in this world anymore.

Rose sat on Olivia's bed, holding her hand in sweaty fingers. The girl didn't speak, only stared at Olivia with concern. Sévère was in his wheeling chair by the window, the heavy curtains drawn aside, pale yellowish light from the streetlamps creeping onto the window sill.

'...cloak the lie in truth, don't you agree? Olivia? Are you listening at all?' He sounded as though he barely controlled his anger.

She sat up and cleared her throat. Tucked a stray lock of

hair behind her ear. 'I apologise for my hysteria. I don't know what came over me.'

'Oh shut your mouth!' he said.

At once, anger boiled to the surface. 'Excuse me?'

His eyes flashed with something that might have been satisfaction. Furious, she stood. 'Will you stop provoking me!'

'You want me to stand idly by while you beat yourself up for the terror caused by the atrocities committed on you? Is that what you'd like me to do?'

She averted her gaze and began straightening her pillows to keep her hands busy and her mind distanced.

'Anyway,' he grumbled. 'Rose, go to bed. I wish to talk to my wife.'

After the girl left for her room, grumbling protests under her breath, Sévère asked, 'What happened, Olivia?'

Damn this man! Could he not leave her in peace for once? Angry, she paced the room. She couldn't even begin to translate the chaos inside her into words.

'I don't know!' she finally said. Truth be told, she wanted to switch off all emotions entirely, and she certainly didn't want to talk about them. But Sévère wouldn't leave her room until she said at least something. 'I couldn't breathe.'

'I saw. You were in a panic. You nearly lost consciousness. I'm not asking you to detail what the Midwife did to you, Olivia. I want to help you feel less scared, less... I don't know. Whatever it is that makes you retreat into yourself.' His voice was dreadfully soft, raising gooseflesh on her arms and back.

With effort, she turned to face him and bit out, 'I helped get you out of Newgate, and so you believe you owe me something. You believe you can pay me back by trying to mend me.' She was breathing heavily, struggling to reign in emotions that rolled over her and through her, tearing down all defences and control. 'Leave me be, Gavriel. Do not attempt to touch my heart or my soul. Those are very dark places.'

Sévère sat back in his chair, looking at her without speaking.

She didn't want to know what he thought or wanted to say so she turned away to sit at the vanity. Unpinning her hair. Running the brush through it like an automaton.

'May I?' he asked.

She froze.

Gently, he took the brush from her hand and began to run it through her locks.

She didn't move.

Her inner turmoil froze, undecided about what part of her he would uproot next.

'The day of my release from Newgate, when we sat on that hill and listened to birdsong, I asked you what you see in me. I hadn't expected you to say "my friend," least of all "my husband." Do you remember what answer you gave me?'

'Solicitor Gavriel Sévère,' she replied without emotion.

'Yes. For a moment, it hurt to be a title, a function, and not a man to you. But then I realised that "a man" might equal "client" or "beast" in your books. It made me angry. I don't fault you for it, Olivia. Had I been abducted as a child, sold off, and ill-used as you were, I'd think the same, if not worse. I can only guess what you've been through, what it felt like to be owned and used. I wish you would trust me but I know this might never be possible. So I'll settle for the next best thing: Use me as your crutch, Olivia.'

Mistrustfully, she eyed him in the mirror. 'Whatever do you mean?'

'Exactly what I said. Use me. Take what you need from me. I don't expect anything in return. You don't have to treat me like a friend or a husband. Use my connections, my anger, my time. But I can't offer you my reputation,' he added with a dark chuckle. 'I don't seem to have one I could show off in good society.'

For several long moments, she said nothing. He ran the brush through her sleek black hair, avoiding her gaze in the mirror.

Then she whispered, 'I cannot rid myself of my past, I cannot get over it, cannot grow out of it. Even if I could, society throws it back in my face. *Whore!* they say, and think they know me. I am nothing to them.'

He opened his mouth to say something, anything, but found no words.

'I know how you must have felt. In your cell with the threat of the noose constantly hovering over you.' She swallowed around the constriction in her throat. 'I can't allow myself to depend on you, Sévère. That would...violate all that I am.'

'What utter nonsense.'

Her nostrils flared. 'Give me the brush and get out of my room.'

'So you can keep hiding? So you can keep lying to yourself?'

'I hate you,' she whispered.

'I know you do.'

He briefly paused in his ministrations, then added, 'There's one thing I need you to know: The money I used to purchase the premises on the Isle of Wight for you wasn't mine. Not a penny of it. It was my father's. Even years after his death, I depend on him. That's one way of looking at it, which I don't. I see it as his gift to me. And I was honouring him by using part of it to help you make your dream come true. Allow yourself to depend on me until you can stand on your own two feet again.'

'That dream is dead.'

'I know. And I am so sorry, Olivia.'

'I can't even be a detective.'

'You are a brilliant detective and you know it. One setback

doesn't define you. You were terrified today. So what? The plan was poorly made anyway. I'm glad we turned around.'

She growled under her breath. This infuriating man! He knew nothing! Fumbled around like a blind man trying to decipher the shape of her dark soul. Whatever for? To get her into his bed?

Use me.

Was that it? Was he hoping she'd want to use his body? She chuffed darkly. If that was his plan, he could wait his entire life and be left wanting.

Then she remembered that he'd killed Frost for her and for Rose. He hadn't even mentioned his plans to her, simply slipped out in the dead of night with his unsteady gait. He'd risked everything — his freedom, perhaps even his life had Frost managed to fight back.

All for her.

Something primal crept through her bones as she recalled the surge of raw power she'd felt when she drilled her thumb into Frost's knife wound.

The memory lit her up like a lightning strike.

Her gaze slid to her palm. *You are a warrior queen.*

She turned her hand and held it out to him. 'How good are you at drawing dragon scales?'

Eight

SÉVÈRE HAD BLACKENED her fingers with ink and a broad goat hair brush, then used a fine sable brush to trace intricate dragon scales from her knuckles to her elbows. 'It's iron gall ink,' he'd warned her. 'It will take days to wash off completely.'

All the better, she thought.

She'd felt strangely vulnerable when they sat on her bed together, her upper body clothed only in a chemise and a corset, revealing her bare shoulders and too much décolletage. Sévère's left hand had rested on her wrist, his right tracing black lines and chasing gooseflesh across her body. He'd noticed her reaction, of course, his keen eyes missing nothing. She didn't want to know what he made of it, and he chose not to comment.

As he drew on her skin with precision, he talked about strategies to find Alice Green. It wasn't much but she had to admit it was better than what she'd cooked up in haste. She was determined not to repeat the spell of weakness, that trembling deep in her bones, the terror of something that could not touch her anymore.

She didn't quite understand why her mind and body had

reacted that way. Why would she suddenly be as weak as a babe? She wasn't a child anymore, for heaven's sake! She didn't have to serve clients, didn't have to be stitched up afterwards or endure an abortion at the hands of that demon.

With a growl, Olivia stoked her anger to a bright fury and left her room.

The servants were asleep but Sévère was still awake. A yellow swath of light sneaked out under his door. She was careful not to tread on treacherous floorboards that would announce her presence as she passed his room, and listened intently for any noise indicating Sévère's approach.

Once she'd left the house, Olivia strode purposefully through the darkened streets, her footsteps echoing dully through the fog. She found a street lamp, its flickering glow casting long shadows on the cobblestones. She pulled off her lace gloves and examined her hands adorned with dragon scales, turning them over in the dim light.

Use me, he'd said with a strange mixture of softness and resolve. He probably didn't expect it would be his drawing skills she'd be using to help pull her armour back around herself.

Olivia's eyes scanned the deserted street as she walked on until she spotted a lone hansom cab. The driver, a hunched figure atop his perch, seemed to have succumbed to the late hour, his chin resting on his chest, an unlit pipe dangling from his furry mouth. The horse stood patiently, shifting its legs, harness jingling softly. A nearby street lamp spilt its yellow light over the sleepy pair, creating an eerily distorted amalgam of man, horse, and carriage in the fog.

Just as he'd done every morning since being released from Newgate prison, Sévère woke up two hours before breakfast with his mind already racing with the day's challenges. He strapped on his brace, the leather creaking as he tightened it. Then he picked up his walking stick and began pacing from his bedroom to his library. It was his daily ritual. Back and forth, back and forth, his footfall soft and silent.

He couldn't bear sitting in his wheeling chair the entire day, pretending he'd entirely lost the use of his legs. The charade was necessary, but it grated on his pride and weakened his body. He used these early hours to exercise, enjoying the strain in his muscles as he pushed himself. He found it easier to plan the day ahead while moving about. The servants knew not to disturb him until twenty minutes before breakfast when he wished to wash and would require an ewer of hot water. This solitude was precious to him, a time to gather his thoughts and steel himself for the challenges that lay ahead.

As he paced, Sévère put his focus on two problems that weighed heavily on his mind. Each step brought new considerations, potential strategies, and the occasional flash of frustration at the complexities he faced.

The first, and perhaps most immediate, was the Midwife. But he put that issue aside until after breakfast.

The other pressing matter was the revision of the Prevention of Crimes Act 1871. Sévère approached this challenge as he would any other complex legal case: with methodical precision and a bird's-eye view. He knew that to effect meaningful change, he must first dissect the problem in its entirety.

He resolved to compile an exhaustive list that would identify every conceivable gap in the protection of underage girls, as well as all individuals — regardless of age — from sexual exploitation. This catalogue of shortcomings would serve as the foundation for his course of action.

Once that task was completed, Sévère would craft a second, equally comprehensive list. This document would propose specific, carefully worded amendments designed to address each and every one of those gaps. He envisioned a watertight legal framework that would leave no room for miscreants to slip through the cracks of justice.

He paused, chiding himself. Making a law watertight was impossible. The law, no matter how well worded, would never be more than a piece of complex text twenty different men could interpret in twenty different ways.

As he rounded his armchair and passed the window, he spotted a cab. And his wife climbing out of it. What the dickens was she—

He wiped the thought away. She was her own woman and neither needed nor wanted him to hover protectively, let alone possessively.

He turned his thoughts back to the matter at hand, wondering how the bloody hell he would be able to protect married women from exploitation by their husbands. That was an impossibility. He scratched that point off his list. His focus had to be on the protection of underage girls and lifting the age of consent from thirteen to sixteen.

That alone would be a monstrous task.

He looked up as he heard Olivia's footfall. She tiptoed up the stairs and past his rooms. As the sound of her movement faded, Sévère felt a pang of concern. He understood her need for independence, her fierce desire to overcome without assistance all the cruelties the world threw at her. Yet, he couldn't help but worry about the toll it was taking on her. He debated whether to follow, to inquire if she needed anything, but ultimately decided against it as he heard the sound of her door shutting softly.

Making an effort to exhale all tension, he scribbled another item to his ever-growing list: Find and propose comprehensive changes to all legal loopholes that allow perpetrators to evade punishment. He envisioned a sweeping reform that would redefine offences, substantially increase penalties for the rape and abduction of underage girls, and introduce robust new provisions to better safeguard the rights of women and children.

The task was Herculean.

The laugh that rolled up his throat caught him by surprise as the sound bounced off the walls of his study. Who did he think he was? Some sort of legal messiah? If he, or any other man for that matter, dared to send such a proposition to the hallowed chamber of the House of Lords, they would take one cursory look at the paper before unceremoniously burning it to ashes. He could almost hear their raucous laughter, picture their powdered wigs shaking with mirth at the audacity of such a suggestion.

No, it was Burroughs, as loath as Sévère was to admit it, who was correct in his assessment. Reforms would forever be blocked and ridiculed as long as men in power saw no direct benefit in the proposed changes. Sévère would have to use the public, that great unwashed mass, as leverage to get what he wanted. He needed an outraged mob, their anger stoked by tales of injustice and corruption. Only then might the lords in their ivory towers find it advisable to listen. The thought exhilarated him.

And it terrified him.

Sévère rubbed his brow and accidentally smeared ink on his forehead.

Perhaps, he mused, the first step was to find a journalist. Someone with a sharp wit and a talent to stir the public's conscience and ignite the flames of outrage.

No. Before you burn all bridges, take a step back, he told himself. Rashness could jeopardise everything they worked for. He needed to approach this problem methodically, with the same careful deliberation he applied to his legal cases.

He was certain that he, Olivia, and Burroughs weren't alone in this seemingly hopeless endeavour. There had to be others out there, potential allies sharing disgust at the current state of affairs, whose determination he could use to effect change.

Stretching his legs and spine, he walked around his desk and added another list to his growing pile: collaborations.

He needed to find other legal experts, advocacy groups, and stakeholders with similar concerns who could help him build support for the proposed amendments. Although he quite disliked such people in general, he saw the benefits of lobbying influential figures within the legal and political spheres.

Perhaps he should meet with members of parliament? The thought made him cringe, but he knew it was a necessary evil if he wanted to change anything at all.

Another chuckle burst from him, tinged with bitter irony. Solicitor Gavriel Sévère, cripple, husband of a notorious ex-prostitute and former inmate of Newgate's condemned ward! Here is a man with an immaculate reputation! Ha!

The absurdity of it all struck him anew. How would he, with his tarnished past and more than unconventional present, ever hope to sway the minds of those in power?

And yet... Wasn't it because of Olivia's experiences that he understood the urgent need for reform better than most men? His wife's perspective would be an asset if only he could find a way to present it without immediately alienating their audience.

However, he had to admit that finding a sympathetic member of parliament to sponsor the amendments, submitting them for consideration during parliamentary sessions, and participating in debates and discussions to advocate for their passage, might be a way to success. He couldn't simply dismiss this option because he hated dealing with politicians. The process would be arduous, no doubt, but it might yield the results he sought.

Alas, it might require a man with a less...tarnished reputation to approach parliament members for support. His own name, he knew all too well, carried with it a weight of scandal that could sink even the most noble of causes before it had a chance to take flight.

He'd have to talk to Burroughs. The man's connections in the legal world might prove invaluable in this endeavour. Perhaps Burroughs knew of someone with the requisite standing and moral fibre to champion their cause.

Hum. Perhaps he could find a prominent social reformer or wealthy philanthropist already advocating for women's rights and social justice. Someone with substantial influence could bolster their campaign. Perhaps one of the more progressive members of the aristocracy could be persuaded to lend his support. Such an alliance could provide the respectability and gravitas his proposal so sorely needed.

Which brought him back to the idea of using newspapermen to reach a broader audience. Once he had secured the support of at least a handful of influential figures, obtaining favourable coverage and editorial support in prominent newspapers would come a great deal easier.

Sévère contemplated the domino effect this could create. A positive press would make it significantly simpler to bring in more politicians, lawmen, and perhaps even wealthy industrialists who might be swayed by the growing momentum. The more money there was in the crowd he assembled, the more influence there would be to wield against the entrenched interests that sought to maintain the status quo.

A grim smile spread across Sévère's face as he considered the potential ramifications of his plan.

He would cause an uproar that would shake the very foundations of the establishment.

Nine

THE BROUGHAM CLATTERED along the streets of Whitechapel, each jolt sending a sharp pain through Sévère's left leg. He clenched his teeth, determined not to display any weakness. Next to him, Olivia remained as still and unmoving as a rock.

He felt a mixture of dread and resolve. They were seeking out a woman who facilitated heinous crimes. Sévère wondered how long he could maintain a facade of civility around the vile creature.

He cast a sideways glance at Olivia, loath to ask her how she was holding up. Her breathing sounded steady, but she held her hat tightly clasped in her lap. Taking a risk of a sharp rebuke, he gently took her hand in his, easing her fingers from the strained grip on her hat.

He remained silent as the brougham continued its rattling journey. Slowly, her fingers lost their tension.

She leaned back and let out a sigh. 'What if she doesn't buy it?'

'Then we gather evidence against her and make sure she rots

in jail. We don't depend on her cooperation to find Alice Green.'

Her hand remained in his. This was new, he thought. What did it mean? If it meant anything at all. Was she merely too fatigued or too anxious to notice? He had anticipated she would swiftly withdraw, sever any physical contact, and perhaps throw an insult his way.

Yet she didn't.

What did it mean?

The carriage lurched to a halt in front of a series of dilapidated buildings. Sévère peered out, taking in the dark windows and peeling paint, and wondered how many girls had been brought to this dismal place.

Without a word, Olivia withdrew her hand from his.

'Ready?' he asked.

'As I'll ever be.'

Sévère knocked on the roof. Higgins jumped off the carriage and onto the rain-slicked cobbles. Their coachman had spent much of the previous day watching the comings and goings of women with girls in tow, the former going in with smiles of assurance, the latter with slight looks of alarm. When they exited, the women were all business, the girls wide-eyed with horror. Once or twice, Higgins had reported, a girl entered the house but didn't leave it. Sévère wondered if they'd been considered too much trouble.

He watched the coachman knock on the front door and broaden his shoulders as he waited. A sliver of yellow fell on the glistening pavement only to be blotted out by a woman stepping into view. Their conversation was brief. Higgins motioned towards the carriage. She paused, made to shut the door. His boot came down. Angry words were exchanged.

But eventually, she made her way to the carriage.

Behind her, Higgins touched the brim of his bowler —

their signal that the woman seemed interested. The game was on.

Sévère opened the carriage door. Thick fog carried odours of mud and rot from the nearby Thames. His left leg throbbed more than usual. He tightened his grip on his cane, inhaled deeply, and glanced back at Higgins.

The man was armed with a revolver, as was Olivia, who held her chin high and her back ramrod straight. No sign of fear. No sign of hesitation.

The strength of this woman never ceased to amaze him.

He tucked his emotions away as the Midwife, a woman in her forties, stepped up to the carriage, her neatly pinned dark hair streaked with silver, a brooch adorning the collar of her pinstriped blouse, and her apron pristinely unwrinkled.

She peered at them over wire-framed spectacles, gaze inquisitive. 'Yes?'

'Good evening, ma'am. Gavriel and Olivia Sévère, private detectives.' He kept his tone neutral, conveying only mild politeness despite the deep aversion boiling in the pit of his stomach. 'We have a proposition for your consideration.'

The Midwife's gaze flitted from Sévère's face to his cane, then to the proffered card. She ignored it, instead scrutinising Olivia from head to toe.

'We'd prefer to discuss this in here,' Sévère added, gesturing for her to climb into the brougham.

She didn't budge. 'What sort of proposition?'

'We have information that might be of interest to you,' he replied.

'I haven't the time for this.' She took a step back, about to turn to leave.

'We're offering a share of our profits and as well as protection should the police become too interested in your...endeavours,' Olivia said.

The Midwife snorted derisively. 'What makes you think I have need of such?'

Olivia glanced at Sévère and smiled. 'As I told you.'

He knew what she meant. The subtle signs of piqued interest. The reluctance to show it.

Olivia turned back to address the woman. 'My apologies. I'd informed my husband earlier that our visit would be fruitless, but he insisted we approach you first anyway.' Olivia twitched a shoulder in feigned regret. 'We'll be on our way. Good evening.'

She reached for the doorknob as if to shut the brougham's door in the Midwife's face.

'I might be able to spare a minute,' the woman conceded, clearing her throat as if to rid herself of some awful taste, then joining them in the carriage.

She folded her hands in her lab and demanded they be brief, maintaining an air of irritation, as though their proposition were an inconvenience to her evening plans.

Olivia gave Sévère a subtle nod, signalling for him to take the lead.

'We've been in contact with parents of missing girls,' he began. 'They have evidence that can put you behind bars.'

He watched the Midwife's face, waiting for any flicker of unease. Unsurprisingly, only a derisive smile crept across her features.

'Is that so? And you think I'm intimidated?'

'I doubt you are, considering the protection afforded by your...associates,' he replied. Olivia had suggested this possibility, and the Midwife's reaction had just confirmed it.

Her eyes glinted in the dim light as she replied coolly, 'If you've come to issue threats, rest assured that you'll soon be crushed like cockroaches should you dare move against me or involve the police. Your supposed evidence, as you suppose it, will vanish, and you and your witnesses will be discredited thoroughly. The gentlemen I serve do not tolerate meddling.'

Pretending mild amusement, Sévère replied, 'I assure you, that wasn't my aim. I'm rather pleased to hear of your protection. It bodes well for our future dealings.'

'You mentioned a proposal. I suggest you get to it,' she snapped.

'Indeed, I have just. However, I needed to ascertain your mettle first. Now, as I was saying, we're in contact with the families of missing girls. Over a hundred families, to be precise. They've entrusted us with their missing daughters' welfare.' Here, he paused, leaning back with a wolfish grin. 'We now have access to their households, their remaining children, as well as their staff and some of their relatives. We can obtain information crucial for a collaborative venture.'

A flicker of interest crossed the Midwife's face. 'Go on.'

'Picture having intimate information about which girls might best suit your clientele. We could furnish particulars on their appearance, disposition, and familial situations. We could even fabricate a farewell note and plant it to make a disappearance less suspicious.'

Sévère paused to let his words sink in. The Midwife remained taciturn, awaiting more.

'It is understood,' Olivia added, 'that we can't be directly involved in any abductions. It would arouse suspicion. But we can supply information to you and your associates, misdirect police investigations, and "discover" letters from the missing girls to substantiate claims of them being runaways. We can identify the most promising candidates, and suggest opportune moments when the girls will be vulnerable.'

Sévère continued, 'We can engineer circumstances to create opportunities. Should the authorities investigate, we can fabricate evidence to mislead them. A family's financial woes or a girl's feelings of neglect or rebellion — all potential pressure points to exploit.'

The Midwife produced a thin smile. 'And what would you stand to gain from this arrangement?'

Sévère mirrored her expression. 'Profits, naturally. Along with certain accommodations.'

'An interesting proposal,' she mused. Her eyes glittered with a blend of wariness and intrigue. 'But how can I be sure you can be trusted?'

Letting her see a glimpse of how little he enjoyed this exchange, Sévère replied, 'As a businesswoman of your mettle, you can't and you shouldn't. However, you and I know your associates would swiftly deal with us should we prove disloyal.' With that, he pushed open the brougham door. 'You have two days to reach a decision. After that, we shall seek another collaborator. Good evening.'

For a moment, she remained motionless. Her gaze darted to Olivia, lingering there. A faint smile played across her lips. Without uttering a word, she slipped from the brougham and shut the door, leaving Olivia and Sévère staring at its polished handle.

Sévère rapped his cane against the roof of the brougham, signalling Higgins to drive. As the carriage jolted forward, he felt a modicum of relief in his taut muscles. He cast a sidelong glance at Olivia, who sat slumped against the backrest, her eyes shut and her face tense.

For a moment, neither of them spoke. The only sounds were the rhythmic clip-clop of horseshoes on cobblestones, the creaking of the carriage, and the rattle of carriage wheels. Sévère's ire rose as he replayed their exchange with the Midwife. He wanted to scrub his mouth clean.

Beside him, Olivia buried her face in her hands, a low groan escaping her. Sévère wanted to reach out and offer some comfort, but before he could move she sat up, rubbed her face, and said with a voice that sent chills across his neck, 'The very thought of having to continue this charade, to feign interest in her despicable dealings, to pretend we're on her side, makes we want to...' She broke off and glanced out the window.

He swallowed. 'This is only the beginning. It will get much worse.'

Although his mind kept searching for alternatives, he was acutely aware that backing out now wasn't an option.

He turned his gaze towards Olivia, wishing he could ease her distress. But what words of comfort could he possibly offer? That at the end of all this, they might save a handful of girls from a life of prostitution?

Ten

HIGGINS WAS CLEANING out the stable when Rose made her entrance, dressed in a pretty green frock, her hair neatly combed and braided, a red ribbon around her throat. Surprised, he raised an eyebrow at the sight, wondering if there was a misunderstanding. Was Rose aware that Mrs Sévère had requested him to apprentice the girl? The dress she'd donned suggested otherwise. She probably had no clue they'd be working around the horses.

On the other hand, it was clear that the apprenticeship was merely a diversion of sorts. Coachmanship was for men, as the name implied, and the girl had brains enough to know she'd never drive the brougham through town.

Was that why she wore a dress? In protest against the patriarchy? A soft snort escaped Higgins. The girl was nine years old for heaven's sake. She'd not think that far at such a young age, surely.

'Morning, Mr Higgins,' Rose chirped, her voice uncharacteristically sugary for someone known to throw stink bombs into the courtyard and hide dead rodents in chamber pots. She twirled once, twice, letting the skirt of her dress flare out around her.

Higgins cleared his throat as discomfort began to wriggle in his guts. 'Morning,' he managed.

Rose beamed at him, her eyes sparkling with a strange light. 'I thought I'd dress up for our first lesson.'

Higgins' thoughts screeched to a halt. His eyes darted to the manure pile at his feet. If Rose thought she could shovel shit in a frilly dress, she was in for a surprise. Or did she expect to skip learning and be a coachman...or coachwoman, from day one?

'You think I'll be letting you drive the brougham around London today?' he scoffed and presented Rose with a shovel. 'First, you learn to muck the stables. Then I'll teach you how to take proper care of the horses, to harness them, and to maintain the carriage and livery.'

Blinking, Rose pushed her lower lip out. 'But I wanted to look pretty for you.'

Higgins choked on his spittle. He staggered a step back and swallowed a torrent of colourful curses. Growling, he pointed a finger at her face. 'I won't stand for your tomfoolery, young lady.'

Her chin quivered. Tears burst from her eyes and spilt down her cheeks onto the pretty silk dress. She turned and fled from the stables, but not without calling him 'such a prude.'

It took him a moment to recover from the shock. It wasn't every day that a girl made an attempt at flirting with him. And a clumsy one at that. Higgins sighed, regretting he'd snapped at Rose. He didn't need much in the way of brains to guess she thought of him as a knight in shining armour after he and Mrs Sévère rescued her from the brothel. The girl had been abducted and sold to a client by her own mother. That same client, it turned out, was later found dead in some filthy corner of Whitechapel. Whoever had done him in, Higgins wished he could congratulate the killer.

He glanced at the stable door left ajar, knowing that he hadn't seen the last of it.

Spitting on the manure, Higgins leaned heavily on the shovel. 'Bloody hell, I need a gin.'

Morning light filtered through lace curtains. From the brightness and silence in the room, Olivia concluded must be past eight in the morning, and Rose must already be up, learning horse lore from Higgins. Which meant Olivia had missed breakfast. She stretched and yawned, recalling the previous night's discussion, and how Sévère's cautious optimism was grating her. Briefly, she wondered if his belief in justice was a front to keep her from falling back into her routine of gazing out of the window and ignoring him.

A bitter laugh rolled up her throat. She'd long ago learned that in this cesspit of a city, justice was served only when it benefitted the wealthy. Why did Sévère refuse to see this?

Well, he'd had a pampered childhood, and he was male. His view of this world was entirely different from hers.

Besides, hadn't *she* asked him to change the law? It had been one of her conditions in their marriage contract. But why had she believed in the first place he could change anything for the better?

She rose from her bed and paused. Should she have told Sévére about her meeting with Betsy? But what would he be able to do? Write a letter to the House of Lords to enquire about a place in Kew where pretty girls were sold to wealthy men?

She snorted.

When Betsy had leaned across the table in the dingy gambling den and murmured foul breath and ill tidings into Olivia's ear, she'd shivered with revulsion.

'Kew,' the old prostitute had whispered. 'that's where they take the pretty ones.'

Olivia padded to the window. The streets below teemed with life, seemingly oblivious to the rot festering beneath London's respectable facade. Her reflection stared back at her, eyes hard with anger. 'Bugger the blasted House of Lords.'

She rang for Netty, who promptly delivered warm water to wash. 'The inspector stopped by earlier,' the housekeeper said in a hushed tone.

'Inspector Height?'

'Yes. He wanted to speak to you both, but Mr Sévére informed him he'd have to return in the afternoon as you were indisposed.' Netty scrutinised her with veiled curiosity.

Olivia felt queasy. Inspector Height's visit could only mean trouble. The last time he'd wanted a moment with them had ended with Sévère in Newgate prison.

She combed and pinned her hair, made her way to the kitchen to enquire about refreshments, then went back up to the ground floor to find Sévère in their private detective agency office.

She settled across from him with a cup of tea in one hand and a buttered muffin in the other. 'What are you working on?'

Startled, he looked up as though he hadn't noticed her entering the room. Dark shadows hung beneath his eyes. She scanned his face, the reddish tinge to his lower lids, the dark pupils. 'Are you in pain?'

He stared at her for a moment longer, then dropped his gaze back to his papers. 'We'll meet Burroughs in the afternoon.'

'And Inspector Height, it seems.'

'Yes, him too.'

'What does he want?'

Sévère kept writing remarks on a list he must have made earlier. 'He has questions about Frost's death.'

The muffin suddenly tasted stale. 'What kind of questions?'

More scribbling, scratching out items on his list, adding more items. 'He said that there was animosity between you and Frost. A history.'

Ice crawled down her back. 'Yes, he asked me about it when you were in Newgate. Frost had... Never mind.'

Finally, Sévère looked up. 'He has no shred of evidence, nothing to investigate, and he's getting desperate because god knows who is putting him under pressure to solve Frost's murder. That's a dangerous combination.'

Olivia's mouth dried up. She drank her tea to wash down the muffin. 'What are we going to tell him?'

'The usual. A combination of truth and lies.'

'Meaning?'

'Frost was your client, was known to many as a man with cruel tastes. One can only suspect he had a long list of enemies.'

She exhaled and nodded slowly. 'What are we going to do about Alice Green?'

Sévère's gaze swung to the sacks of letters. 'We call them all in and gather information.'

Olivia leaned back, her mind scanning the options. They were approaching Alice Green's abduction from a broader angle — not just to find the girl but to put a dent into London's flesh market. 'The return on investment is over a thousand per cent, did you know?'

'For maidens?'

She nodded toward the sacks. 'I'll read them all and sort them according to urgency. How big a crowd do you want in your office?'

'*Our* office. And no, I don't want a crowd. We'll meet one family at a time.'

'That will take...'

'Weeks, yes. That's why you'll send them a letter asking for specific information, tell them about our rates, and suggest a day and time to meet us here.'

She cocked her head. 'Are we having financial problems?'

He lifted his eyebrows. 'Why do you ask?'

'By telling them our rates you're turning away anyone who can't pay. Which might be more than half of them.'

'We can't save them all, Olivia. And we won't help anyone if we don't take payment for our work.'

A bitter taste settled on her tongue. 'And by asking for specific information in our first letter, we might gain insights even from the impoverished parents, which might help the girls of wealthier parents.'

'Which in turn might help everyone else because we're not only searching for abducted girls. We're hunting those who abduct them.'

Olivia paused, considering. 'If half of them,' she made a motion towards the sacks of letters, 'are able and willing to pay three guineas up front, you'll have earned three hundred and fifteen pounds in a couple of weeks. If you meet ten parents every day, five days a week.'

'*We*, dear wife. We will have taken in three hundred and fifteen pounds. But make no mistake, we'll need most of that money to bribe hoodlums and officials of the Crown.'

She huffed. 'The only distinguishing characteristic between the two is a powdered wig.'

'Well...'

Well!' She brushed muffin crumbs off her dress and stood. 'I better get to it, then.'

'How are you planning to sort them?' he asked.

'The letters? Hum, I was thinking that the more recent the disappearance, the higher the chances we'll find the girl. Letters that indicate the involvement of a seductress, especially if they mentioned the Virtuous Maiden Society or Aurelia Pembroke will also be a priority.'

He nodded. 'Look for unique identifiers, patterns, and commonalities that can help narrow our search. Write down all ideas and questions that come up while you're reading. Even if they seem silly. They might be useful later.' After a pause he added, 'And make sure all those letters are spread out when Height returns. I want him to be aware of what we're doing. A police inspector sympathetic to our cause might be useful one day.'

Soon after, much of the office floor was covered in letters, some sorted into neat stacks, others spread and awaiting their fate. Olivia crouched amidst them, pencil poised over her notebook, brow furrowed in concentration. Across the room, Sévère was working silently on his strategy list when the quiet scratchings of pen on paper were interrupted by the sudden sound of Rose's angry footsteps stomping past the office door.

Olivia's head snapped up, her gaze meeting Sévère's. His expression mirrored her own confusion.

Concerned, she rose and hurried out of the office, following the girl up the stairs, her worry growing with each step. When she reached her room, the door was slammed in her face.

Tamping down her irritation, she pushed open the door to find Rose face down on her bed, sobbing into her pillow, her green dress crumpled and her braids undone.

Olivia approached cautiously and rested a comforting hand on the girl's back.

'What's wrong?' she asked.

Rose shook her head, her sobs muffled by the pillow.

'Did Higgins upset you?'

The sobs intensified as she remained stubbornly silent.

'I will get to the bottom of the matter. And if that man has done something to you, I will make him pay.' With that, Olivia stood and marched out of the room. She descended the stairs, her skirts swishing angrily around her ankles as she made her way to the stables.

She found Higgins mucking out a stall, his face set in a grim expression. He glanced up as she approached. Unease flashed in his eyes.

'Higgins,' Olivia began, her voice sharp with barely contained anger, 'would you care to explain why Rose is crying her heart out?'

The coachman avoided her gaze. His nostrils flared in irritation. 'I'm not entirely sure, Mrs Sévère. The girl showed up dressed in her finery, probably hoping she could drive the brougham around town. When I told her she'd have to muck the stables, she ran off crying.'

Olivia sensed there was much more to the story than he was letting on. 'And that's all?'

He nodded, still refusing to meet her eyes. 'That's all, Mrs Sévère.'

With suspicion and dread mounting, Olivia studied him for a moment, then snarled, 'Have you laid hand on the girl?'

His gaze hardened as he finally looked at her. 'I would *never* harm a child!'

'So you claim. I will speak with Rose, and if there is even a hint that you have violated her trust, I swear I will make you wish you had never been born.'

With anger roiling in her belly, Olivia made her way back into the house. As she passed the office, she was met by a familiar voice, stopping her in her tracks. She paused, taking a deep breath to compose herself before pushing at the door.

Sévère and Inspector Height looked up as she entered.

Olivia forced a polite smile, shoving down her unease and frustration.

'Mrs Sévère, I hope you are well,' Height said. 'If you allow, I would like to ask you a few questions regarding your...former occupation.'

'To what end?' Her tone was frosty.

'I am investigating the murder of Chief Magistrate Frost, and I believe—'

'How does that concern me?'

He drew a breath and inclined his head. 'As I was attempting to explain, the man appears to have patronised brothels rather...frequently.' Height fidgeted with a waistcoat button, then cast an uneasy look at Sévère. 'Perhaps the lady would prefer to discuss this privately?'

'My husband is fully aware of my former profession,' she retorted. 'As is all of London. Obviously.'

Heights sighed and massaged his brown. 'I am deeply sorry for the trouble I've caused you.'

Sévere barked a laugh. '*Trouble?* My wife's reputation is in tatters, as are my health and career. But by all means, call it *trouble*, Inspector. Let's set aside this trifling matter, shall we, and examine why you've come here. Is it to gather information or to unearth yet another imaginary killer in my home? What are you planning to destroy this time?'

Olivia walked up to Height, stared him in the eye, and said coldly, 'As I'm sure you're aware, many brothel owners knew of Frost's... proclivities. His taste for maidens was hardly a secret in certain circles. Isn't it strange that the police showed not the least interest in Frost's activities until the man turned up dead? Have you considered that a father or a brother of all the little girls Frost had abducted and drugged for his pleasure has finally knifed the disgusting pig?'

Height's expression tightened. 'We're exploring all avenues.

If you hear any rumours about someone boasting about the murder, I'd appreciate you letting me know.'

Olivia's lips curled with disgust. 'Why would I condemn a man who took down a monster?'

She gestured to the piles of letters strewn across the floor. 'These are all cries for help, Inspector Height. Many of these missing girls, likely all, have been sold into prostitution. Perhaps your efforts would be better spent on living victims rather than avenging a dead predator.'

Height fell silent, his gaze sweeping over the letters. When he finally spoke, his voice was subdued. 'I wasn't aware...'

'Oh shut your mouth!' she snarled, entirely fed up with the man.

Height cleared his throat. 'Perhaps we could help each other. If I learn anything about those missing girls, I'll pass it on to you. Send me a list of their names. In return, if you hear anything about Frost's murder...'

Considering, she chewed the inside of her cheek. 'Have you ever heard of a place in Kew where young girls are sold?'

Height's expression darkened. 'I've heard whispers of a house of horrors there. Another inspector mentioned it. I won't name him. All investigations into it have been stalled or shut down.'

Olivia scanned Height's face. 'And what does that tell you, Inspector?'

He swallowed, thumbed his waistcoat buttons, and replied with a hoarse voice, 'Corruption on all levels of law enforcement.'

She smiled bitterly. 'And what are you going to do about it?'

Eleven

OLIVIA FLEXED her fingers and shook out a persistent cramp in her hand. She and Sèvere had been working well into the night. William had been occupied at court, unable to join them for a discussion. At least Olivia had managed to respond to all the correspondence. Her mind felt as limp as an old lettuce but her anger continued to simmer beneath the surface.

She could no longer bear being confined to the office, doing nothing but pleading for information, penning one letter after another after another, spitting angrily at Inspector Height, and hoping someone would take action to help these girls.

Olivia couldn't remember a single occasion when the authorities had stepped in to help her or any of the women society deemed 'fallen' when they were desperately seeking a life free from abuse.

Why was she even wasting her time hoping that anything would ever change?

Sighing, Olivia prepared for bed and cinched her robe around her waist, then left her private quarters and rapped on Sévère's door.

A muffled, 'Who's there?'

'It's me.'

A moment's hesitation. 'Come in.'

She entered the room and closed the door softly. His gaze touched on her face and the items she cradled in her hands: a bottle of ink and a fine brush.

He perched on the bed in his nightclothes, wrapped in a faint haze of smoke. A long pipe rested on the nightstand, a ribbon of grey rising from its bowl.

'Am I intruding?' she asked.

He shook his head.

She ventured further into the room. 'Would you...paint wings on me?'

For a moment, he appeared at a loss. His throat worked as he gave her a curt nod.

Olivia advanced another step, her gaze darting to the pipe. 'But I... I don't want to be a bother.'

'You're not. Would you care to sit?'

'There?' She gestured towards the bed. 'If it's all right?'

He shifted and turned down the covers to make room for her.

Hesitantly, she settled on the edge, her back to him.

The mattress sagged a little as he settled behind her. Quietly, he asked for the brush and the ink.

She held the requested items out to him. Then she eased her robe and nightgown down to her waist. Her movements felt too clumsy, her breathing too loud.

'Your pain, how bad is it?' she whispered. She thought she'd smelled opium on him the previous day, but the whiff she'd caught was so weak, she couldn't be certain. Now, her worries were confirmed.

He didn't reply.

She heard his measured intake of breath, the soft pop of the ink bottle opening. Glancing back, she watched him searching for a place to put the cork. As he leaned toward the nightstand, the cork slipped from his fingers and dropped to the floor.

Olivia gathered her long tresses and pulled them over her shoulders, exposing her back.

He froze.

'Are you all right?' she asked.

'Are you?'

'I am...nervous,' she admitted.

'As am I,' he whispered, then even softer, 'Olivia?'

'Yes?'

'Would you like dragon wings?'

She nodded as warmth rushed through her belly.

'You don't opt for pretty. You choose ferocious and deadly.'

She tucked her secrets closer to herself, and pressed through her teeth, 'Beauty serves no purpose.'

'Neither does ugliness.'

'It can provide protection.'

'And beauty can open doors.'

'Are you drawing dragon wings now or gazing at my back?'

He sighed. 'I'm trying to figure out how to *not* make them look like bat wings.'

'Oh.'

'Have you considered bird's wings?'

She snorted. 'Something pretty, you mean?'

'Something formidable.'

She scoffed. 'Such as?'

'Perhaps raven wings?'

'Perhaps...' she said, uncertain.

'Ravens are highly intelligent. They are fiercely loyal and mate for life. And beautiful, I think. Your hair. It's the colour of raven wings.'

'I didn't know you are so fond of ravens.'

'I am. Very much.' It sounded as though he meant to add, *now*.

She sensed his gaze on her bare shoulders, illuminated by the soft candlelight.

She cocked her head, not looking at him, just letting him know that she wondered what made him hesitate. After a moment, she asked, 'What's on your mind?'

'I'm uncertain where to start.'

'The beginning is usually a good place,' she offered.

Still, he remained motionless.

'Perhaps above the heart,' Olivia whispered.

A hush descended as he drew a deep breath, dipped the brush in ink, and touched it to her skin.

She felt him tracing a sweeping line up to her shoulder and down, down, down to her hip. He outlined the large feathers of a wing and then the smaller ones. Gooseflesh rippled with each brushstroke, and she wondered if he could hear her thundering heartbeat.

Once more, he began at the centre of her back, sweeping up towards her shoulder and down again to her hip, creating the other wing with its array of many feathers.

He continued until the candle began to sputter, his hand finally coming to rest. 'Why do you trust me with this?' he asked.

'Because I have wings now,' she answered. 'Are they finished?'

'Yes, but give the ink a moment to dry.'

'Hm.' She felt more exposed and vulnerable now than she had when she bared her back to him. 'How is your pain, Gavriel?'

He sucked in a breath as he often did when she used his given name. As though she were threatening to slip a knife between his ribs.

'Tolerable. The dosage is relatively low but enough to help me sleep.'

'I could read to you if that would help.'

In response, he gently pulled her nightgown and robe back into place, his hand lingering briefly on her clothed back. 'Not tonight,' he murmured.

She turned, an unfamiliar sensation stirring within her, and found his gaze fixed on her, his eyes so dark she felt she might drown in their depths.

'I must go,' she croaked and staggered to her feet. 'Good night.'

She fled his rooms, down the stairs, down, down, and into the kitchen. She kicked off her slippers and pressed her feet against the chilly flagstones, shut her eyes, and steadied her breathing.

'It will pass,' she whispered. 'It will pass.'

Fog muffled Olivia's footsteps on the damp cobblestones as she trailed the man through Whitechapel's streets. Cigar smoke and the faint scent of expensive perfume lingered in his wake. His careless swagger only fuelled the anger churning within her. Etched into the back of her eyelids was the image of a young face peering through a second-floor window of the brothel the man had exited a few minutes earlier.

She skirted the yellowish pools of light cast by street lamps, her mind sifting through options. How could she prove his guilt? Witness statements held no sway, dismissed by the police as easily as swatting away an annoying insect. Physical evidence was a rarity. She'd have to drag the police to the scene to catch the man in the act of violating an underage girl. But even then, he'd likely extricate himself with a bellowed, 'My dear sirs, I had no idea the girl was younger than thirteen! She was certainly willing to accept my advances!' which would promptly be corroborated by the brothel keeper.

The word of a rape victim had no weight in court.

There would never be justice for these girls. Not through legal channels. The system was rigged, corrupt to its core.

Her gaze fixed on the man's back as he sauntered down the street, seemingly without a worry in the world. If she had the tools, she could end his life right here, right now. A garrotte or a knife — it would be simple to disguise it as a mugging gone awry.

But one more death wouldn't suffice.

She'd already had a hand in Frost's demise that Sévère had made appear so effortless. Would she have enough strength to plunge a knife deep into a man's chest?

There were dozens like him, hundreds perhaps, preying on the vulnerable with no fear of retribution. A series of 'muggings' might raise suspicion, but if timed carefully and with variations in method, perhaps...

Her connections and street knowledge could be put to good use. She could gather information and track these men's movements, striking when they least expected it. An unfortunate tumble down the stairs here, a bout of food poisoning there — it would demand time and patience, but she could whittle away at their numbers.

She huffed. What was she even thinking? Murder a hundred men? It was madness. And yet, as she watched the man disappear around a corner, she couldn't shake the feeling that this might be the only viable solution.

She paused, gazing at a patch of lamplight playing in a murky puddle. If she succeeded in killing only one before the police caught her, she would have to ensure the man was the most despicable of his kind.

The death of a single monster could mean safety for more than a dozen girls.

Twelve

OLIVIA GAZED into the looking glass, fastening the buttons of her high-collared blouse. She noted the dark shadows under her eyes and told herself to make a serious attempt at catching more sleep. She could do without awkward questions from Sévère as to why she appeared so exhausted every damn day.

A commotion startled her. Rose burst through the adjoining door, her cheeks flushed, her eyes narrowed in frustration.

'I have nothing to wear!' she wailed, and flung herself onto Olivia's bed.

'I've just tidied that, first mate! What's all this fuss about?'

Rose's only response was a dramatic groan.

'What special outfit could you possibly need for your lessons with Higgins? Where are your trousers and shirt? The ones you use for your secret excursions?'

Rose draped an arm across her face. 'I can't possibly wear them. They make me look plain.'

Taken aback, Olivia scrutinised the girl. This preoccupation with appearance for stable work struck her as more than peculiar. 'Rose,' she said, her tone stern but not unkind, 'you're to learn horsemanship, not dancing.'

Rose sat up, her lower lip jutting out in a pout. 'But—'

'No buts,' Olivia cut her off. 'Put on something practical. At once.'

With a huff, Rose stomped out of the room. Olivia watched her go, a knot of unease in her stomach. This concern about appearance was a strange side to Rose, one she'd not seen before. Where had it come from all of a sudden? And why the dickens did she want to look pretty for Higgins? The girl was nine!

Mistrust began to bubble to the surface. Olivia would need to have a frank conversation with the coachman once his lessons were concluded for the day. Something had occurred between him and Rose, and Olivia would get to the bottom of it.

Across the desk, William lounged in an armchair, balancing a plate of biscuits on his thigh and holding a teacup in his hand. Crumbs peppered his front from whiskers to lap. His gaze flitted between Sévère and Olivia, as the former recounted their investigation into Alice Green's disappearance and outlined proposals for amending criminal law.

Familiar with the details, Olivia's thoughts drifted to her clandestine exploits in Whitechapel and what she could possibly accomplish. Supposing she could accomplish anything at all. As her gaze came to rest on Sévère, the weight of her secrets settled heavily on her shoulders.

But some matters were best kept private, even from allies.

Olivia's attention snapped back to the conversation between the two men as William let out a hoarse chuckle. 'Leave the lobbying to me, Mr Sévère. And I'll keep an ear to the ground for any whispers about the Midwife or this,' he stuck a biscuit into his mouth and twirled a hand in the air, as though to reel in a length of tangled yarn, 'this Virtuous Maiden Society.'

Olivia leaned forward. 'Have you caught wind of a house in Kew? We've got word that it's where the prettier girls are brought. Height called it a house of horrors. It might be where they are broken in and auctioned off.'

William shook his head. 'I've not heard of it. But I'll make discreet inquiries. Now, what's your strategy for undermining the Midwife and locating Miss Green?'

Methodically Sèvère lit a cigar and placed it on the rim of a crystal ashtray. He leaned back in his wheeling chair and folded his hands over his belly. 'We all know that evidence alone won't be enough. We need a policeman on our side. Someone whose word will be believed beyond a doubt by judge and jury.'

William brushed crumbs from his lapels and wiggled a thick finger at Olivia and Sévère. 'The irony of it! *You* of all people are thinking of involving the police?'

'You make it sound as though we're criminals,' Sévèred replied dryly.

Olivia coughed. 'Well...'

William's finger kept wagging in their direction. 'You, dear Olivia, will always be considered questionable, to put it mildly, because of your past. And you, Mr Sévère will always be the husband of said questionable individual as well as a man led to trial for murder.' He set the teacup on the desk with a bang. 'But you know how to use this to your advantage. That's why you do the dirty work behind the scenes while I butter up fat Lords and wealthy industrials.' With a satisfied grin, William shoved another biscuit past his teeth.

'There's hope Inspector Height feels remorse for arresting

you for a murder you didn't commit and may genuinely wish to help us,' Olivia grumbled in Sévère's direction.

'Not to be relied on,' Sévère said.

'No. That would be foolish.' Olivia rubbed her tired eyes and sighed. 'I trust him only as far as I would trust a wet alley cat. But we could use him as a source of information. He'll expect something in return, though. I have an inkling what that something might be.'

Sévère eyed her, an understanding passing between them. 'Are you sure?' he asked.

She gave him a nod.

'Might I be included in your little tête-à-tête?' William asked.

She turned to William. 'Height seeks information on Frost's shady activities. He doesn't seem to believe it was a mugging gone wrong. He's looking for a motive and I intend to provide one.'

William stroked his moustache, twirling a corner between his fingers. 'Hmm... Risky.'

'We'll also feed him hand-picked information from our investigation into the disappearances of these girls.' Sévère gestured toward the neat stacks of letters on a shelf.

'In hopes he'll reciprocate with updates on all active cases of missing girls?' William asked, eyebrows raised.

Sévère shook his head. 'That would be rather naive, Mr Burroughs. We're well aware that relying on the police to investigate such matters is pointless. No, what I want is to rub Height's nose into this stinking pile of injustice. I want him riled enough to take action. Our good inspector isn't stupid enough to believe the police and the magistrates can or will do anything about this.'

'You think he'd go against his chief? Take the law in his own hands?' William asked.

'What law?' Olivia snarled back. 'There *is* no such law he or I could take in our own hands!' Abruptly, she paused, her mind stumbling over a potential ally. Someone who could offer her not only help but a solution.

Her gaze slid to Sévère. She'd have to find a way to keep this from him. He was too perceptive. While she was certain he was aware of her nightly excursions, she was equally confident he didn't know their exact nature.

Now, she needed only to—

'Olivia?' Sévère's voice pulled her back to the present.

'Yes?'

He regarded her with a frown. 'Have you been listening?'

'My apologies. You were saying?'

'How do you suggest we approach Height?'

Olivia chewed her cheek, considering how to kill two flies in one strike. She looked at Sévère and grinned. 'I'll pay him a visit and propose a trade of information.'

She watched his throat work as he lowered his gaze, a wry smile on his lips. That was how it had begun between Olivia and him: a trade of information.

A soft knock at the door cut through her thoughts. Netty stepped into the office with a letter in her hand. 'This was delivered by a gentleman. He didn't give his name.' She sniffed, glanced at William and the empty plates, and asked if more refreshments were required.

'No, thank you. You may leave,' Sévère said as he slit open the letter with a pen knife.

When Netty had left the office, he offered the missive to Olivia.

We have a deal. Meet me at Cannon and Shadwell tonight at eleven o'clock.

'And so it begins,' he murmured.

Olivia entered the police station and came to an abrupt halt. What only weeks prior had been a worm-eaten wood floor was now covered in shiny black-and-white checkered linoleum. The walls, though, still bore the same old peeling wallpaper in questionable colours. The funds must have run out or some higher-up had decided that one improvement per decade was sufficient for Division H Headquarters.

Her heels clicked across the new flooring as she approached Inspector Height's office. She knocked at the door, counted to three, and without invitation turned the knob and stepped inside. Stale air, saturated with cigarette smoke and scents of hardboiled eggs and cold cabbage smacked her in the face. The detective himself looked up from his desk, stacks of papers flanking a checkered handkerchief with four eggs and a sandwich. His hand holding a peeled egg hung frozen before his mouth.

'Mrs Sévère,' he said with annoyance in his tone. 'I was under the impression that a closed door can't be mistaken for an invitation to enter.' He ate the egg without offering her a seat.

'I believe we can help each other, Inspector.' She pulled out a chair and took a seat across from him, her gloved hands resting on a well-worn armrest.

Height raised an eyebrow. 'You might think I owe you, given... Well, given that I arrested your innocent husband. But—'

She made a sharp motion with her hand. 'I didn't come to stoke any feelings of guilt you might have. I'm willing to provide you with... insights into the late Chief Magistrate Frost's affairs.'

He wiped his hands and sat up straighter. 'Go on.'

'In exchange, I'd like information on corrupt officials involved in the white slave trade, and any information the police have on our missing girls. We've sorted through all the letters we received, and now have more than a hundred sixty cases of suspected abductions, more than half of them of underage girls.'

Height ran his fingers over his moustache, his expression darkening. '*A hundred and sixty*? How are you going to... never mind. What makes you think I have access to that kind of information? I investigate homicides.'

Olivia's smile was a thin, calculated line. 'I believe you're a man who likes to keep his ears open and consider all angles, Inspector. I'm even willing to bet you have more integrity than most of your colleagues.'

Height's gaze lingered on hers. Finally, he spoke, his words measured. 'I'll share what I can. But I must warn you, it's not much. I'll look into Kew. From what I've heard, the house in Kew is something of a clearing centre for London's white slave trade. But I can't conduct an official investigation, do you understand that?'

Olivia's eyes flashed with anger, 'And why would that be, I wonder.'

Height sighed and lowered his voice to a whisper, 'It's protected by... men. And I'm not just talking about police.'

'And what are you going to do about it, Inspector?'

Height's face twisted with a mixture of shame and frustration. 'It's not a battle I'm equipped to win.' His eyes locked onto hers. 'If I do this, I want everything you have on Frost, everything you can dig up. And I need your discretion.'

He held out his hand. She grasped it and said, 'Likewise.'

'We will not discuss this here. Invite me to your office in the next couple of days. I will expect details on the Chief Magistrate.'

'And I will expect details on these missing girls. Here's a list with their names and addresses, and the dates and circumstances of their disappearance.' She placed an envelope on his desk.

Nodding once, Height picked up another egg and began peeling off the shell. 'Now, if you will let me finish my lunch, I'd be much obliged.'

She had mixed feelings when she left the police station but tucked all emotions away to consider her and Sévère's evening plans for meeting the Midwife. They would need to discuss tactics for infiltrating the Midwife's network of associates to identify and locate the woman who abducted Alice Green. The next meeting with Height had to happen soon. They'd have to provide the Midwife with genuine information on ongoing cases of missing girls. But was this the fastest way to gain her trust? They couldn't inform Height of their undercover work. To involve a policeman in their actual plans would be much too risky.

But what about...

Oh, but of course! Olivia made a sharp turn and hailed a cab to Percy Circus.

She rang the bell at a corner house just across from Baptist Church. A servant admitted her and led her to the parlour, letting her know that Mrs Muir would be with her shortly. The room was as crammed with paraphernalia as it had been the first time she'd visited. Vases bore artificial flowers. Familiar porcelain figurines and ebony statues still populated the floor, the mantelpiece, cupboards and window sills. Large masks hung on all four walls, each with bristly hair and the smile of a shark.

'Didn't think I'd have the pleasure of seeing you again, Mrs

Sévère.' A small, thin woman in a chair was wheeled into the room. 'I brought Addie.' She patted the hand of the young maid who was pushing her chair, then waved bony fingers at Olivia. 'Please, sit, sit.'

'Mrs Muir, Miss Shepherd, I'm...' With a sigh, Olivia brushed wrinkles from her skirt, looked at Addie Shepherd, and cleared her throat. 'I am sorry I... I don't even know how to begin. He's a murderer, yes, but also a good friend of yours and he's in jail because of me. And for that, I am truly sorry.'

Addie Sheperd looked slightly confused.

Mrs Muir smiled. 'Well, well. It was either him or your innocent husband. You did the right thing.' She spoke to Olivia in a tone one usually reserved for a child.

'He's made a deal with the magistrates,' Miss Shepherd said. 'He's not allowed to work as a dye chemist anymore, not that anyone would have him after what he did, but he's free. He helped put more than a dozen murderers away.'

Olivia nodded. She knew as much but she couldn't afford to ask Height or any other official as to the whereabouts of Albert Perkin, a convicted serial poisoner who'd turned on his clients in exchange for freedom. Although one could argue that he merely fashioned poison chemises and that they, like any knife, were but a tool. Do we put all blacksmiths in jail? Of course not.

If Perkin had only made poison undergarments, a jury might not have found him guilty of murder. But there was the small detail of him attempting the murder of Mrs Appleton — the housekeeper of his half-sister. The man ended up accidentally overdosing the chemise, which had not reached his intended target but had instead found his half-sister, resulting in her death and that of Sévère's friend Dr Johnston, who had attended to the dying woman. Much to the chagrin of Perkin, Mrs Appleton was left unscathed.

Had Sévère not been jailed for Johnston's murder, Perkin might never have been caught.

And now, Olivia needed the help of the man she had put in chains. Chances were he'd turn her away or report her to the police.

Thirteen

THE WINDOWS of the brougham were streaked with rain, making it nearly impossible to see if anyone was approaching from the darkness. Olivia felt trapped. Impatience made her skin itch.

Sévère checked his watch. 'Ten past eleven,' he grumbled.

'We should leave,' she said. 'We don't want to give her the impression we're desperate.'

He snapped his watch shut and slipped it back into his waistcoat pocket. 'Back home,' he called up to Higgins as he knocked his cane against the brougham's roof.

Just as Higgins clicked his tongue and the chestnuts leaned their weight into their harnesses, Olivia spotted a stout figure step into the lamplight outside, waving an arm. 'Stop!' Olivia called to Higgins and pointed Sévère's gaze at the Midwife hurrying toward them.

Breathing heavily, the woman clambered into the carriage and sat across from them. She brushed droplets from her sleeves and wiped her wet hands on a kerchief. 'Well, then. What have you got for me?'

Olivia said, 'You are late.'

'So?' Raised eyebrows. An expression that told them she'd not apologise for such a trifle.

'We have established trust with over a hundred mothers who have daughters aged between nine and eighteen, all of them virgins. We know that you take twenty shillings for examining a girl and writing a certificate of intact maidenhood. We offer twenty-two shillings per head if you help us find buyers for the girls.' Sévère's tone was matter-of-fact as though talking about the sale of livestock. Which, in the eyes of some, it probably was.

The Midwife blinked once, tucked away her kerchief, and replied, 'I can't get you buyers for that many girls.'

Olivia snorted. 'Come now. I've been in the trade long enough to know the constant demand for fresh faces. Especially now with military deployments affecting business. Young men about to leave and fight for Queen and country wish for a special kind of entertainment before they die.'

'And we all know that your side of the business is flourishing since vamped-up virgins have started glutting the market,' Sévère added, looking bored.

The Midwife paused, eyed them with a flash of appreciation in her eyes, and nodded slowly. 'I'll see what I can do. But my customers usually like to know how these girls are recruited.' She looked expectantly at Olivia. It was always women who procured girls.

'Oh, I have my methods.' Olivia smiled mildly. 'Advertisements for housemaids, promises of etiquette lessons, invitations to exclusive tea parties. You know how easily young girls are lured by the promise of a better life, a new dress, a pretty hat, or a cheap piece of jewellery. Once they're in, they rarely leave. Ruined, no money, no friends in the city, nowhere to turn.' She shrugged.

'You seem to understand the business well enough,' the Midwife said. 'Now, about your methods — how do you ensure the girls are... suitable?'

'Ah-ah,' Sévère interrupted, gaze reprimanding. 'We agreed to an exchange of services and information. We did a lot of talking. It's your turn now, Mrs...?'

'Edith Sharpe,' she replied without hesitation.

Sévère gave her a look that said he wasn't naive enough to believe she'd given her real name. 'Let us discuss clients, then. We are looking for regulars. Gentlemen who would take one or two maidens a month are preferred. But we're also willing to supply girls to Kew. We've heard the payment is better.'

The Midwife leaned back, her face now hidden in shadow. 'I might be able to be of assistance there if you can handle... reluctant merchandise.'

Olivia gazed out the rain-streaked window at the blurry spots of lit street lamps in the darkness. She forced a bored tone into her voice. 'Reluctant girls are part of the business. Nothing a little persuasion can't handle. You know that as well as I do. You're wasting our time, *Mrs Sharpe*.'

The Midwife cleared her throat but before she could reply, Olivia cut across her. 'How many girls can you examine with two days' notice?'

After a moment of silence, the woman replied, 'Easily a dozen in an afternoon.'

'That should suffice. Now about the other issue. We told you we can provide you with information on ongoing police investigations. There's one you might be interested in. But we want something in return,' Olivia said, then motioned to Sévère.

He waited for the Midwife to give him a nod before he said, 'Procuresses who claim to be members of the Virtuous Maiden Society are currently being investigated by the police for the recent disappearance of a girl by the name of Alice Green. You, too, are under investigation. While we would be able — with the right motivation of course — to nudge the attention away from you, the police have their teeth in the Virtuous Maiden Society as they were involved in the disappearance of another girl who is the daughter of a police sergeant. You should consider doing yourself the favour of giving away the procuresses. We'll provide your information to the right man at Scotland Yard while ensuring you are protected. What we want from you in return is to find Alice Green. If we can show to all those concerned mothers that the Sévère & Sévère private detective agency is trustworthy and skilled in retrieving missing girls quickly, we'll find dozens more mothers willing to allow us into their homes and entrust us with the safety of their girls.'

'Which means more profit for all of us,' Olivia added with a smile.

'I don't know anything about this Alice Green,' the Midwife said a little too quickly.

Olivia sighed, looked at Sévère and said, 'Then we are finished here.'

'Yes, we are, darling.' He pushed open the carriage door with a nod at the Midwife.

The woman hesitated for a moment, chuckled, and said, 'We'll see.' Then she stepped out onto the street and walked away without another word.

Sévère knocked his cane against the roof. 'It's time, Higgins.'

The brougham lurched forward, then came to a halt after turning a corner. Higgins jumped down on the street and disappeared as Olivia climbed up to his seat and grabbed the reins. She'd done this only twice under supervision and never without Higgins.

Holding her breath, she tapped the whip to the horses' backs.

Olivia felt as though she'd barely slept when she woke the next morning and hurried through her breakfast with a stoic Sévère as her companion.

He held his head high and maintained a sharp arrogance in his glare when Higgins helped him down the flights of stairs and into the wheeling chair on the ground floor, where the usually quiet waiting room was overflowing with grieving and desperate families. Most of them kept their gaze politely averted when they spotted Sévère in Higgin's arms, but all ogled him when he wheeled his chair past the waiting room and into the office.

Olivia took a seat next to him and asked Higgins to call in the first client.

First, Mrs Miller — a gaunt mother clutching a worn rag doll. 'Emily never went anywhere without this. Until that day,' she said, eyes hard as marble, and went on to describe a woman with a 'kind face' who'd offered Emily a job as a maid.

Next, Mrs Thomson, hands red and cracked from laundering, recounted how her daughter Sarah was approached outside her school by a well-dressed lady offering lessons in etiquette.

And on it went, this parade of grief flowing through the office doors of Sévère & Sévère Private Detective Agency.

The Coopers: twin sisters, one missing. The remaining twin, hollow-eyed, described a woman with a 'hypnotic voice' who promised the sisters fame on the stage.

The Blackwoods: a brother, barely containing his anger, spoke of his sister's fascination with a new dress shop that had opened in their neighbourhood. 'The owner always had the prettiest dresses in the window,' he seethed. 'And *that* woman offered her one of them for a 'little game with a gentleman.' I warned her and now she's gone!'

The Fosters: a mother, twisting her handkerchief, described how her daughter had received an invitation to an exclusive tea party. 'We thought it was her chance to move up in society,' she sobbed.

The Clarks: a stoic father recounted how his daughter was offered a position as a lady's maid. 'The woman spoke so eloquently, we never suspected...'

The Wrights: a young boy, the missing girl's brother, piped up. 'I saw her get into a carriage. It had a strange symbol on the door, like a bird in a cage.'

When at last Netty entered to tell them they had no more clients for the day, Olivia sagged in her chair and groaned. 'This is hopeless!' She rubbed her burning eyes and cast a glance at Sévère.

'It seems these procuresses are cut from the same cloth. They present themselves as well-heeled ladies, dangling promises of a better life before their unsuspecting victims. And they're clever in their choice of hunting grounds,' he said to Olivia. 'I'd be most grateful if you could send for Higgins to help me to my private quarters now.'

Olivia noticed Sévère's growing unease, which seemed to be more than emotional exhaustion. She cast a look at the windows, to the waning daylight, and realised that he must be as famished as she was. Or perhaps his pain had returned?

As Sévère and Higgins were leaving the office, Olivia suddenly recalled Inspector Height's impending arrival. 'Oh, blast it!' She hastened to catch up with the two men and said to Sévère, 'Height will be here shortly. Shall we have a quick bite in your library?'

Sévère's only response was a tired nod.

As night settled in, Olivia found herself at her desk, facing Inspector Height with his hat in his lap and a glass of brandy in his hand.

He shifted uncomfortably in his chair, his eyes darting once to the door and then back to Olivia.

She leaned forward, her elbows on the desk, fingers steepled. 'My husband is occupied elsewhere. You're here about Frost. Shall we begin?'

Height's tension eased somewhat. 'You mentioned having information about his...activities.'

'Frost was a regular patron of several brothels in Whitechapel. If he went elsewhere, I have no information about that. He was known to have a particular preference for very young girls. Children, to be specific.'

Height's nostrils flared. He ran a finger across his dark moustache, eyes unfocused.

Olivia continued, 'I could provide specifics, such as locations and names. But we both know that this will never result in anything but further abuse of the victims, this time under the pretence of a murder inquiry.'

She kept staring at him, allowing the silence to linger.

He cleared his throat, shifting uncomfortably before speaking. 'Are you telling me to stop, Mrs Sévère? Wouldn't that make you look just a bit too suspicious?'

'Do you know how many girls Linton Frost raped, Inspector?'

'I couldn't say. Perhaps a dozen?'

She offered him a chilling smile. 'He already had a reputation when I was only nine, so it's reasonable to assume that he's been doing this for more than a decade. It is also quite reasonable to assume that he's been abusing one underage girl each week, every week, for ten years. Care to calculate the total?'

Height blanched.

Olivia stood and leaned across the desk, her fists digging into the polished mahogany. Her voice was cold and precise as she delivered her chilling advice to the inspector.

'Your suspect is among the families of the roughly five hundred girls Frost violated. Consider them all. Don't disregard from your investigation those he assaulted years ago. I can assure you...' She fixed Height with an unwavering stare. 'We *never* forget what has been done to us.'

The inspector's face drained of all colour. He swallowed hard as if struggling against an invisible grip on his throat. Revulsion and shame shone in his dark eyes. 'I... I had no idea it was so widespread.'

'Didn't you?' Olivia shot at him. 'Or did you choose not to see, just like all your dear colleagues?'

Height's shoulders sagged. When he met her gaze again, a trace of vulnerability flickered in his expression. 'The law...,' he began hesitantly. 'It's not equipped to handle this.'

Olivia leaned back, her expression softening a touch. 'And that's why Frost's killer did the world a service. That monster would have kept raping girls, and no one — not you, not any policeman, jury, judge or magistrate — would have held him accountable. Ever.'

'We're talking about murder, Mrs Sévère! I cannot simply disregard—'

'Do you have any idea how many girls take their own lives after men like Frost are through with them?' she growled.

'I investigate murders, not suicides.'

'By all means, continue hiding behind your precious equivocations!'

He smacked his hat against the desk. 'Blast it all! Do you

imagine I'm satisfied with the current state of the law? It's letting these girls down, yes! It's failing those without influence or means, for pity's sake!'

She watched him as a tiny smile curled the corners of her mouth. 'And what are you going to do about it?'

'Why do you keep asking me this?'

'Are you not a man of the law?' she countered, her tone challenging.

Noting his puzzled expression, she said, 'It makes you the only person with a voice, Inspector. I don't have one. None of these girls have one. Prostitutes certainly don't have one. Women in general don't. You sit in my office, making demands. You complain about the law's inadequacies. Why don't you stop moaning and start doing something?'

'And what would you have me do?'

She placed her elbows back on the desk, fixing Height with an intense gaze. 'Use your murder investigation as a cover to help us find the people responsible for the recent abductions of more than a hundred girls.'

Part Three

As I was in bed
Some little forths gave in my head.
I forth of one, I forth of two;
But first of all I forth of you.

Letter of a thirteen-year-old Derby girl to her alcoholic mother who sold her into prostitution for three pounds sterling. Published by W.T. Stead in the Pall Mall Gazette, 1885

Fourteen

THE DARK INTERIOR of the hansom cab, the steady clip-clop of hooves on wet cobblestones, the gentle patter of rain, and the inky darkness outside — all matched Olivia's sombre mood as she journeyed towards Albert Perkins' residence. Her mind still dwelled on the faces and desperate pleas of the family members of the missing girls, each tale more heart-wrenching than the last.

A dozen families, a dozen abducted daughters. The weight of their anguish left Olivia drained in body and spirit. She and Sévère had listened to their stories, seeking a common thread that could help them solve the case, but there was only the most obvious link: pretty women with silver tongues and their promises of respectable work, adventure, and an escape from the day-to-day drudgery. Beyond this, no clear pattern had emerged. They'd hoped for a mention of the Virtuous Maiden Society or the Midwife, but neither had surfaced in the families' testimonies.

. . .

The cab bounced over a pothole, jolting Olivia from her thoughts. With doubt gnawing at her, she stared out at the rain-slicked streets. Would they ever find any of these girls? The vastness of London seemed to swallow them whole. When Olivia was a prostitute, more than half of the working girls she knew were underage. Most of those pretty, young faces disappeared after three or four years. Suicide or disease took them. Many men believed that raping an untouched child would cure them of venereal disease. And so they spread it further and further. In this damned city, the murder of young girls was committed inch by excruciating inch.

The more Olivia thought about the task ahead, the more insurmountable it appeared. How does one change an entire society?

Certainly not by adhering to etiquette. Which, in her case, meant keeping her mouth shut.

Forever.

Angry, she kicked at the dashboard. The cabbie grumbled an insult at her.

She ignored him.

Giving up wasn't an option. These families had placed their trust in her and Sévère, their last hope after the police failed them. Olivia rubbed her brow in frustration. She had to believe there was a way, no matter how elusive it seemed at the moment.

She thought of Sévère, how he'd spent the day listening to their clients, his jaw clenched in pain. She hadn't known how serious his pain was until the previous night when she entered his bedroom to ask if he could trace the raven's wings on her back again. After knocking and not receiving an answer, she'd stepped inside cautiously, her footsteps muffled by the thick rug.

The room was dimly lit by a single oil lamp, its flame casting long, undulating shadows across the walls. A thin veil of opium smoke hung in the air. He lay on his bed, eyes half-closed, lost in a haze of pain and drugs. His usual sharp, controlled demeanour had melted away, replaced by a vulnerable softness that tugged at something in her chest.

'Sévère,' she'd whispered, cautiously approaching the bed. 'Are you all right?'

His eyes fluttered open and rolled toward her but didn't seem to be able to find focus. A wince of pain as he attempted to sit up. 'I'm sorry, my dear,' he murmured, his words soft and stretching. 'I'm afraid I'm in no state for marital gymnastics.'

'Really, Sévère. Your humour knows only one direction.'

Seeing him like this, she felt a pang of concern and frustration. Part of her wanted to scold him for not asking for her help, while another part knew why he hadn't: She wasn't someone to lean on.

Her eyes drifted to the nightstand, where a small stack of books sat. She approached, ran her fingers along their spines and selected a collection of Whitman's poetry. The choice felt bold, even rebellious — Whitman's free verse and celebration of the self seemed at odds with her world, yet strangely fitting for their unconventional relationship.

She hesitated a moment, then gingerly lowered herself onto the bed next to him, aware of his vulnerable state, the heat radiating from his body, the soft sound of his breathing.

'Shall I read to you?' she whispered.

There was a long pause before he said, 'If you wish.'

She opened the book and began to read, her voice low and soothing, 'I am not contained between my hat and boots, I have said that the soul is not more than the body, and I have said that the body is not more than the soul, and nothing, not God, is greater to one than one's self is.'

As she read, his breathing grew deeper, more regular. She

became overly aware of every small movement, every shift of his body.

Here, in his room, on his bed, Whitman's words seemed to take on a new meaning, speaking to their complicated relationship, the barriers she'd built, and the connections she tried to deny.

Olivia continued reading until he had fallen asleep, her voice a gentle whisper. When she finally rose and slipped out of the room, she made herself leave her profound sense of companionship behind.

She would not allow herself to be weak around a man.

Never again.

Casting reverie aside as the cab rattled on through the dreary night, she steeled herself for her encounter with Albert Perkins. With any luck, he would provide the insights she needed. If not, she would find another way.

She didn't know what she'd expected but the small pang of disappointment on seeing Albert Perkin sporting a beard certainly wasn't it.

He caught her gaze snagging on his mouth. 'Good evening, Mrs Sévère. Addie informed me to expect you. If you're curious about the facial hair — it serves to conceal my harelip. And my notoriety, for which I owe you no small measure of gratitude.'

And there it was: the bitterness she had expected. 'I don't know if you me or yourself to thank for your current predicament.' She kept her voice as light as if extending an invitation to dance.

A flash of a smile crossed his face. 'Well, I'd always meant to invite you for tea. Shall we?' He motioned for her to step into a small room that served as his living quarters — a combined kitchen, sitting area, and bedroom.

They sat on worm-eaten stools. He poured tea into two mismatched cups.

With her eyes fixed on Perkin's face, she began. 'I'm aware that you might be the last person willing to help me, but there is no one else with your expertise I can ask.'

He snorted. 'Are you planning to kill your husband and need my help?'

She burst out chuckling. 'Dear god, no! I actually like the man, much to my surprise.' She bit her tongue, took a sip of her tea, and started spinning a tale to extract information from the notorious poison murderer, 'Six women, all dead within a year. Each different, yet connected by a thread the police conveniently ignore.'

'And you think I did it. Are you mad? I was in gaol only recently.'

'I am quite aware of your incarceration, Mr Perkin.' She stood and paced the room, her skirts rustling. 'The six women were prostitutes, and I knew them all. Mary Beth, food poisoning, they said. Louisa fell from a window. Sarah drowned in the Thames. Eliza had a heart attack. Catherine choked on her vomit. And poor Agnes was found face down in a puddle, no cause of death given.'

His brow wrinkled in confusion. 'The police—'

'Couldn't give a fig,' she spat. 'Just more whores off the streets, as far as they're concerned.'

'But you think...what precisely?'

'I suspect someone's killing us off, one by one. And I'm trying *not* to be next.'

'Would you please stop running around the room like a headless chicken?'

Groaning, she sat back down and wrapped her hands around her teacup.

Perkin leaned forward, elbows on the tabletop. 'What makes you so sure they were murdered?'

She tapped her index finger against the table's worn surface as she spoke, 'Instinct. These women were survivors. They didn't make stupid mistakes. They don't jump into rivers or fall out windows. And we all knew each other.'

'Have you seen the police reports? The coroner's findings?'

Olivia barked a laugh. 'A woman like me taken seriously by the police and shown evidence or reports?'

'So you came to me? For what exactly?'

'You're the expert in... shall we say, unconventional methods of dispatch.'

His fingers travelled to the scar on his upper lip, his gaze focused on her cup. For a brief, terrifying moment she wondered if he'd poisoned the tea. But Addie knew that she was here, and Perkin knew Addie knew. He would not resort to such clumsiness if he wanted Olivia out of the way.

'It's possible, I suppose,' he said. 'But to kill six women in such varied ways...'

'If someone wanted to hide a pattern, that's how they'd do it, don't you think?'

Perkin nodded slowly. 'True enough. But how to administer it, if it was indeed poison? In their food? Their drink? What would have been used?' He spoke more to himself than to her.

Olivia replied, 'I don't know. That's why I'm asking you.'

Perkin's eyes narrowed. 'There are ways,' he murmured but did not elaborate. He paused, looked up at her, and asked, 'A poisoning during the business transaction would be most likely. Something slipped into their food or drink should be easy.'

'I doubt it,' Olivia cut him off before he could follow that line of thought any further. 'These women were experienced.

They wouldn't have taken anything the client offered. All food and drink are purchased through the brothel. Bringing your own is as preposterous as showing your naked arse on Victoria Station.'

'Is it? I had no clue. Then how?'

Her mind raced. She needed to steer the conversation without arousing suspicion. 'What about...contact poisons?'

He tilted his head, gifting her a sardonic smile. 'That's not going to work.'

'Why not?'

'Well, if the murderer has a death wish, then certainly. I'd highly recommend contact poison for unclothed, sweaty, whole-body interaction.' He didn't even blush.

Olivia grew more cautious. 'But then it must have been...I don't know. Could one use a tiny needle?'

He dug his fingers through his beard. 'Possibly. But injecting someone without them noticing? That's quite a challenge.'

She inhaled, then held her breath as if on the cusp of sharing an idea but hesitating. Averting her eyes, she murmured, 'Hmm. I came across something... Well. It might sound far-fetched. Then again...if someone had told me a year ago that a chemise could be used as a murder weapon, I would have laughed.' She swung her gaze back to him. 'I read about a poison ring with a concealed needle. Coated in a substance like snake venom. One quick jab — easily disguised as an accidental scratch — and the poison enters the bloodstream.'

Something bloomed in his expression. She couldn't quite place it.

'Ah, I see where you're heading,' he said with a hint of amusement. 'A ring with a little needle and a concealed compartment, filled with a swift-acting toxin. It's a romanticised notion, and rather impractical. Consider the limited amount of poison a ring can hold and the risk of self-poisoning during application. I doubt this was the method of murder. Curious, though. I hadn't pegged you as someone to put stock in fanciful ideas.'

Olivia bristled at his dismissive tone. She rose, pushing her empty cup aside with more force than necessary. 'Don't lecture me about impracticality There must be poisons that mimic natural causes of death. You've used one yourself, for heaven's sake!'

Unfazed by her outburst, he leaned back and regarded her. 'Very well. Let's entertain your theory. Suppose your killer used cyanide. He'd need to create a superficial scratch on the victim's skin and apply cyanide salt. To ensure success, he'd require one and a half grains. Do you believe a prostitute wouldn't notice that quantity of salt in a wound? No, I thought not. However, dissolving less than a tenth of that in a small volume of water and injecting it directly into the bloodstream? Yes, that would do.'

She returned to her seat. 'So I'd have to find out if the bodies have injection marks. Wouldn't the police have caught it?'

He shrugged. 'Not necessarily. You said the police don't give a fig about the deaths of prostitutes. Besides, the injection site needn't be conspicuous.'

'So a tiny needle, dissolved cyanide, and...injected in an area with dense body hair — armpit, groin — that could be the killer's method?'

Perkin inclined his head in agreement, but there was a flicker of suspicion in his gaze. 'Or any number of other possibilities. It's late, Mrs Sévère. You should return home, lest your husband think we're having an affair.'

A rather abrupt request to leave, she thought. But she nodded and thanked him for his time. Before stepping out onto the street, she turned back to face him. 'Wouldn't the purchase of cyanide salts require special authorisation? There should be records.'

'Not necessarily. Any jeweller or photographer could procure a few grains from an apothecary.' His gaze sharpened and held hers.

'Just like aconitine,' she replied. It was that substance Perkin had used to fashion his contact poison murder weapon Her words had the intended effect: His face darkened, and his interest in Olivia's peculiar line of questioning guttered.

Fifteen

OLIVIA STOOD BEFORE HER VANITY, her fingers flying over the buttons of her blouse. Early morning light filtered through the curtains and cast a pale glow across her cheekbones. She paused, her gaze fixed on her reflection, wondering if determination alone would get her anywhere.

Her attention drifted to the drawer where she kept a fake moustache and mutton chops. Should she put on the disguise of a male assistant to a jeweller to be granted access to the tools she needed without arousing suspicion? Or would the so-called weaker sex be less suspicious when purchasing poison?

She'd need two stops: one for half a grain of cyanide salt, another for a small syringe with the finest needle available. Simple items that, if combined and shoved into the armpit of a monster, would improve the lives of a handful of girls.

She finished dressing, smoothed down her skirts, and paused. What she was about to do wasn't like Frost's murder — a death she'd been involved in, yes, but not caused directly.

This would be different. This would be done by her hand and only her's, plain and simple. Without Sévère's knowledge.

While most days, her fury gave her the certainty she could kill a man, today wasn't filled with such surety.

Her doubts didn't stem from the consequences of her actions. She was prepared to face gaol, the gallows, or transportation to the colonies — it mattered little. What mattered was finally being free of feeling like a victim. Finally feeling that she could make a difference in this world.

But who would be her mark? Olivia paced the room, her mind sifting through a rogues' gallery of despicable men she'd encountered in her life. It had to be someone whose death would send shock waves through London's upper crust, and someone whose absence would make the world safer for girls and women like herself.

She paused by the window, gazing out at the awakening city. She would choose carefully. And then she would show no mercy.

As she pinned up her hair, she caught her gaze in the looking glass once more. The woman staring back at her seemed changed, harder somehow.

Smiling, she whispered, 'Never relent.'

Olivia knew she stood on the precipice of an irrevocable decision, about to venture into uncharted moral territory. But as she thought of the law that had failed to protect the vulnerable time and again — because it was never intended to protect the weak, only the powerful — she felt not a flicker of remorse.

She only hoped she had the skill and strength to carry out the task.

Before making her way to the dining room, she gathered herself, mentally rehearsing her ruse for the apothecary she would visit later that day.

~

Olivia gazed across the breakfast table at her husband, noting the deep lines around his eyes and the slight tremor in his hand as he lifted a teacup to his mouth. His usual proud posture had given way to a subtle slump.

'I've been considering offering Higgins another raise,' he announced, voice rough. 'The man's taken on a fair bit more responsibility than that of a coachman.'

Olivia nodded as she pushed a piece of toast around her plate, a greasy trail of butter in its wake. The clink of silverware against porcelain filled the silence between them.

'He's practically my steward now, not to mention his work as our assistant detective,' Sévère continued. 'We should compensate him accordingly.'

'I agree,' she said, her gaze drifting to the empty chair where Rose should have been seated. The girl had taken to eating in her room more often than not these days, another of her new behaviours Olivia found increasingly worrying.

Sévère's gaze narrowed. 'What's troubling you?'

She blinked. 'Nothing in particular. I agree with you about Higgins. He's certainly earned it.'

As Sévère fell into silence, Olivia wondered when she'd last had a proper conversation with Rose. The girl had turned to haunting their home, flitting from room to room and speaking in short bursts of anger.

Rose had never been the same since her mother sold her to Linton Frost. Even after her rescue, she remained withdrawn, and though their stay at the Isle of Wight had brightened her spirits, they'd darkened again once she returned to London, and grew even more erratic when she began her apprenticeship with Higgins.

Rose trudged through her days, finding joy neither in her lessons with the coachman nor at school. Was this normal for a nine-year-old? Or was this the inevitable aftermath of a child rescued from a brothel? Each attempt to reach out was met with single-word answers, downcast eyes, and the sharp retort of a slammed door.

Sévère pushed his plate aside, wiped his mouth on a napkin, and checked the time on his pocket watch. 'Forty minutes until we meet our first client. Time to talk about Higgin's discovery.'

She nodded and popped a bite of breakfast into her mouth without tasting it, her thoughts on the coachman's uncomfortable shifting and sudden fascination with his boots whenever she tried to discuss Rose's strange reaction to her apprenticeship.

'I've made a list,' Sévère continued as he unfolded a piece of paper he'd pulled from his trouser pocket. 'I'll ask Higgins to copy the White Lilly's public records and financial statements.'

When they'd met the Midwife two nights ago, Higgins had followed the woman to the northern end of Commercial Street — one of the few affluent areas in Whitechapel. He saw her entering a house bearing a bronze plaque engraved 'The White Lilly Foundation.' She hadn't exited until more than two hours later.

The next day, Sévère learned that the White Lilly was a registered charity for orphaned girls.

Olivia couldn't shake her worries about Rose. She barely got two words out of her these days.

'...all board members and major donors should be mentioned in there. Then we trace larger financial transactions between the White Lilly and other registered charities and businesses...'

Twice she'd followed the girl, lurking in the shadows to spy on Higgins' teaching methods. There was nothing untoward in the coachman's patient instruction. But tonight she would have answers.

'...and especially all orphanages they work with. *That* is

where they get their girls. Undereducated, desperate for attention and a decent meal, and easy to lure into prostitution because I'm sure they've been told from the very start how worthless they are, most having been born out of wedlock. Olivia?' Sévère's voice cut through her reverie. 'Why are you torturing the napkin?'

She dropped the napkin she'd been folding into a compact square and looked up at Sévère. 'I'm worried about Rose.'

Sévère leaned back in his chair, wincing slightly as he shifted. 'The girl has been through a great deal.'

There was no use in asking his opinion on this matter. Olivia stood and said, 'I'll spend a few nights watching the White Lilly. See who's coming and going.'

'I'd like Higgins to—'

'No. Not for this. He doesn't know anyone in this business. I do. We need names.'

Someone bumped into Olivia's shoulder, jostling her from her thoughts.

'Excuse me!' a man grumbled and pushed past her into the apothecary. She realised with a start that she'd been rooted to the spot, staring at the door for god knows how long. Her mind had been circling around methods of murder, and the risk of being apprehended before she could act. All because she'd been foolish enough to seek advice from a known serial poisoner who was now cooperating with the police.

Had she left her wits in the gutters? Why on earth had she entertained the notion that Perkin, of all people, could be trusted? Desperation for justice — or revenge to be perfectly honest — had clouded her judgement, leaving her to act impulsively rather than strategically. The urge to slap herself for such recklessness was overwhelming. Consulting Perkin while keeping everything hidden from Sévère? Purchasing a lethal poison and a syringe — incriminating, to say the least — before she was even certain about her mark's identity?

Olivia turned away from the storefront and made her way back home, admonishing herself for behaving like a lunatic. She was a detective, for heaven's sake! A businesswoman. Her keen intellect had always been a source of pride. Her wits had saved her countless times. Whenever she lost them, she'd become...

She stopped. The throng of pedestrians parted around her. A stream of men, women, and children oblivious to her dark thoughts.

Rage simmered within her.

A victim.

Whenever she allowed fear to take over, allowed her wits to falter, she became a victim. Again. All it had taken was the sting of a bee and a mouthful of cold words from her mother.

Olivia shook out her clenched fingers, set her jaw, and decided to resume her target practice.

The heavy curtains were drawn, hiding condensation running down the window panes and muffling the clatter of hooves and wheels and the murmur of pedestrians on the street outside the office. Sévère sat in his high-backed leather chair, feigning mild curiosity as Inspector Height paced before them. Olivia leaned against the mahogany desk, her dark eyes following the man's movement.

'Two more reports of wealthy gentlemen being stalked here in Whitechapel,' Height said. 'This mysterious figure... I hope he's only a stalker and not the man who stabbed Chief Magistrate Frost to death. Otherwise, we may have a serial murderer on our hands who could be planning his next kill.'

Olivia felt Sévère's sharp gaze upon her. Their eyes met for a heartbeat before he turned back to Height.

'That's certainly concerning, Inspector,' Sévère replied. 'Have you any leads?'

Height shook his head. 'Nothing concrete.' Then he narrowed a considering glance at Sévère. Everyone in the room knew the words sitting on Height's tongue. *You have a motive. Where were you on the night of Frost's death?*

Olivia's fingers tightened on the edge of the desk. 'Well, I doubt we can be of any help.'

With some effort, Height faked an understanding smile.

Sévère knocked once on the wooden armrest of his chair. 'While this is undoubtedly important for you, Inspector, we have little to add. We should discuss our ongoing investigation into the missing girls.'

'Of course. Have you made any progress?'

Olivia straightened, grateful for the change in subject. Before she could reply, Sévère said, 'We've traced several disappearances to a common source. We're currently collecting evidence against that person.'

'Do you have names?' Height asked.

'Aliases,' Olivia replied curtly. She caught Sévère's glance. They'd agreed to keep Height at arm's length and reveal only what was absolutely necessary. Their plans and methods, their use of the Midwife as an informant, Sévère's work with William to suggest amendments to the law — all of it off-limits.

The Inspector could not be trusted to keep their secrets.

'I see.' Height pinched the bridge of his nose, sighing. 'We're on the same side, Mr and Mrs Sévère. I was under the assumption you'd share information with me.' He threw a measuring glance at Olivia.

She bit back a sharp retort. The same side? The man was either dangerously naive or wilfully blind to the corruption in his own ranks.

'Of course,' Sévère replied smoothly. 'But you'll understand that we can only trust you so far. Everyone in this room knows the police are part of the problem.'

Height pressed his mouth to a line. 'There's something that might interest you. An investigative journalist has been digging into the white slave trade for the past three or four years. He might be willing to share information.'

'Who is he?' Olivia exchanged a glance with Sévère, seeing her cautious interest mirrored in his eyes.

'Name's Winston Fairfax,' Height replied. 'Quite the rabble-rouser, but undeniably committed. Been causing quite a stir with his articles in the Pall Mall Gazette.'

Sévère leaned forward. 'And what, in your opinion, would this journalist be able to do for us?'

Height shrugged. 'He seems genuinely dedicated to exposing these crimes and those responsible. However... I recommend you exercise caution. His approach is rather too indiscriminate for my liking.'

Sévère looked perplexed.

'Makes accusations with scant evidence. Has been taken to court for libel twice already, but managed to escape with a metaphorical black eye.'

Olivia exchanged a glance with Sévère. An ally in the press could be valuable. But a man with an agenda and a loose mouth would be too risky to associate with.

'We'll consider approaching him,' Sévère said, closing the discussion.

Height nodded and consulted his pocket watch. 'I've been looking through the list you gave me, Mrs Sévère,' he said to Olivia. 'I cross-referenced it against active cases of missing persons.' He paused, then added in a sombre tone. 'Only three of the disappearances are under investigation.'

Olivia nodded. 'Why is that not surprising? Were reasons given for abandoning the other hundred sixty cases?'

Another shrug, tinged with guilt this time. 'The police usually assume these girls know what they are doing. That they ran away from home to earn money, out to seduce men.'

'Of course. Such thinking makes your life a lot easier, doesn't it?' she asked bitterly.

He avoided her gaze as he replied, 'There's a reason I investigate homicides rather than sexual offences.'

Olivia tilted her head, waiting for him to elaborate.

'I have daughters,' Height explained, his voice trailing off. 'I can't bear to...' He shook his head, unable to finish.

'Understandable but pathetic,' she bit out. 'Have you any information on the clearing house in Kew?'

The inspector coughed into his hand, then slowly wiped his palm on his trousers, collecting his thoughts. 'I'm making progress. My colleague is reluctant to divulge details, but he alluded to the involvement of at least three members of the House of Lords. And even royalty.' He frowned at Olivia and Sévère. 'This doesn't come as a shock to you? Why? What have you discovered?'

'Nothing definitive yet,' Sévère replied. 'Does the involvement of the powerful astonish you, Inspector? How else would you run a highly illegal and highly profitable business offering luxury commodities to the wealthy?'

Height exhaled a hiss, seemingly poised to deliver a caustic retort. But he only rubbed his chin and said, 'I ought to be on my way.'

'Indeed, it's getting late. Thank you for your insights,' Sevére said pleasantly.

Olivia remained silent.

As the door closed behind Height, a momentary hush descended upon the office. She felt the weight of Sévère's gaze on her.

'Olivia,' he said. 'We need to talk about these stalking reports.'

She turned to face him, chin lifted. 'Do we?'

His eyes held a blend of concern and wry amusement. 'You're well aware that we do. Should Height piece it together...'

'He won't. I'm careful.'

'You've drawn the attention of the police already. This is dangerous terrain you're treading.'

Olivia offered a nonchalant one-shouldered shrug. 'And what would you have me do? Stand idly by?'

Sighing, Sévère raked his fingers through his unruly hair. 'Of course not. On a separate note: This journalist could be a valuable source of information.'

'Or a liability. He'll expect information in return.'

'True enough. But having a voice in the press could help sway public opinion, put pressure on the right people.'

Olivia considered this. 'Perhaps. I'll give it some thought.'

Sévère moved his chair to stand beside her. 'Agreed. We'll approach him carefully, assess his motives. And in the meantime...'

'In the meantime, we continue our work," Olivia finished. 'We find out who's running the house in Kew, who's behind the Virtuous Maiden Society, and who are the Midwife's main customers. And we bring them all to justice. One way or another. By whatever means are to hand.'

After a soft knock, Olivia entered Sévère's quarters. She walked through his private office and library and paused at the threshold of his bedroom. He was seated in his bed, reading a book. The soft light of an oil lamp illuminated half of his face.

'Hello.' She hesitated, unsure what to say next.

His gaze fell on the ink bottle and small brush in her hand. 'Raven wings?'

'I think something faster than a raven would be more... fitting.'

'A bird of prey?' he asked as she approached his bed. He placed the book on his nightstand and moved aside to make space for her.

'An eagle?'

'Impressive birds, certainly. But not the fastest.' His gaze followed her as she sat down on the mattress by his side.

'What is the fastest bird?'

'The peregrine falcon. It can even catch swifts.'

'Oh. I didn't know.'

'I've never seen one myself. But I read that the peregrine falcon dives with such high speed that when it strikes high up in the air, you can hear the impact from the ground. It's almost like a gunshot. The peregrine's prey is killed instantly by the force of the impact. A bird as fast and as powerful as a bullet.'

'Her prey never sees her coming.' She murmured. Smiling, she turned her back to him, and let her nightdress slip off her shoulders. 'Would you draw peregrine wings from my shoulders down my arms? Perhaps with the tips reaching down to my fingers?'

He fell silent for several long moments before answering, 'I'll do my best. May I start with your wrists?'

She held out her left hand. 'Why the wrists?'

'You'll see,' he said softly.

She turned toward him, covering her bare breasts with her right arm and extending her left to him.

'Don't look,' he said.

'Nor you,' she countered, her gaze following the lazy flicker of the oil lamp's flame.

When he switched to the other wrist, he paused, inhaled deeply, and said, 'Promise me you'll only watch them. Collect information. Promise me you'll tell me before you go out to kill a man.'

There was a long silence before she answered, 'Promise me you won't try to change my mind or hold me back.'

He continued drawing on her right wrist. 'I promise.'

She waited until he was finished with both wrists and began drawing the first wing on her right shoulder. 'I promise,' she whispered, then lifted her hands toward the glow of the oil lamp.

On her left wrist, he'd written, *courageous.*

And on the other, *cherished.*

Sixteen

THE TIMES, **7th September, 1887**

MYSTERIOUS FIGURE ALARMS GENTLEMEN IN WHITECHAPEL

Reports have reached this office of most peculiar occurrences in the East End. Several respected gentlemen of means have encountered a shadowy figure whilst traversing the streets of Whitechapel in the late hours. The mysterious man, described as tall and cloaked, has been observed following these upstanding citizens as they conduct their business.

A prominent banker who does not wish to be named, recounts, 'I felt eyes upon me as I quit an establishment. When I turned, I glimpsed a dark silhouette holding a knife.'

Inspector Height of Scotland Yard advises caution but assures the public that investigations are underway.

Sévère placed the newspaper aside and glanced across the breakfast table at his wife. She was tall, yes. But he had doubts she'd be clumsy enough to be seen sneaking through the night while holding a knife in plain view.

Chewing on his next words, he pulled another newspaper from the stack and leafed through it, searching for more reports on the stalker but found none.

'When you follow these men, do you wear a cloak and hold a knife?' he asked as though talking about the dryness of the muffin on his plate before him.

'Excuse me?'

He pushed The Times toward her.

She read the brief mention of the stalker, and looked up at him, frowning. 'These men must have a terrible memory, poor vision, or the stalker is someone else. I'm neither wearing a cloak nor do I carry a knife on me. Not visibly, that is.'

'From now on, you'll carry your revolver at all times. And you'll take up target practice with Higgins. Better yet if you take the man with you when you go out.'

A smile flitted past her lips as she glanced down onto the back of her hands, adorned with peregrine feathers in black ink. 'I shot an old pillow in the basement last night.'

'Did you, now. How many shots did it take to kill it?'

She sighed. 'Five. Two wine bottles suffered horrible deaths before I managed to bring down the culprit.'

He snorted. 'How far away from you was it?'

'Let's change the topic, shall we?'

An hour later, they sat in their office with the mother and brother of Maggies Bradys — a missing seventeen-year-old girl who'd wanted to follow in her mother's footsteps and become a washerwoman for an esteemed household. Both were haggard with worries about their financial situation and the well-being of the missing girl.

When Olivia heard Rose's footfalls in the hall, she excused herself and left the office, passing two families in the waiting room without paying them any attention. She rushed upstairs, into her private quarters, and knocked on Rose's half-open door before stepping through. With a screech, the girl crossed her arms over her chest and nonexistent bosom. Blood stood high on her cheeks. Her chin was set, eyes on fire.

Olivia's suspicion was stoked to a new intensity. 'What in the blazes is going on?'

'Can't you knock?' Rose turned her back, reaching for an undershirt and hastily pulling it over her head.

'What is Higgins doing to you, Rose?' Olivia tried to soften her voice but mostly failed.

'What?' The girl whirled around, eyes wide with shock.

'I swear, I'm going to kill him for this.'

'What?! Are you mad?'

'Your lessons with Higgins are finished. You'll never have to see him again. I'll take care of the matter. This man won't so much as take a *look* at a woman anymore. Stay in your room until I tell you it's safe.'

She reached out to touch Rose's wet cheek but the girl withdrew abruptly, gulped a shuddering breath, and threw herself onto her bed without another word.

Rose didn't want to talk. She hadn't wanted to talk about anything or with anyone since the night she was sold to Chief Magistrate Frost. So Olivia silently stepped back and shut the door.

'In my own house,' she murmured. 'In Rose's own home! Can't a girl be safe anywhere in this world?' Fury burned bright red. She had to make an effort not to run down to the stables like a bull with his balls on fire. With precision, she loaded her revolver and hid it in a fold of her dress on the way down the stairs, past the waiting room, through the hall and out to the stables.

Higgins was brushing down the horses that stood calmly with their eyes half closed. He turned just in time to see her lift the revolver. It took him a heartbeat or two to grasp that a loaded weapon was pointed at his head and that the one pointing it was furious.

'If there were any chance you'd hold still long enough, I'd cut off your balls and spare your life,' Olivia snarled.

Higgins slowly raised his hands and stepped away from the horses.

'You think I'd let you run, you bastard?'

'I'm trying to keep the horses safe.'

His nonchalance only infuriated Olivia further. 'I don't want to know why you did it, so don't even think about what excuses or reasons you could come up with to save your skin. You're all the same, after all. But you *are* going to tell me how far you went with her.'

Slowly, he blinked. 'Her?' Blinked again, threw a glance at the door at Olivia's back, and blurted out, 'You can't possibly mean Rose!'

Having had enough of this charade, she approached the coachman, all too ready to shove the muzzle of the revolver against his chest, and only realised her mistake when she'd taken one step too close, and the weapon was flung one way and she another.

The horses shied, kicked the walls and whinnied. Higgins murmured something to them and laid a gentle hand on a shiny brown coat. Olivia rightened herself and scanned the floor for the revolver, but saw no sign of it. The stables were too ill-lit.

Higgins stepped into her line of sight, arms akimbo. 'Did Rose accuse me of molesting her?'

'She didn't need to say it! It was obvious!' Olivia spat.

'I imagine it would be,' he snarled back, 'Had I actually laid hand on the girl. The truth is, I would *never* force myself onto anyone, least of all a child!'

Olivia scoffed. 'You are no longer welcome in this house. You have one hour to pack your things and leave.'

Sighing, he turned away from her to scoop oats from a burlap sack with his coarse hand. He held them out to the two horses who politely nibbled the grain off his palm. 'Talk to your husband.'

Snorting, she knocked the dirt off her skirts. 'I don't need my husband's permission to throw you out of my house.'

Without looking her way, he said in a low voice, 'Talk to him. Ask him how I came to be in his service.' With that, Higgins marched from the stables and shut the door in her face.

'He was sentenced to hard labour for committing acts of gross indecency with a man. His lover sold him out. For two years, he dredged the Thames during the day and was abused by inmates during the night. It happens to most who go in for sodomy. Strange isn't it? Two consenting adults having relations is illegal when said adults are both male. But take a rough man and an unwilling woman and the law turns a blind eye.'

Olivia felt nauseous. She sank onto a chair as Sévère continued. 'Higgins learned to defend himself fairly decently. That was one of the reasons I offered him the position.'

'What were the others?'

A wolfish smile cut across Sévère's face. 'His sense for justice. He was known to protect the weaker inmates. Got him into a pickle often enough, but he kept on with it.' He looked up at her with a hard expression. 'Higgins is neither interested in women nor in exploiting the weak. While I do understand where your fear and aversion are coming from, you can't be running around accusing men of rape.'

Olivia pressed a fist to the pit of her stomach. 'I need to talk to Rose.'

'No. You need to apologise to Higgins.'

'I know!' She spat and jumped from her seat. And then softer, 'I know. But I need to find out what happened. I need to talk to Rose first.'

He nodded once. 'I'll talk to our next clients alone. You go talk to the girl.'

The silence in the waiting room felt hollow as she passed through. A woman looked up at her, at first hopeful it would finally be her turn, then downcast as Olivia walked past without a word.

She was halfway up the stairs when Netty called, 'Excuse me, Mistress, but your presence is needed.'

Annoyed, Olivia threw over her shoulder, 'Not now, Netty.'

'It's about your maid.' Netty rushed up the stairs to Olivia and whispered, 'She attacked Alf with a knife.'

Finally, Olivia took in Netty's state. Her cap was not perfectly centred atop her head. A few strands of greying hair had escaped the knot. The housekeeper's hands were, as so often when she was distressed, kneading her apron.

'A knife?'

'You better come quick.'

'Is the boy injured? Should we call for a physician?' Olivia asked as they rushed down the stone steps to the kitchens.

'Not a scratch on him, thank goodness.'

Scents of rosemary and fried garlic in butter made Olivia's mouth water as she stepped into the kitchen. A wave of heat billowed toward her. And there amongst the pots and pans stood a girl with pigtails, a bruise on her right cheek, and a pushed-out bottom lip.

Using Cook as a meaty shield, Alf lurked in the back. He wiped a grin off his face the moment Olivia appeared. She marched up to him, grabbed him by the collar and dragged him toward Rose. Pressing both children down on a bench, she demanded to know what the bloody hell had happened.

'She pulled my ear!'

'He boxed my face!'

'She almost stabbed me to death with a butcher knife!'

'Oh don't be so melodramatic, you ass! Surely, you were about to—' Rose broke off, biting her lip.

Alf used the beat of silence to add with enough volume to shatter glass, 'She started it! And then she tried to kill me!'

Calmly, Olivia asked Rose if she indeed planned on killing the kitchen boy. Rose's only answer was to cross her arms over her chest and push up her chin as if to say, 'If necessary, I would have.'

Alf was not impressed. 'See!' he screeched.

'Quiet! You,' Olivia poked an index finger at the boy's sternum, 'You will cease punching Rose, or I'll personally throw you out and find another kitchen boy.'

'But—'

'But nothing!' Turning to Rose she snapped, 'If you ever pull a knife on somebody, you should be absolutely certain you know the consequences of your actions and are willing to bear them. But a bruised cheek does not justify such violence, young lady!'

Facing Alf once more, she added, 'Attend to your duties. We'll talk again tomorrow.' And to Rose, 'You and I will talk now. In your room.'

Once there, Rose threw herself on her bed, face pressed into a pillow. Olivia tore it away from her and dumped it on the rug. 'No more hiding. Sit up.'

Wide-eyed, Rose sat and wiped at her eyes.

'Tell me about your lessons with Higgins.'

'This is a madhouse.' Olivia sank onto a chair. She recoiled as her hand made contact with a tacky substance on the armrest. 'Ugh!'

'It's probably snot,' Sévère supplied.

'Disgusting.' Grimacing, she rubbed her palm on her skirt.

'Mrs Miller was weeping the entire time.' The shadows under his eyes seemed darker than usual, and there was an air of fragility around his shoulders that made her aware of just how much they'd been working in these past weeks.

Closing his notebook with a snap, he continued, 'I've read up on Fairfax's writing for the Pall Mall Gazette. That's a man with an agenda. He's ruthless, loud, and engages in frequent undercover work. He pretends to buy maidens by the dozens to get into contact with procuresses. His articles are causing a modest buzz. There's potential if the larger papers weren't intent on smothering him. I haven't seen any explicit mention of the Midwife or the Virtuous Maiden Society, but that doesn't mean he knows nothing about them. We should approach him.'

She nodded once. 'I think Higgins believes Rose is flirting with him.'

Sévère looked up sharply.

'She told me she wants him to be fond of her,' she added.

'I beg your pardon? A nine-year-old girl?'

She sighed, plucking at loose threads on the armrest. 'You have to understand that growing up in a brothel we learn there's only one way to interact with men. Two, if you count kicking them in the balls to get rid of them. She doesn't understand that her behaviour isn't exactly appropriate... Well, unless one is an *ordinary* adult who's courting. She doesn't even know what she's doing is being perceived as flirtatious, let alone the implications.'

'Has she explained what she means by wanting him to be "fond" of her?'

'I think what she's looking for is a father figure.'

Sévère choked on a laugh. 'Higgins? Of *all* people?'

'Why not? You should have seen him blasting through Madame Rosseau's to rescue the girl. You should see him with the horses. And you are too terrifying to be a good father for her.'

Silence came crashing down.

'I'm sorry. That was thoughtless of me,' she said quietly.

'No need to fret. I've no desire to play father to anyone,' he grumbled. 'Do speak with Higgins, though. The poor man must think we're giving him the boot or reporting him to the authorities.'

Awkwardly, she cleared her throat. 'Well, I actually...'

'You already told him to leave?'

Olivia rose from her seat. 'I'll talk to him straight away.'

They took a late supper in Sévère's bedroom with him reclining on the bed, an opium pipe nearby and soup cradled in his arm.

'Last night, I talked to most of the prostitutes who wrote to us for help,' she began before she noticed fresh signs of pain and exhaustion in his face. 'You look terrible. I'll tell you about it tomorrow morning.' She glanced at the opium pipe and his heavy-lidded gaze. 'Have you consulted a physician about your pain?'

'Yes. They all say the same,' he replied dryly. 'I'll soon depend entirely on opium for sleep. The drug will make me stupid and forgetful, and the wheeling chair will leave me lazy and weak. I'll become more useless each month. In four or five years' time, you can roll me atop a rubbish pile and leave me there, and I won't even notice the difference.' He let out a bitter chuckle.

Worried, Olivia perched beside him. 'Did they propose any alternatives to opium?'

Snorting, he replied, 'Hot compresses and friction treatment.'

'Then that's precisely what we'll do. Along with an opium unguent. You once told me you hate smoking. Has that changed?'

'No. I still hate it. But you're not my nurse.' He sat up and finished the bowl of soup that had begun to grow cold.

'No, I'm not. I'm your friend.' She stood, took his empty bowl and her own and said, 'I'll be back in a moment.'

She returned with an ewer of hot water and clean flannels. 'Do you still have your aconitum ointment?'

Grumbling, he rummaged in his nightstand and found a small jar with white lard and aconitum.

'Tell me about William's progress,' she said to distract him as she pushed aside the duvet and raised his nightshirt to expose the length of his left leg.

He coughed. 'Olivia...'

'It's only a leg.' She wrung the hot water from a flannel and applied it to his thigh. 'Would you like me to guess or will you tell me where the pain is?'

He clapped a hand over his eyes. 'Olivia. I have neuralgia of the femoral nerve. It means —'

'The femoral nerve extends from the lower spine through the front of the pelvis and thigh. You're likely experiencing pain in the front of your thigh, groin area, and possibly down to your knee.'

Astonished, he looked up at her. 'How on earth do you know that?'

'One of my clients, Simon, was a medical student. I would read anatomy books to him whilst he...examined my physique. I often quizzed him before exams. I was quite good at it.'

He cleared his throat. 'I see. However, this is still my leg, groin, and pelvis, not Simon's.'

'I promise I won't ravish you.' She placed a second hot flannel on his thigh and handed him a third. 'For your groin.'

'Perhaps another time.'

Her eyes sparkled with mischief as she asked, 'Would you prefer to grow addled, or would you rather apply this warm flannel to your groin, lovingly prepared by your devoted wife?'

'I'll be damned,' he groaned, closing his eyes as he slipped the warm compress beneath the duvet. 'I'll have you know I still possess a modicum of dignity.'

'And that, my dear husband, is why you will not smoke yourself into oblivion, but instead endure the torment of being tended to by a young, beautiful woman.' She placed a fresh hot flannel on his thigh. 'Now then, pray tell, what did the physicians mean by recommending friction treatment?'

'Bloody hell, Olivia!'

'Massage or birching?'

'They weren't forthcoming with details, and I refrained from inquiring further.' He removed the cooled flannel from his nether regions and tossed it into the ewer in her lap. His gaze was sharp and reproachful. 'I'm still a man. Don't treat me like a neutered simpleton.'

She froze. 'I apologise. I didn't mean to give the impression… I was joking to try to make the situation less awkward. And I truly don't want you to be in pain.'

With a weary sigh, he pinched the bridge of his nose. 'Perhaps you could bring compresses and hot water in the evenings, and I'll apply them myself while we discuss our clients and ongoing investigations.'

'All right.' She proffered fresh flannel. 'Did William say anything about his progress?'

Sévère placed the hot cloth on his leg which was now safely hidden under the duvet cover. 'Without exception, Mr Burroughs' proposals for legal reforms are rebuffed by the House of Lords.'

Frustrated, she huffed. 'Let's return to the matter of the prostitutes I mentioned earlier.'

'How many did you meet last night?'

'About a dozen. I compensated the street girls for their time and charged a guinea from the others.' She wrung out another warm compress and passed it to him. 'In hindsight, these women should have been our primary focus. Not the countless families. The working girls have far more valuable information. I've compiled a list of names. But the disappointing news is that no one's heard of the Virtuous Maiden Society or a procuress named Aurelia Pembroke.'

'So they are aliases?'

'It would seem so. I suspect the White Lily and the Virtuous Maiden Society are one and the same. The procuresses fabricate new names for themselves each time they prepare the abduction of another girl.'

'Makes sense. It's what I would do,' he said, easing himself down with a soft groan to lie flat on his back.

'How's the pain?'

'I might be able to convince myself it's improving slightly.'

She watched his expression, the tension around his eyes and the fleeting glance he cast at the opium pipe on his nightstand.

'You're faced with two options, Gavriel,' she said gently. 'You can choose the path of least resistance and pay the price in a year or two when your body demands opium simply to keep breathing. Or you can face your challenges head-on, enduring the pain day and night in manageable increments. They may seem overwhelming at times, but I assure you, during those nights, you can lean on me.'

He threw her an irritated glance. One that asked, *what could you possibly know?* Only to shutter with the realisation that she did indeed know everything about pain.

'I learned all about pain as a child, Gavriel. You did as well. You've simply forgotten.' She reached out and took his hand in hers. 'Would you like me to stay?'

'No chasing after villains tonight?'

She offered him a small smile. 'Even I need to sleep occasionally.'

'Very well,' he said cautiously. 'But do tell me what you learned last night.'

She fluffed up a pillow and slid under the covers, placing a hand on Sévère's breastbone and asking if he was comfortable. Then she said, 'They gave me two names of members of the House of Lords, several names of government officials, and names of high-ranking military and police officers who ensure the clearing house in Kew keeps running. And the name of the woman who owns the business, who supplies wealthy men with innocents of all colours and circumstances, and of both sexes.'

'Bloody hell, woman! Why didn't you say anything the entire day?'

'I was undecided as the whether to go out tonight and shoot a handful of them, but then I realised it might be better to buy enough ammunition and find out where they live first.'

She chuckled, yawned, and added, 'I'm sorry. I was too angry and tired to think straight.'

He groaned. 'By the gods, woman. You are going to give me nightmares.'

'It does distract from your pain, though, doesn't it?'

'Until you mentioned it again, yes, I was very distracted.'

'Would you like me to read Whitman to you?'

'I think you should rest. You haven't had a good night's sleep in...how long?'

'I can't remember.'

'Well, there you go. Should I read Whitman to you?' he asked, half amused.

'Just put your hand in mine. There, like that.' She yawned again. 'I'll return to my rooms once you're asleep.'

He didn't say anything for a long while. Only breathed quietly beside her. Occasionally, a tremor ran through his limbs but she was too exhausted to ask if his pain was bearable.

Seventeen

SÉVÈRE SLUMPED IN HIS CHAIR, his nerves frayed and his body aching. It had been a mere seven days since he'd been abstaining from opium use, and it felt like an eternity. Each day brought forth new waves of irritability and cravings. He knew he should be counting his blessings but his mind grew fixated on the dulling of pain a smoke could provide. Just one day into his newly opium-deprived life, and he'd grown irritable. Two days in, and he broke out in a sweat at the mere thought of the drug. The third and fourth days weren't much better. Now, on his seventh day, he was as much on edge as he'd been when prosecuting his very first trial.

All that would have been manageable if not for pain that had doubly intensified. Without Olivia by his side, he might have succumbed to the damned drug on day six, latest.

He never spoke to her of his struggles but was certain she sensed his deteriorating state. Each night, she brought hot compresses, and read to him until he pretended to fall into a fitful sleep. But the truth was, the pain and his cravings wouldn't let him rest.

There was one night when exhaustion overtook her. She fell asleep by his side, too worn out from long, sleepless nights. Waking up with a start the next morning, he made sure she found him turned away from her, a silent gesture to reassure her that he would never take advantage of her kindness.

They hadn't spoken of it since, and she had not repeated her overnight stay.

He couldn't fathom how she managed these long nights. First, staying with him into the late hours, then changing into men's clothing to watch the comings and goings at the White Lily. At least now, she brought Higgins along.

Sévère felt like a burden, a cripple who was unable to contribute to the ongoing investigation or life in general.

He'd ceased any thought of accompanying her. The only distance he managed to walk these days was from his library to his bed.

How he abhorred what the recurrence of poliomyelitis had wrought with his body!

And so he threw himself with every scrap of his limited energy into strategizing. A law needed amending, clues needed connecting, and culprits identified and brought to justice.

But more immediately, there was the matter of the upcoming 'ball.' Earlier that morning, an invitation had arrived, embellished with gilded letters on thick, ornate paper. Neither Sévère nor Olivia had expected the Midwife to make good on her promise, not after the abruptness with which she'd ended their last meeting.

A sense of foreboding gripped him. He needed to be on top of his game — one more good reason to abandon the opium pipe and keep his mind sharp. The Midwife was a cunning adversary, one who kept all her secrets close to her chest, feeding the two of them only the smallest morsels of information with a cold smile plastered to her face.

Sévère didn't trust a single word coming from that woman's mouth.

'The girl was brought to Kew,' the Midwife had said. 'Find another one to publicly rescue. From what you've told me, you have hundreds to choose from.'

They'd sat in their brougham across from her. The sun had dipped low, shrouded by clouds heavy with rain.

Sévère had felt Olivia's gaze on him as he replied nonchalantly, 'Very well, we'll choose another. Any will do. Although...' He paused, feigning contemplation before turning to his wife. 'The police inspector's daughter is not one of our cases but we'd do well to "accidentally" stumble on her whereabouts. A stroke of fortune. Or better yet—'

'The Virtuous Maiden Society,' Olivia interjected, aware of his train of thoughts. She swivelled her gaze to the Midwife, who regarded them with narrowed eyes and a hard expression. 'If we can deliver her to the police, any lingering doubts they might have about us would be thoroughly extinguished. We need the police to take us into their confidence. Planting evidence at the home of every abducted child requires more than just a handful of coppers in your pocket.'

The Midwife maintained her silence. She had contributed little during their meeting. That was when Olivia reached her limit. She slammed a fist against the carriage wall. 'Oh, hang the blasted Queen's unmentionables! If I learned anything in my years as a businesswoman, *darling*, it's to never sell myself under value.' With that, she shoved open the carriage door. 'We're done here. Get out.'

The Midwife held Olivia's gaze, a hint of a smile crawling across her mouth. 'As you wish. Expect invitations to the upcoming function.'

‘Function?’ Sévère enquired.

‘A ball in Cheswick. Well, the ball is a cover for an auction, of course. You’ll find all you need there.’

‘Except Alice Green,’ Sévère muttered, returning his thoughts to the present.

‘Did you say something?’ Olivia asked from across the desk.

'We have to tell the Greens their daughter isn’t coming home.'

'Hm.'

'You don't agree?'

She cocked her head, staring at the notes in front of her. 'I think you're right, but perhaps not yet. There's still a small chance she hasn't been shipped off to the continent. I doubt all girls who are sent to Kew end up abroad.'

Sévère felt as though a wet, icy cloak was pressing down on his shoulders. A shiver ran through him. His health was deteriorating fast. The evening they’d met the Midwife, he’d barely been able to make it to the brougham and then back into the house, even though Higgins had supported most of Sévère’s weight.

'Are you all right?' she asked.

He nodded briefly, although his backside was killing him. 'I need to move about. Would you mind helping me up?'

She went to lock the door, then helped him out of his wheeling chair. He tried not to lean too heavily on her but mostly failed.

'We need to be precise and systematic, but I fear our lack of sleep won't improve this...,’ he waved a hand at the scattered notes, ‘this chaos. Let's comb through everything again, all evidence, statements, hypotheses. Let's spread out all you've gathered on the floor. Then we add what we've learned from the families of the missing girls and the public records of the White Lilly.'

He used the backrest of a chair as a crutch as he stretched his aching legs and back.

Olivia began to arrange the paper scraps that held the names of men, the organisations they were affiliated with professionally and privately, and their connections to the white slave trade. At the centre of the puzzle was Catherine Burnham — a woman who ran a network of exclusive brothels that catered to the wealthy and influential, even to the nobility and members of the House of Lords, according to witness statements Olivia had taken from the prostitutes who had come forward for help to find a missing friend or sister.

'Did they say how many of the girls brought to Kew are sold abroad?' he asked.

She sat back on her haunches. 'No, I forgot to ask. But I assume it would be most profitable to sell the girls' maidenhoods here in London, and then ship them off after they'd lost value.' She looked up at him, her eyes black. 'From what I've heard, the girls are drugged, bound, and then stuffed into coffins for export to the continent, usually Brussels.'

Sévère felt a yawning emptiness spread inside his chest. 'I am not looking forward to telling little Miss Green that her sister is currently undertaking a journey of two hundred miles in a coffin.'

'*If* they shipped her off. But that's not all, Sévère. Burnham runs a network of exclusive brothels for the nobility here in London that cater to unusual desires.' Her intense gaze held his, measuring. 'Including torture.'

The clock on the mantle ticked away the silence. Sévère leaned forward, knuckles white on the armrest. 'No need to remind me. Let's move on to Burnham's clients. Lord Reginald Ashworth, especially. He's a member of the House of Lords.

Your informants said he's known for his philanthropic work with orphanages. Seems his interest in children only pretends to be charitable, one of the things he has in common with most of Burnham's clients.' He nodded toward a note labelled "The White Lilly" his wife had placed close to the scrap bearing Burnham's name.

'The worst monsters often wear the most convincing masks,' she mused. 'No one would think what this man is truly about when he donates to orphanages. And he's not just interested in girls. Boys, too. Very young boys.'

Sévère spotted a note with a name that was unfamiliar to him. He pointed at it. 'Who's this?'

'Sir Edward Blackwood, heir to the Blackwood shipping fortune. A regular at Burnham's establishments, with a penchant for flogging.'

Sneering, Sévère indicated a sheet of paper bearing three names. 'I've heard of those three. And to think they're all called *gentlemen*.'

She snorted. 'Don't you know? It's the same with costermongers and eating halls. When the sign says, "Best Baked Potatoes in London," you can be sure the exact opposite is true.'

He grunted. 'The Duke of Harlington, Lord Percival Mountbatten, and Baron Thaddeus Winthrop — all members of the House of Lords. If we could collect sufficient evidence against those three, the public uproar would be enormous. Enough to pressure the House of Lords into agreeing to our law amendments.'

'Hm... With a bit of luck, one of them will be at the ball,' she said absentmindedly.

He waited for her to follow her train of thought to the end, which was usually going along several intersecting tracks simultaneously before arriving at a conclusion or hypothesis.

'Four high-ranking military officers,' she murmured. 'Major

Alistair Cunningham, Rear Admiral Horatio Farnsworth, Colonel Everett Sinclair, and Brigadier Archibald Whitaker.' With her eyes on fire, she gazed up at him. 'These men are protecting Burnham's business. Even if we manage to collect evidence against them, they won't be prosecuted.'

Sévère began pacing the room, heavily limping, the chair serving as a crutch in his iron grip. 'But even if one-tenth of the information we've collected here can be proven, the implications are staggering. And yet, I am still waiting to be surprised by any of this.' He threw his arm out toward the notes on the floor and almost lost his balance. 'Bloody damn,' he grumbled.

'What are we even going to do with all this?' Olivia asked, her eyes following his restless movement.

Sévère paused, gazing out the window at the gaslit street below. 'We must proceed with utmost caution. These allegations need to be confirmed beyond a shadow of a doubt. We cannot afford to make accusations without irrefutable evidence.'

He turned back to face Olivia, 'The ball is an opportunity. If we can confirm the presence of even half of these men, it would lend credence to our suspicions and potentially provide us with the means to gather more concrete proof.'

Olivia stood, carefully stepping around the papers strewn across the floor. 'And if we do find them there? What then? Neither you nor I are particularly believable when it's the words of several respected, powerful men against that of a former prostitute and a coroner who's fallen from grace.' She walked up to him and softly dipped her fingers to his chest. 'Catherine Burnham cannot be allowed to keep running her business.'

Sévère's eyes met hers, a dangerous glint in their dark blue depths. 'We will gut these worthless blaggards.'

She raised her eyebrows. 'Figuratively or literally?'

'I honestly don't give a fig anymore.'

Eighteen

THE WEATHER WASN'T SUITING Olivia's dark mood at all. A lingering sunset gilded the Thames as they travelled along quiet, tree-lined streets, shaded by towering oaks and chestnut trees. The bruised sky peeked through the leaves, casting the entire landscape in a serene, amber glow. The air carried a warm, earthy scent, mingling with the sweet fragrance of late-blooming flowers in the well-tended gardens of nearby estates.

They'd been travelling for nearly two hours. Higgins had stopped once to water the horses and allow them to graze on a particularly lush stretch of the roadside. Now, the first signs of Chiswick peeked through the trees. Stately homes lined a riverbank, some modern, others Georgian in style. The dying sun created a halo on their slate roofs.

Nausea hit Olivia when the brougham passed through intricate wrought-iron gates and turned onto a gravel driveway. The sound of crunching stones was sharp in her ears. Where others might have seen a grand entrance, framed by well-maintained gardens, where flowerbeds burst with the vibrant colours of late-summer blooms, she only saw the gate to the hell that had been her childhood.

Here, behind the facade of wealth and influence, her nightmares waited.

'Hold my hand,' she croaked, her breath failing.

Sévère complied at once.

Dusk began to settle as they arrived at the main entrance where the warm glow of lanterns dropped onto a row of black carriages.

Sévère bent forward and gently touched her face. 'We are both armed. No one can hurt you. If you can't bear it anymore, you only need to say it and I'll get you out of there. You are the *last* person in this world to be held responsible for bringing these monsters to justice.'

She laughed. A short burst of bitter amusement. 'Can we stop calling it that? Justice is in the hands of a few wealthy men.' She pointed her chin at the mansion. 'These men. Calling what we're justice doing seems to...taint all our efforts.'

Sévère gazed at her for a long moment.

Slowly, she sucked in a breath and squared her shoulders. Cold seeped into her gaze as she let go of his hand. 'We won't bring them justice. We'll bring them a reckoning.'

He flashed a wolfish grin as he leaned back, pride and admiration in his gaze.

Higgins hopped off the driver's seat, pushed an approaching servant aside, folded down the stairs and opened the carriage door. Unspeaking, he held out a hand to Olivia. And she did what she'd always done in the company of monsters: She left herself behind.

Her right foot found the steps.

I

Her left foot hit the gravel.

feel

Higgins let go of her hand to attend to Sévère.

nothing

Getting the chair out of the brougham involved a lot of pulling and grunting, and drew the attention of guests and servants alike. When they'd finally brought it up the front steps of the house, Sévère experienced two sensations as he looked up at his wife.

One was relief, seeing that she had her emotions under control.

The other was an eerie sense of loss as he realised she wasn't quite there. All that made Olivia Olivia had been left in the carriage.

He swallowed, fingered his lapels, and nodded at Higgins. The man would be nearby, the horses ready.

He took in the elegant carriages pulling away as gentlemen in evening attire and the occasional lady in a flowing gown, a shawl draped around her shoulders to guard against the cool evening breeze, disembarked.

Olivia was dressed in mint green silk. Her sleek black hair glittered with the small pearl pins she'd worn for their wedding. His mind touched on the memory of unpinning her hair and brushing it. He quickly shut down his stray thoughts. *Not now, not here.*

They were received in the grand drawing room, where a warm glow from crystal chandeliers cast reflections across gilded mirrors and the rich, dark wood panelling of the walls. High ceilings were adorned with intricate plasterwork. Velvet drapes framed tall windows. Men clustered in small groups around mahogany armchairs and tables, speaking in low tones.

A handful of women were present, dressed in elegant silk

gowns. Sévère wondered if the ladies were mostly ornamental and if they knew what their men were about. The women sat or stood to the side, speaking quietly among themselves, offering polite smiles when noticed.

As fine brandy was served in crystal glasses, Sévère noticed the guests throwing occasional glances at a set of tall, gilded double doors to one side of the room.

Olivia moved closer to his side, placed a hand on his shoulder and gave it a gentle squeeze. And then another. And another. Another.

Her signal to him that she recognised four people in the room. And they hadn't seen even half of the faces of those present. This pressure on his shoulder, more than all the dark thoughts this so-called ball had brought to the surface, this pressure made him yearn for a blade. He wondered when he'd become so protective. He used to pride himself on keeping all emotions at arm's length.

'This bodes well,' he murmured, the sarcasm veiled in his voice.

She threw him a sharp glance, her eyes empty of all that was Olivia.

A shiver ran down his spine.

She put a polite smile on her face, bent down to correct his impeccable white bowtie and whispered, 'No symbols of rank anywhere.'

'I noticed. And they all seem to know each other.'

'Of course they do.' She smiled again, brushed a finger along his collar and turned her attention back to the room. 'Are you coming, dear?'

He couldn't help but grin. Her words asked him to politely mingle while her tone wished for a bloodbath.

Sévère moved his chair through the opulent drawing room, picking up bits and pieces of conversation. The murmur of voices was punctuated by an occasional trill of laughter or clink of crystal. Olivia walked slowly and with purpose at his side, but his attention remained fixed on the crowd around them.

Servants walked through the crowd, bearing trays with canapè, wine, and brandy. Sévère held his head high as though he were towering above everyone, ignoring the bulk of the wheeling chair he'd come to hate even more than his weakened leg.

The layer of ice shrouding his wife was palpable. He hoped she wouldn't attempt scouting out servants' stairwells, attics, and basements. The thought of her sneaking away, sticking knives into old men's hearts and rescuing children put him on edge. They couldn't afford suspicion. They needed names. Heroics had to be postponed to another day.

A cluster of men to his left caught his eye. Their proud postures, thrown-back shoulders, and sharp gazes hinted at years of military discipline. One man with a silver beard and slicked-back hair, gestured emphatically as he spoke. 'The situation in the colonies demands immediate attention. We cannot afford to appear weak.'

Sévère turned his attention to another group of gentlemen, their waistcoats straining against evidence of prosperity. 'Johnson's new steel mill is a gold mine,' one wheezed. 'If we pool our resources, we could have a controlling interest by year's end.'

'Capital idea,' another replied, his jowls quivering with excitement. 'Let's discuss the particulars over brandy later. Away from prying ears, eh? And let's not forget...'

Olivia kept moving and so did Sévère. The machinations of wealth churned on. He scanned the crowd. Surely, some members of the House of Lords must be in attendance. But try as he might, he couldn't spot a single familiar face. Reining in his impatience, he reminded himself that he knew only a handful of members of parliament. It didn't help much, though. Frustration and anger blended to a bitter taste in his mouth.

His wife's steps slowed, and Sévère found himself halting before a man who stood apart from the main throng of guests, leaning against the backrest of an armchair that a young woman occupied. Probably his mistress. The stranger was of unremarkable height, perhaps an inch or two shorter than Olivia. His face bore the weathered lines of a man in his fifties who had indulged in too many cigars and too much fine brandy.

The man's tailcoat was of the finest black wool and silk, impeccably cut to flatter his somewhat paunchy frame. A waistcoat of deep burgundy silk peeked out beneath, adorned with a gold watch chain that winked in the light of the chandeliers.

It was the man's eyes, however, that captured Sévère's attention. They were a pale, watery blue, set deep within a face that seemed perpetually on the verge of a smirk. Those eyes held a cold intelligence, assessing Sévère and Olivia with a calculating gaze that made the hairs on the back of Sévère's neck prickle.

'Ah, what a pleasant surprise,' the man purred. 'How delightful to see you this evening. What may I call you today, my dear?'

Sévère felt the coldness emanating from Olivia. The stranger must have felt it, too. She replied, 'May I introduce my husband, Gavriel Sévère. You might have read about us in the papers.'

A bold move, Sévère thought. But a good one. Someone was bound to recognise them. Besides, they couldn't be telling one lie to the Midwife and an entirely different one to these people here.

The man extended a hand to Olivia. His fingers were adorned with several heavy gold rings. 'Of course, of course! My sincerest apologies. I merely wished to grant you... discretion, should that have been your wish.' Turning to Sévère, he added,

‘Allow me to introduce myself, Mr Sévère. Lord Augustus Blackwood.'

Ah, yes, he’d heard about the man. It was whispered in the corridors of power and the back rooms of gentlemen's clubs. A rising star in the House of Lords, known for his shrewd political manoeuvrings.

Sévère did not extend his hand to accept Blackwood’s, pretending his arms were as lazy as his legs. 'A pleasure, Lord Blackwood. I've heard much about your work in Parliament.'

Blackwood's lips quirked in a half-smile. ‘Good things, I hope?'

'Opinions vary,' Sévère replied.

Blackwood chuckled. 'As they often do in our line of work.' His eyes glittered as he turned to Olivia. 'What brings you here, dearest, if I may ask?'

'You will cease with the endearments, Blackwood,' Sévère ground out.

'Of course, of course!' He took a sip from his crystal tumbler and wiped a droplet from his beard. Then he narrowed his gaze at Olivia. 'Well?'

'Why am I getting the impression I am being interrogated by the police?' she replied cooly.

At the mention of ‘police,’ Blackwood's nostrils flared. The conversations around them dimmed to a hush.

A gong sounded. ‘Refreshments will now be served in the ballroom,’ a servant announced.

Barely concealed *ohs* and *ahs* travelled through the crowd. Men smiled in anticipation. Here and there, so did a few women.

Blackwood gifted them a false smile and left.

Sévère made to move his chair in the direction of the ballroom. ‘Are you abandoning me already, dear?’ Olivia said in a voice so sugary, he began to feel sick. Smiling, she bent down to kiss his cheek, and whispered into his ear, 'Remember that you can't simply walk the girls out of here.'

He wrapped a hand around the base of her neck. 'I know. And I am glad we're not expected to place a bid.'

She huffed. 'Be careful, though. There's likely a small room nearby where merchandise is sampled. If you get anywhere near *that*, you'll be expected to engage.'

He sighed, took her hand in his, and pressed it to his chest. With a nod, he let go.

She straightened up, slid a pleasant facade over her expression and moved with the crowd toward the double doors.

Nineteen

AS THEY MOVED with the throng into the grand ballroom, Sévère kept his attention on the guests. He registered the extravagant décor, the exorbitant cost it must have entailed. His attention snagged on the intricately carved mahogany walls, their gold-framed inlays depicting idyllic countryside scenes. The contrived innocence irked him.

Olivia, a smiling ghost at his side, seemed to freeze for the briefest moment, and that's when he noticed it, too: The ladies, who'd seemed mere decorative fixtures, suddenly took on an air of purpose.

Sévère exhaled a measured breath and watched as the women spread across the ballroom. Their faces, previously adorned with vapid smiles, now wore expressions of gentle authority. It reminded him unsettlingly of his childhood tutors.

A door swung open, and in rushed perhaps three dozen children. The smallest girls wore white silk, while those nearing adolescence were dressed in lavender. Miniature tailcoats, black trousers, low-cut waistcoats, crisp dress shirts, and little white bowties adorned the boys — all of them tiny, innocent replicas of the adults present. Each child had a number affixed to their right shoulder.

Their eyes sparkled with excitement and curiosity, their small bodies brimming with energy as they fidgeted with their attire and gazed around the opulent room in wonder.

'They haven't a clue,' Olivia murmured.

He watched, growing sicker by the moment, as the ladies gracefully gathered the children into small groups. Each woman was the epitome of kindness, their voices gentle and encouraging as they guided their charges towards the waiting gentlemen.

Small hands, trembling with nerves, presented bouquets, sweets, and hopeful smiles to these perfectly groomed luminaries of society, who in their finely tailored suits tried and failed to preserve a semblance of nonchalance.

'Clever bastards,' Sévère muttered under his breath. He had to admire the sheer audacity and cunning of it all, even as it filled him with a revulsion he'd never before experienced in his life. Every element had been painstakingly orchestrated, every aspect of the charade skilfully constructed to maintain a veneer of innocence.

Were the police to raid this mansion, all they would discover were upstanding men and women engaged in the seemingly innocuous pursuit of selecting their next lady's maid or steward's assistant.

It was flawless. Not a single law had been broken, provided the guests feigned ignorance of Mrs Burnham's dealings. Undoubtedly, they would. And Mrs Burnham would maintain that her sole purpose was ensuring her young wards found suitable homes.

The guests moved about the room, laughing when a child amused them, engaging in conversation with any who seemed particularly charming.

Sévère found himself searching the faces of the men, committing each one to memory. He wished his limited drawing skills extended beyond ridiculous dragons, knights, and birds. He wished he could create accurate portraits, have them printed with appropriate captioning, and plaster them throughout London. Let everyone see the true nature of mankind.

A young girl, no more than twelve, stumbled as she approached a portly gentleman near the fireplace. he steadied her with a hand on her shoulder, his touch lingering a moment too long. Sévère's fingers curled around his armrest, the urge to hurl a knife overwhelming.

Olivia pressed a hand to his shoulder, squeezing trice more. Three more were identified.

The pressure helped remind him they couldn't act, not here and not yet. He knew they needed irrefutable evidence, and so he forced his gaze away from the girl and her 'benefactor.' *Names, connections, the entire network*, he silently told himself.

The evening stretched on, an endless procession of innocence being led to hell. Sévère felt each moment like a blow to his innards. He had seen much in his years as a coroner and solicitor, but this calculated exploitation of the most vulnerable was starting to crack his carefully maintained facade.

'The bidding begins,' Olivia said to him.

He could no longer bear her empty smile. Instead, his gaze trailed after the servants moving silently through the room, impeccably dressed in black and white, offering trays that held not refreshments, but a roster. Men perused the list, whispered something, and the servant jotted down a number before moving on.

Olivia began to move through the crowd, leaving him no choice but to follow and keep playing his part. Sévère couldn't help but wonder how many other such gatherings were taking place across London.

His wife soon made her way toward a woman who stood aloof from the crowd. Although there was nothing remarkable about her, her keen observation of the proceedings and the deferential nods she received from many attendees set her apart.

Olivia's demeanour shifted as she addressed the woman, her usual sharp-tongued confidence replaced by a demure, almost timid air. 'I must confess, I'm thoroughly impressed. A brilliantly organised event. And the merchandise appears exceptionally well-maintained.'

It was at this moment that Sévère's suspicion was confirmed beyond a doubt. They have found Mrs Burnham.

The woman's eyes twinkled with amusement. 'Whatever do you mean?'

Olivia did not introduce herself and Sévère. She said, 'If you don't mind me asking, I wonder if a mutual acquaintance might have mentioned us and our...particular offerings?'

Interesting, Sévère thought. Everyone on a tightrope, pretending they were treading solid ground.

Mrs Burnham's gaze shifted to Sévère, her eyes astute and calculating. 'Your murder trial caused quite a commotion. The condemned ward of Newgate must have been an enlightening experience for a man of your standing.'

'Not precisely comfortable, but instructive.'

'You're lucky your wife caught the real killer. Quite the feat.' She paused, her eyes roaming over his wheeling chair. 'There are whispers, you know. Some say your need for that chair is a ploy. They believe you exacted your revenge on Chief Magistrate Frost, the man who had had his way with your wife for many years before you found her. Word is, he played a part in your wrongful arrest and even assaulted her in the courtroom.'

Sévère's skin grew ice cold. He knew she was trying to provoke him, hoping for an outburst that would reveal information he wanted to keep from her. At the very least, she wanted to test his mettle. Did she realise she had struck at the core of the truth?

He gifted her a mild smile and said in a tone a man might reserve for his wayward grandchildren, 'It must be challenging to manage your enterprise whilst placing faith in the murmurs of every Tom, Dick, and Harry.'

Mrs Burnham's smile widened, revealing teeth that seemed too well-maintained for a woman in her fifties. 'In my line of work, information is currency. And I assure you, I am exceedingly wealthy.'

Sévère smiled back. 'Then you know why we're here.'

Higgins slipped into the bustling kitchen. The air was stifling warm and thick with scents of roasted meats and fresh pastries. Servants scurried about, their faces flushed from exertion and the heat of the ovens.

He seated himself between two other coachmen, his posture relaxed, expression amiable. A maid, her apron and hands dusted with flour, slammed a steaming cup of tea in front of him. He accepted with a nod, his eyes scanning the room.

'Quite the to-do upstairs, eh?' he remarked casually.

A kitchen boy paused in his task of polishing silver. 'Aye, Mrs Burnham's gatherings always are. This one's no grander than most.'

Higgins took a sip of tea. 'That so? Must be nice, working in a house with such important guests.'

A scullery maid let out a giggle. 'Oh, you've no idea. Why, just last month, we had Lord—'

'Hush, Mary,' a footman cut in. 'You know we're not to gossip about the guests.'

Higgins arched an eyebrow. 'Come now, what's the harm? It's not as if I'm likely to cross paths with such fine folk. Besides, I'm in the market for a new position. My current mistress, she's...' He trailed off, cleared his throat, and added, 'Besides, the pay leaves much to be desired.'

The servants exchanged knowing looks. The cook, a portly woman with greying hair, joined them at the table. 'Ah, we've all been there. No shame in looking for greener pastures.'

Leaning in closer, Higgins lowered his voice to a conspiratorial whisper. 'Just between us, then. Who might a fellow turn to for employment in these parts?'

As the evening wore on, names and snippets of conversation flowed freely. Lord this, Lady that, a member of Parliament whose proclivities brought about raised eyebrows and stifled laughter. Higgins tried hard to commit each detail to memory, wishing he had a piece of paper and a pencil to write down this flood of information.

The peal of a bell set off a frenzy of motion. Servants rushed to and fro, balancing trays laden with delicacies and decanters of fine spirits. In the lull that followed, Higgins steered the conversation back to Mrs Burnham's gatherings.

'Monthly affairs, eh?' he inquired, his tone light. 'So we'll be seeing each other regular-like.'

The cook nodded. 'Like clockwork. Though next month's might be something special. Mrs Burnham's been in quite a fluster about it.'

Higgins tried not to appear too eager. 'Special? How so?'

But before the cook could respond, the kitchen door swung

open. A lanky man with a stern demeanour swept in, his eyes narrowing as they fell upon Higgins.

'And who might you be?' he demanded.

Higgins stood and picked up his bowler. 'Merely the coachman of one of your esteemed guests. I was hoping for a cup of tea and a few minutes by the fire.'

The man's lips thinned. 'I see. Now that you got what you were looking for, it's time you return to your horses.'

Higgins nodded meekly and bid a polite farewell to the servants who'd shared their table. 'Much obliged for the hospitality.'

Faint strains of music from the grand ballroom drifted down the corridor and into the lavish office. Sévère's eyes swept over the rows of antique books lining the walls, the cold fireplace. Something was missing but he couldn't quite put his finger on it. Despite the scents of polished wood and old paper, this space smelled too clean.

Unused.

'You came to discuss business. Let's get to it, then.' Mrs Burnham settled behind a mahogany desk.

'We understand you're in a unique position to find suitable customers for the merchandise we have at our disposal,' Sévère began.

Mrs Burnham's eyebrow arched. 'And what sort of merchandise might that be?'

'Don't play coy,' Olivia cut in. 'You're selling young girls and boys. We have connections that could prove quite lucrative for your enterprise. And ours, of course.'

He suppressed a wince at her bluntness. He'd hoped for a

more subtle approach, but there was no reining in his wife once she'd set her mind to something.

Mrs Burnham scoffed. 'My, my. You certainly don't mince words, do you? And what, pray tell, makes you think I'd be interested in such an arrangement?'

Olivia picked up a golden letter opener, hefted it in her hand, and examined it in the lamplight. 'Higher profits.'

'Not to mention, we can provide protection. We are in a unique position to alter evidence. Make it appear or...disappear,' Sévère added. As he talked, he pushed his wheeling chair around the office, pretending to admire the floor-to-ceiling collection of old books. His gaze searched for anything that might serve as incriminating evidence — a ledger, a stray note, anything to expose connections and activities of Mrs Burnham's network. But the office was immaculate. In fact, upon closer look, it was more a library with a desk as a decoration than an office.

A front.

Mrs Burnham leaned back in her armchair, studying them. 'Regrettably, I must decline. My business is entirely legitimate, I assure you.'

Olivia scoffed. 'You and I know that's not the case.'

'Do we?' Mrs Burnham's voice took on a dangerous edge. 'I'd be careful making such accusations without proof.'

Attempting to diffuse the tension, Sévère said, 'Perhaps we have misunderstood the nature of your establishment. We meant no disrespect.'

A soft knock sounded at the door, and a willowy butler entered without waiting for an invitation.

'Pardon me, madam, but there's a message for you.' He leaned towards Mrs Burnham's ear and murmured urgently.

Sévère overheard the word 'driver.'

'Thank you, Samuel. You may leave,' Mrs Burnham replied. Her gaze snapped back to Sévère and Olivia. 'It seems your coachman has been asking all sorts of questions about my guests.'

Part Four

A bridge of silver wings
stretches from the dead ashes
of an unforgiving nightmare

Aberjhani

Twenty

THE INNKEEPER COULDN'T CONCEAL his disdain at having to accommodate a cripple. Each subtle sneer at the wheeling chair made Sévère's fists itch. He ground his teeth in frustration, longing for the days when he could walk on both legs, unencumbered by this wretched contraption that had become his prison.

Higgins' voice boomed through the small lobby. 'Now listen here, man. I'm certain you can understand the importance of accommodating this gentleman with the room I booked for him.'

The innkeeper, a short man with a receding hairline and shifting gaze, spoke as though he were in great pain. 'You're late. I've let the room to a family of four. Can't very well turn them out now, can I?'

Higgins leaned in, face hard. 'You'll bloody well find a way, or you'll be dealing with more than just a late arrival and tardy customers. We paid good money for that room, and we expect it to be available.'

The innkeeper's gaze flickered from Higgins to Sévère.

'Well, I might be able to find something, but it'll cost extra. Can't just give away rooms for cheap, you understand.'

Higgins' voice dropped to a growl. 'You'll take what we've already paid, and you'll be grateful for it. Or do you want me to let everyone know how you treat paying customers?'

'Fine, fine. I'll see what I can do. Though, at this late hour...'

After an uncomfortable pause and a good amount of hemming and hawing from the innkeeper, Sévère relented. If the man insisted on having his hands greased before they could finally retire, so be it. 'Perhaps, you might consider offering the family an upgrade to a larger room upstairs. At my expense, of course.'

The innkeeper's eyes glittered. 'Well, I suppose that could be arranged. Though it would be quite inconvenient for them, moving all their belongings...'

Ah, so the man wanted even more money. But Sévère had had enough. 'I'm certain you'll manage. Higgins, kindly assist our host with the arrangements.'

As his coachman followed the innkeeper towards the back chambers, Sévère consulted his pocket watch. Twenty minutes past midnight. He worried about Olivia, who was presently hiding behind an immaculately trimmed hedge, watching Mrs Burnham's establishment in hopes of gathering evidence to see the woman and her clients thrown in prison.

Bloody hell! How he longed to be of practical use in gathering evidence or following suspects. Alas, he could scarcely traverse a gravel path without assistance, much less manage the shortest flight of stairs. He could manage it, truthfully, on most days —at least so far — but doing so would risk his carefully constructed alibi.

'Pull yourself together, you spineless fool,' he grumbled under his breath.

Voices drifted down from the upper floor — the innkeeper's placating tones mixed with the whining of sleepy children. Sévère shut his eyes, focusing on the task at hand. Mrs Burnham's operation needed to be shut down, and he couldn't allow his little problems to stand in the way.

Higgins appeared, gesturing towards their quarters. 'All sorted. Let's get you settled in.'

Sévère nodded, forcing a thin smile. 'Thank you, Higgins. I'd be lost without your help.'

Although true, the words left a trace of gall in his mouth. Relying on others for the most basic of tasks was an experience he could do without.

The narrow corridor proved treacherous — his chair's wheels snagged repeatedly along warped floorboards and on rumpled rugs. Their allocated room was rather cramped: a single large bed with their luggage at its foot, two small pallets, a basic washstand, and a covered bucket serving as a chamber pot. His heart sank at the sight.

'I should be leaving,' Higgins said. 'Is there anything else you need?'

Sévère shook his head. 'Just keep her safe.'

With a grunt of acknowledgement, Higgins left.

Sévère woke with a start. The empty silence of the room sent a spike of anxiety through him.

He hauled himself upright, wincing as his left leg protested. His concern for Olivia churned in his gut, and he found himself unexpectedly troubled by Higgins's absence as well. As he washed with cold water and dressed in rumpled clothes, each passing moment fed his darkest fears for Olivia's safety.

Sévère manoeuvred his chair out of the room and down the corridor. Scents of frying bacon, scrambled eggs and toast wafted up from the kitchen, but his hunger was overshadowed by unease.

The innkeeper stood behind the front desk, poring over a ledger.

'Pardon me. Has there been any word from—' Sévère stopped mid-sentence at the sound of a familiar grumpy voice.

'Morning.'

Turning, he found his wife and Higgins framed in the doorway. They appeared thoroughly spent, their clothing dishevelled and mud-spattered.

'Please send breakfast to our room,' Olivia said gruffly to the innkeeper before he could comment on the men's clothing she was wearing.

'Are you well?' Sévère asked.

Olivia nodded wearily. 'Nothing a hot meal and some rest won't cure.'

Once they were all settled in their room, balancing plates on the bed for lack of table and chairs, Sévère studied Olivia's face. There was a tension around her eyes, a rigid set to her jaw that spoke of disappointment and frustration. Higgins didn't look much better.

'I gather the nocturnal adventures continue to be difficult?' Sévère said, as he filled everyone's mugs with piping hot tea.

Olivia retrieved several creased papers from her pocket and laid them between the breakfast dishes. 'Most of what we have are fragments. Names without faces and faces without names.'

'I'll recognise them next time I see them,' Higgins announced with a yawn.

Nodding, Olivia briefly touched his wrist. 'Good. We shall outfit you most elegantly, find you some opera glasses, and secure your entry to the next parliamentary session.'

Higgins' bushy eyebrows shot upward.

There was newfound ease between the pair that spoke of

late-night confidences, Sévère observed. 'You do realise how this sounds?' he said with a smirk.

Olivia shrugged. 'It's common knowledge that the real criminals are in high places, not prison cells.'

Higgins nearly choked on his scrambled eggs.

'It's not enough.' Frustrated, she swept the notes aside. 'We can't prove anything. We have no witnesses, no evidence. As far as the law is concerned, Mrs Burnham could be a sweet elderly lady, looking out for orphans.'

'They didn't move any of the children,' Higgins reported. 'At least not from what we saw. By three o`clock, the last guests left. By four, lights were out.'

Sévère chewed thoughtfully on his buttered toast. It tasted more like papermaché than bread. 'We will follow the money. I'll cross-reference your notes with the financial records of the White Lilly, their associates and orphanages.'

'And I'll take a nap while Higgins drives us home,' Olivia grumbled.

The private detective agency's office resembled a paper maelstrom. Financial records from the White Lily, lists of board members, transaction logs, names and locations of orphanages, names of guests from the previous evening, and notes on his hypotheses littered the floor.

Looking at the chaos, Sévère was certain that soon he wouldn't be able to manoeuvre his chair through the office without destroying the picture he was creating.

He resumed scribbling theories, drew lines between page items that might or might not be related, noted names appearing in multiple places, and circled others for which they needed considerably more information. For the first time in weeks, he felt useful. And he relished the challenge before him.

The gentle protest of floorboards drew his attention.

Olivia lingered in the doorway, her gaze trailing over the sea of notes. 'Any progress?'

Sévère leaned back in his chair, stretching his neck until it crackled. 'Some. Let's start over there.' He pointed toward a window. 'Dates of abductions, all more or less evenly distributed over the past three months. Anything older, and they are thinning out. We don't see those cases because families have given up. Lost hope, I assume.'

Olivia circled the place on the floor he had indicated.

'The locations of the abductions tell us more,' he continued. 'Train stations feature prominently. Each time, a woman offers to keep an eye on the children and luggage whilst parents purchased tickets. In half the reports, witnesses describe someone maternal in her fifties or sixties, elegant, silver-haired. But with an oddly youthful smile.'

'Like Mrs Burnham. She has all her teeth. And they are strangely white and straight. Does that mean we have our first useful witnesses?'

'For abductions, possibly. We're far from proving her role in London's white slave trade.' He rubbed his chin, eyes flying over his notes littering the floor. 'Let's get to the statements of the prostitutes.' He pointed toward the cold fireplace. 'Three members of parliament: the Duke of Harlington, Lord Percival Mountbatten, and Baron Thaddeus Winthrop. I should have connected all of this with string,' he motioned to the entire mess of papers on the floor, 'but then I'd never be able to roll myself out of this office.'

Clearing his throat, he pressed on. 'Higgins confirms both Winthrop and Mountbatten attended last evening's "ball." Both serve on the White Lilly's board and contribute substantial sums to its orphanages. In all of this, several names appear with suspicious frequency, like this Lord Ashworth.' Sévère pointed toward a paper shrapnel. 'He seems to have his fingers in multiple pies. Ashworth's name crops up as one of the White Lily's directors whilst bankrolling three separate orphanages.'

Olivia's lips thinned. 'Convenient.'

'He's not alone. I found at least five others with comparable connections.'

Olivia began to pace. 'Each day we delay—'

'I know.' Sévère's tone was gentle but firm. 'I know. But we must tread carefully. These men are powerful and well-connected. We've only just started and our evidence is circumstantial at best. One misstep and we could lose everything. All we can prove so far beyond a doubt is that kindly gentlemen are pouring their money into good causes.'

She lifted her gaze. 'I'll visit the orphanages. We need to compare how many children went missing before the White Lilly's involvement.'

He shook his head. 'Direct inquiries from the two of us would alert them. Mr Burroughs is better positioned to make these investigations.'

She cocked her head, brow furrowed. 'Is he getting anywhere at all with the House of Lords?'

Sévère sighed, pinching the bridge of his nose. 'For every step forward in the engagement of a few, the mass of parliament pushes him two steps back. We need public attention on this... this... I don't even have the words anymore.'

She nodded once and pointed at a trail of papers. 'Let's put William's part aside for now. What are these here?'

'Shipment records.'

She bent down and picked up a list. 'Steamships sailing from Dover and London to Antwerp. This is a long list, Sévère. She's shipping girls out every two weeks?'

'Don't forget the boys,' he said.

'I don't. Have you found any way to trace these records back to her? Perhaps through...what's this name here?' She squinted at the list, turning it sideways to read what he'd written in the margins. 'You've listed all the steamships that carry coffins as cargo?'

'Yes and no. We can't connect shipments to her directly. Indirectly, hum... Circumstantial connections are tenuous at best.' He pointed at another note near her feet. 'Quincy Casket Company has a monopoly on all casket exports to Belgium. And they may be the sole casket maker in London with major investors.'

Her gaze snapped from the note at her feet to Sévère.

'Blackwood and Winthrop,' he said.

Hope flared in her expression. 'Is Burnham's name mentioned anywhere in these documents?'

He shook his head. 'Pick up that one next.' He motioned toward her right. 'Yes, that one. Major Cunningham, Rear Admiral Farnsworth, Colonel Sinclair, and Brigadier Whitaker — all present at last night's gathering at Mrs Burnham's mansion. They're the ones safeguarding the shipments to Belgium.'

'How?'

'Higgins managed to corner Whitaker's driver by the stables last night. The fellow was deep in his cups. He bragged about having privileged information on diplomatic cargo meant to strengthen Anglo-Belgian relations and ensure continued alliance support.'

'What?'

He groaned. 'Yes. Any policeman not in their pockets won't get within sight of those caskets.'

'And neither will we.'

'Exactly.'

'Bloody hell.' Olivia looked around the room, trying to find a place to sit without treading on the sea of papers.

'Would you help me up, please? I need to stretch my legs.'

She did at once, and he felt deeply ashamed at having to lean so heavily on her. He cleared his throat and said, 'I'll pen a message to Burroughs, asking him to find out more about the White Lilly's orphanages. Specifically, any physicians on payroll and records of runaways.'

While Sévère stretched his aching limbs, Olivia silently stared at the empty fireplace.

When he had finished his letter to William Burroughs, she turned to him with a calculating grin. 'I'll get you your public outcry.'

Twenty-One

THE PALL MALL GAZETTE

Editor's Note: We received this letter the previous evening and believe its claims to be genuine. We have therefore decided to publish it in the interest of public awareness and the pursuit of justice. We would furthermore like to request that Justice R.T. Peregrine contact our editorial offices for an anonymous interview.

We, the jury, having duly considered the evidence presented before us, find Chief Magistrate Linton Frost guilty of the following heinous offences:

1. The violation of no fewer than four hundred girls, most below the age of consent, said acts being perpetrated with the utmost cruelty and disregard for human dignity.

2. The wilful and malicious aiding and abetting in the abduction, drugging, and rape of these innocent children, thereby causing immeasurable suffering to the victims and their families.

3. The chief magistrate's gross abuse of his position to conceal his nefarious activities and obstruct the course of justice.

Having weighed the gravity and multitude of these offences, and in consideration of the irreparable harm inflicted upon countless innocent souls, we, the jury, have decreed that the only fitting punishment for such egregious crimes is death.

We therefore rule that the execution of Chief Magistrate Linton Frost on July 21, 1881, by means of a knife to the heart was justified, and fitting in manner for the pain he inflicted upon the hearts of his countless victims.

Let it be known that this verdict has been reached with the utmost solemnity and in the interest of true justice, which the accused has for so long denied to others.

Let it be known that we are watching you, men of law, money, and power. You can no longer hide your heinous crimes from us.

Signed

Raphael Thorne Peregrine

Lord Chief Justice of the People's Court, London

'The Daily Telegraph printed an excerpt of your letter, and The Sentinel mentioned it.' Sévère looked up from the newspaper and across the breakfast table. He tapped at the page in front of him. 'And then of course the Pall Mall Gazette. They printed it in full.'

'I am aware,' Olivia said with a quirk of a smile. 'I'll have words with that journalist...Winston something or other.'

'Winston Fairfax.' Sévère attacked his boiled egg with rather more force than necessary. 'I'd caution against the meeting were I delusional enough to think you'd heed my advice in the matter.'

'I'm quite safe. I'm a woman, you see. The weaker sex.' She

spread butter on a slice of warm toast and watched it melt. 'And I'm not foolish enough to make an appointment with the man. A chance encounter would serve far better.'

'What do you hope to achieve?' He caught the edge in his voice and tamped down on his bad mood.

Olivia noticed his discomfort, of course, but did not enquire about today's level of pain. They reserved such conversations for the late evenings. Instead, she said, 'I want his insights. He's been investigating the white slave trade for years. He might know something that could help us connect Mrs Burnham directly with the White Lilly, or to the casket shipments to Belgium and her men in the military.'

With a shake of his head, Sévère lifted his teacup and drained it. 'He'll demand information in exchange for anything useful.'

'I can always fabricate something suitable,' she replied, dabbing her mouth with a napkin as she rose. 'I'll join you at the office shortly. I promised Rose I would braid her hair.' With that, she left him to his breakfast and climbed the stairs to her chambers.

The girl was perched at the vanity, absently picking at the bristles of a hairbrush.

She took the brush from Rose's hands and undid her unruly braids. 'You're aware that the man who raped you is dead and can't hurt you anymore.' Not a question, a statement.

Wide-eyed, Rose nodded.

For several long moments, Olivia studied Rose's reflection in the mirror. The girl's expression grew bewildered, and then, very slowly, turned to shock. With a gentle smile, Olivia gave a single nod.

'We share an understanding, first mate. At least that's how it used to be between us. Since your mother sold you and that man violated you, you've drawn back into a shell. They made you believe you were to blame. They made you believe you are to bear the shame of their actions. Perhaps they even convinced you that you can't confide in anyone, ever. Not even me.' She held Rose's gaze in the mirror. 'I wish you could trust me more, I truly do. I went through the same torture. Frost was the man who took my innocence by force, and he returned every week until I left and married Sévère.'

'Does he make you do these things? Mr Sévère?' An abashed whisper.

'No, he demands nothing from me but my honesty and my help in solving cases.' As she said this, she realised once more how absurd it sounded. This arrangement was unlike any other marriage.

'Why?' Rose asked.

'Because we are friends and he holds me in high regard.' It struck Olivia how explaining this to Rose made it all the harder to deny. 'And I hold you in high regard, too. I wish with all my heart that you'd never had to go through this pain, and I promise I'll do everything in my power to protect you.'

'I have nightmares,' Rose whispered.

'I know. I'm so sorry. You can sleep in my bed if that makes it better.'

Rose dropped her gaze with a shrug.

'Talk to me, Rose. *Please*. I want to help. And I *can* help, I promise.'

'Can I ask you something?'

'Of course.'

'Did they take you to a dreadful woman who forced her fingers into your...quim?'

'Yes,' Olivia said darkly. 'The Midwife.'

Rose's gaze snapped up. 'Are there others like her?'

'There are many who offer this so-called "service," but only one is known as the Midwife. Was she the one your mother summoned?'

Rose's watery gaze darted away. She produced a nod. Her throat was working.

Olivia placed a comforting hand on Rose's shoulder. 'Sévère and I are collecting evidence against this horrible creature and all her accomplices. Our office is filled with notes and observations. We will get her, Rose. She won't escape the consequences much longer. But if you remember anything your mother discussed with the Midwife, or any detail no matter how small, it might help us lock her up.'

'Mother, too?'

Olivia paused, trying to analyse the strange mix of hardness and vulnerability she saw in Rose's face. 'If you want that, yes, absolutely. But if you don't want that, I'll find a way around it.'

Rose swallowed, scraped tears from her cheeks and said, 'I want them all to hurt.'

Olivia paced the length of Sévère's office. A fire crackled in the hearth. Sévère sat with his feet up on a footstool. Dust motes danced through the milky early afternoon light that stretched its fingers through the lace curtains.

'Rose talked about Frost this morning.' Olivia paused by the windows. 'It's the first time she's opened up about the rape.'

Higgins stood with his shoulder leaning against a bookshelf, his bowler hat loosely held in his hands. 'Will she be all right?'

'I believe so,' Olivia replied. 'She also told me her mother arranged for the Midwife to examine her. That wretched woman cashed in on her own daughter's rape and intended to sell her to

Burnham afterwards. The Midwife deemed her unsuitable for what she called "the Kent operation." Too plain, apparently.'

Sévère stared at the fire near his feet and asked without looking up, 'Is she willing to testify?'

'Yes.'

'The oath of underage children holds little weight at court,' Sévère continued. 'One of many reasons why creatures like Mrs Burnham don't fear prison.'

Pensive, Olivia chewed on her cheek and murmured, 'We need the Midwife to turn against Burnham. But how do we convince her?'

'I could rough her up some.' Higgins flipped his bowler onto the bookshelf, crossed his arms and showed his teeth. 'Or resort to blackmail.'

'Difficult,' Sévère grumbled, picking lint from his knee and flicking it into the fire.

Abruptly, Olivia turned to face to room as a memory hit her like a bucket of ice water. 'Alexander Easy.'

A wistful smile crossed Sévère's features. 'The man is long gone.'

'You don't say,' she replied, eyebrows at a dangerously sardonic angle. Alexander Easy had breathed his last in Olivia's company when she'd been a prostitute, known as Miss Mary. After calling for help in a panicked frenzy, her madam and Bobby — the burly guard — had dismissed Olivia with promises of taking care of 'the problem.' Which, it turned out, was to discard Alexander Easy in the Thames.

Two days later, Olivia found herself apprehended by Inspector Height and the Coroner of Eastern Middlesex – Sévère. That was how they'd met. And heavens, had she hated him then.

With a devilish smile, she turned to Higgins, who had no

clue what she was talking about. She said, 'Alexander Easy was a client. He suffered a heart malady in my bed. I implored Madam Rosseau and Bobby to help him. They simply disposed of the poor man.'

Theatrically, she tapped her lower lip. 'Come to think of it, Alexander might have been still breathing when they took him. Which means the madam and Bobby are responsible for his demise.'

Sévère cast a frown her way, a sharp glint in his eyes.

Olivia shrugged. 'And it appears I'm the only one who can attest to their guilt.'

Higgins chimed in, 'A little roughing up and a lot of blackmailing? I like it. When do we leave?'

Grinning, Sévère turned his gaze back to the fire. 'A hefty sentence awaits them if you were to testify. The question is, would the prospect frighten them enough?'

'They would do anything to avoid prison, including testifying against the Midwife and Burnham.'

'They'd risk crossing Burnham and her powerful allies?' Sévère asked.

'Their first priority is self-preservation. At least one of them will speak up. I intend to break them both.'

Rain hammered against the brougham. People hurried past, some without an umbrella or newspaper to protect against the deluge.

The Midwife took her seat across from Olivia and Sévère. Water trickled from the woman's hat onto the floor.

'Good evening,' Sévère said, with a welcoming expression plastered to his face.

Olivia's fingers tightened around the pistol hidden in the folds of her skirt.

The Midwife's mouth thinned. 'Your message said it was urgent.'

'Indeed. We'd like to offer you an option.' Sévère kept his voice barely above the patter of rain. 'Two, in fact. Face trial for your part in Mrs Burnham's enterprise, or assist us in bringing it down.'

A burst of laughter escaped her. 'Oh dear me. What makes you think I'd ever betray that woman?'

Olivia leaned in. 'We have amassed detailed witness accounts of your illicit dealings. What we require from you are the names of your clients and allies, and all records of your operations and those of the White Lilly.'

The Midwife snorted, her gaze drifting out the window as though entirely uninterested in the conversation. Yet her fingers anxiously fidgeted with her skirts.

'Our evidence is sufficient to have you sent to the colonies. Two decades of hard labour in the unforgiving Australian desert awaits you. For someone like you, that's a death sentence.' She paused for effect. 'Unless, of course, you cooperate.'

Silence fell.

'Assuming I were to consider this...' the Midwife hesitated. 'How can you ensure your witnesses stay silent?'

Sévère replied, 'They'll all comply with our demands, or face a lengthy sojourn in the colonies. Should you choose to cooperate, be sure to retrieve your records and those of the White Lilly so there's ample evidence to stop Mrs Burnham and her cronies from continuing their sordid business. And kindly take Mr Higgins along for the ride, he's quite amicable if one follows his instructions.'

All air seemed to leave the Midwife when she said, 'They'll kill me if they discover I've betrayed them.'

'Then see to it you're not discovered,' Olivia shot back.

The Midwife's mouth compressed. 'My records are in my house. Hidden.'

Olivia swung open the brougham door. 'Mr Higgins, it's time.'

The coachman dropped from his perch, a rivulet of rain sliding off his bowler. Olivia's gaze followed his and the Midwife's path across the street, then she unfurled her umbrella, folded up the collar of her coat and climbed up on the brougham. The horses fidgeted; she surmised it was due to Higgins' absence or perhaps her presence. The animals sensed her unease behind the reins and mirrored it.

Olivia kept a hand on her pistol. Sévère had his own gun ready, as did Higgins. But all of the world's weapons would not quell her unease.

The situation was critical.

Without the Midwife's cooperation, the likelihood of an arrest, let alone a trial, was slim.

Olivia kept watch over the Midwife's home, guarding Higgins' back, prepared to threaten anyone who would dare enter the building while the coachman was inside.

The downpour began to lessen. It made no difference. Olivia's coat was already soaked.

The door to the Midwife's house was pushed open, and Higgins stepped out. He tapped a finger to his bowler, signalling that he had what they needed. The Midwife appeared behind him, and they both made their way to the brougham.

'You all right up there?' Higgins asked cheerily.

'Why wouldn't I be? The weather is splendid.' Olivia mentioning the splendid weather was her signal to Higgins that no one had attempted to enter the house while he was inside.

They traded places. Olivia and the Midwife entered the carriage, and the brougham began moving. It wasn't far to the White Lilly, a journey of roughly a quarter of an hour. Sévère lit an oil lamp and perused the Midwife's ledger in silence, then closed it without a word and dimmed the flame.

His eyes bore into the Midwife. 'Your records are incomplete. You are trying to play us.'

'I keep *her* name out. As we all do.'

Casually, he folded his hands in his lap. 'And why, pray tell, should we be on the way to the White Lilly if not the slightest trace of Mrs Burham's activities is to be found anywhere?'

She mirrored his gesture. 'Your coachman is armed, is he not? The proof of Catherine Burnham's control of London's white slave trade is in her office. And that's at the White Lilly. I'll show you the way. Gaining entry is your own affair.'

Amused, Sévère showed his teeth. 'Oh, believe me, *Mrs Sharpe*, I am making it your affair.'

Twenty-Two

THROUGH THE BROUGHAM'S WINDOW, gas lamps reflected on the White Lily's rain-soaked facade. Tension in the carriage was palpable. The leather creaked as Sévère shifted in his seat and fixed his gaze on Olivia. 'Bloody hell, do you think I'm not aware of the risks? That I wouldn't stay out of your way if that helped? But the evidence must stand up in court. You know how little value a woman's testimony holds, a former convict's even less.' He cast a glance through the driver's hatch toward Higgins, who kept an eye on the surroundings while they discussed their burglary of the White Lilly.

'We have to get in and out fast. If anyone discovers us, we need to run. You will only slow us down.' Olivia's words cut him to the quick.

The Midwife sat opposite them, not in the least interested in hiding her sardonic grin.

'Higgins.' Sévère rapped his cane against the roof. 'Your thoughts?'

'Begging your pardon, but Mrs Sévère has a point.' Higgins'

voice drifted down through the hatch. 'I can support you, you know that. And if we have to leg it, I can carry you for a bit. But *this* one,' he pointed a rude finger at the Midwife, 'she's a liability. We can't just leave her. So it's either I dispatch her now, or we bring her along and I shoot her as soon as she starts causing trouble. Which she will do. Might as well be done with it now.'

'What? We had an agreement! You can't possibly expect to drag me into this?'

'You dragged yourself into it without our help,' Olivia snapped just as Sévère said to Higgins, 'I can manage, thank you very much. And I will keep watch over our esteemed guest.'

'Which you can do effortlessly while staying put right here, while Higgins and I gather evidence,' Olivia countered.

Sévère leaned in. 'I recognise crucial evidence when I see it. We can't afford to miss anything vital, and all the evidence will have to be properly documented. The chain of custody must be established. One procedural mistake and the entire case falls apart. I'm joining you. End of discussion.' Sévère knew he was risking his alibi for Frost's death with the Midwife present.

Olivia groaned. 'We won't have any evidence if we're caught because you can't move fast enough. All because you're being stubborn!'

'I'm being practical.'

'You're being proud.'

The Midwife's grin widened. 'Such domestic discord. Delightful.'

Sévère drew his revolver and aimed it at her chest. 'Should I hear another word from the woman who makes a living with the systematic rape of children, I'll demonstrate how charming I truly am.'

'I cannot fathom why you are in such a flurry over this matter. If a girl is to be seduced, better she's with a gentleman who can offer money and nice things, rather than a bumbling youth who gives her nothing in return.'

Sévère lifted his revolver higher, aiming at the wretched woman's face.

Olivia clenched her fists and took a deep breath to steady herself. 'Continue telling yourself that if it eases your conscience, but stop pretending you are anything more than a self-serving opportunist. And if you have any sense of self-preservation, please do shut your mouth.'

'The house looks empty,' Higgins interrupted. 'But we could scout the area first, make sure we know all the exits, check for noisy neighbours.'

Sévère glanced out of the window and nodded. 'And while you're scouting I'll have a little chat with our guest.'

He wasn't quite sure if he wanted to prove to himself or Olivia that he wasn't a useless cripple, and that he had a modicum of pride and self-respect left in his bones. Above all, he felt an unshakable need to protect her. Knowing he wouldn't be able to convince her to stay behind, he took the next best option: join her and guard her back.

'A copper is patrolling the area,' Higgins whispered, a little winded from scouting the vicinity. 'But no signs of life in the house. We might just be able to saunter in and leisurely search the place.'

The coachman steadied Sévère's descent from the carriage, then passed him the crutch. 'Easy now,' Higgins said, his firm grip anchoring Sévère as pain shot through his weakened leg.

Bloody hell, how Sévère loathed his treacherous body!

The White Lily loomed in the drizzle before them. They skirted the pools of lamplight cast across the cobbles.

'Get moving.' Olivia jabbed her revolver at the Midwife's back, who grumbled in protest.

Sévère's crutch bit into his armpit as they made their way through a dark alley to the back of the house. Each step sent ripples of torment through his hip, but he refused to slow down.

Olivia nudged the Midwife aside and gave Higgins a nod. He promptly aimed his revolver at their guest. Scrutinising the facade, Olivia decided that the servants' quarters lay in the attic, as the basement had no windows, just a hatch for coal.

A cat yowled in the distance.

'Tools, please,' she said to Higgins. He handed over the farrier's hammer and a thin strip of iron he kept in the brougham's toolbox. She forced the latch of the coal chute and disappeared.

'How on earth is she going to find her way in the blackness down there?' Higgins whispered.

'Valid question,' Sévère mumbled. His heartbeat lurched when he heard the scraping of the backdoor latch.

'Coming?' Olivia appeared in the door frame, a grin on her face. Her expression turned hard when her gaze fell on the Midwife. 'You're with me. Show us where Burnham keeps her secrets and you'll be free to go.'

As they slipped through the scullery, Olivia gestured towards her right. 'The coal cellar. If we get separated and you need to run and the exits are blocked.' Sévère nodded, searching the darkness for any signs of movement.

Higgins shifted next to him, subtly motioning towards the house's front. 'Someone's there,' he whispered.

Sévère followed Higgins' gaze and saw only darkness. But he thought he heard a faint rustling of footsteps. He touched a hand on the Midwife's shoulder to get her attention. 'Where is it?' he whispered.

She pointed to the first floor. Sévère suppressed a groan. When they'd walked through the scullery and kitchen, he hadn't found a service staircase. To reach the first floor, they'd have to get through the entrance hall and up the main staircase. He knew there was no way to ascend the staircase without alerting whoever was guarding the house.

The entrance hall stretched before them, thick with shadows. When he heard a soft cough ahead of them, he glanced at Higgins and signalled for his coachman to lean closer. Sévère whispered into his ear, 'How many?' pointed ahead, and moved to lean against a wall for support.

Higgins didn't bother to reply. He slipped away.

Somewhere nearby, a clock ticked away the seconds. Then, minutes.

His heart leapt into his mouth when his coachman reappeared. 'Just one guard. Managed to convince him to take a nap. Swaddled and tucked in, nice and tidy. Let's move.' He draped an arm around Sévère's back, and they proceeded through the entrance hall and up the flight of stairs to the first floor, every groan of the floorboards echoing like thunder in the silence. Sévère's leg threatened to buckle with each step.

When they reached the landing, the Midwife whispered, 'You're making a terrible mistake.'

'I've made many, but this isn't one of them,' Olivia replied. 'Carry on. Lead the way.'

At the end of the hallway, they paused before a door. 'This is her office,' The Midwife said.

'You failed to mention the guard. What else are you keeping from us?' Olivia asked in a hushed tone. When no reply came, she pressed the muzzle of her revolver against the Midwife's neck. 'Your usefulness lies solely in providing us with information and ensuring we're not discovered. Make no mistake, *Mrs Sharpe*, I'll use you as a shield if we run into anyone. And I don't give a fig about the number of holes you sustain in the process.'

'There's only one guard, I swear. I must have forgotten he was here!'

'Open the door, then. Quietly.' Olivia kept the revolver pressed to the woman's neck.

Sévère didn't believe a word the Midwife was uttering, and he didn't expect Olivia to, either.

They entered the room and shut the door quietly.

'Find a lamp and light it,' Sévère whispered to Higgins. Moments later, a soft glow illuminated the room, revealing an office akin to Burnham's study in Chiswick. But here, the desk bore stacks of writing paper and envelopes, an inkstand with pens and nibs, a stub of sealing wax, a letter opener.

Sévère addressed the Midwife, 'You know what we came here for. Point us to it. The faster we're done, the sooner you can return home.'

The woman crossed her arms and remained silent.

Higgins moved around to light candles, approached the door and pressed his ear to it, then returned to Sévère's side. 'Where do you want me?'

'Convince our guest that cooperation is to her advantage.' He turned to the desk and rummaged through its contents, looking for anything with names, locations and financial transactions.

'Fine, fine!' the Midwife hissed.

He looked up. Higgins had her at gunpoint. The man did not look happy. With a tremble in her arm, she pointed at a carpet in front of the desk. Olivia stepped aside, flipped the carpet, and ran her hands over the exposed floorboards. Higgins moved an oil lamp closer to provide better light. Tapping his crutch against the floor, Sévère probed for the hollow sound of a hidden compartment.

'Try there,' Olivia said.

The soft creak of a floorboard came just a moment too late. Sévère felt a sharp crack against the back of his head.

He staggered forward.

The desk approached with alarming speed.

Twenty-Three

THE DIMLY LIT room swayed around Sévère as he struggled to regain his bearings. Two blows to his head, one from...what was it? A chair? Another from the desk when his head had struck it with a nauseating thud. Pain radiated through his skull. His left leg and hip ached fiercely. He must have twisted it when he fell.

Olivia was at his side in an instant, her hands cupping his face, gaze analysing and urgent. 'Can you hear me?'

'I'm not deaf,' he grumbled.

Her fingers probed the back of his head and came away bloody. 'This scullery-drudging, sodding hag!' she cursed.

'I take it my brain is still inside my skull.' Sévère tried for humour to lighten the mood as a fresh wave of pain washed through him. 'I'm all right,' he managed, patting Olivia's hand that was still cradling his face.

Higgins burst into the room, breathless and frustrated. 'She gave me the slip.'

'Gutter-crawling doxy!' Olivia stood, rubbed her face, and kicked at the desk. 'Ow.'

'It can't be helped now. Let's focus on our search. Higgins, lend me a hand, will you? I'd like to sit on that chair over there,' Sévère said through clenched teeth.

His coachman obliged, and Olivia pulled a candle closer to the floorboards they'd been examining. She ran her fingernails along the edges while Higgins tried to wedge the pointed end of his farrier's hammer into the cracks.

'Nothing,' she said.

'No surprise there,' Higgins grumbled.

Sévère clapped his palms on the armrests of his chair. 'We are here now and will make the best of it. Olivia, hand me those ledgers. I'll go through them. Higgins, try your hammer on that desk. Quietly, if possible. There must be something here we can use.'

Time flew by, the silence broken only by the rustle of paper, the creak of wood when Higgins pried open locked drawers, and Olivia's murmured oaths. They worked methodically, searching every inch of Burnham's office for any small piece of evidence they could use against her.

Sévère's attention was focused on the documents in his lap, but everything they'd found was in code. There was a pattern here, a cadence to the letters and numbers that evaded him. He could feel it, just out of reach, like a hint of a thought at the edge of his consciousness.

'No false bottoms or hidden compartments in any of the drawers or parts of the desk,' Higgins said, dusting off his palms.

Olivia rummaged through shelves, scrutinising each book for concealed notes. 'Blast it! Would Burnham leave something important where it could be easily found?'

Sévère looked up, his eyes meeting hers. 'All of this is in code.' He indicated his stack of ledgers. 'Useless without the key.'

Olivia kicked the desk again. 'I shouldn't have taken my eyes off that fucking arse-licking witch!'

Higgins choked on his spittle.

Sévère cleared his throat. Hearing his wife swear like a sailor felt...refreshing in an odd way. 'We need to be smarter than her.'

'And we obviously aren't,' she replied.

She scoured the floor, angrily flipping rugs and tapping floorboards. Sévère scanned the office, trying to see it as Burham would: a sanctuary for secrets.

His leg and hip were throbbing sharply. He pushed the pain aside, focusing on the task at hand. They were close, he could feel it. They just needed to find the key that would make everything fall into place.

He spotted a box on the top shelf and asked Higgins to pass it to him. 'Hmm, locked,' his coachman said, set the pointed end of his hammer to the lock and cracked it like an egg.

Sévère set the box on his lap. The lid had mother-of-pearl inlays depicting a caged bird. He ran a fingertip over it as something tugged at his memory. It was just out of reach. He opened the lid and paused, processing what he saw.

'We're leaving,' he said, his voice hoarse. 'Higgins, take all of this down to the brougham. My wife and I will follow.'

'We're not cleaning up?' Higgins eyed the bunched-up rugs, the cracked-open desk, the floor strewn with books and papers.

'No. We're going to drag Inspector Height out of his bed.'

'What did you find?' Olivia asked.

'The key.' At her frown, he added, 'I'll explain later.'

A faint pop echoed from the stairwell. They froze. The hair on Sévère's neck snapped to attention. He pulled his revolver as Higgins, doing the same, crept toward the door and listened. Wide-eyed, the coachman turned back to them, pressing a finger to his mouth.

Taking one look at Olivia, Sévère reached a decision in the blink of an eye. 'You'll leave. I'll create a distraction.'

'Absolutely not!' Her expression brooked no argument.

'It's the only way. Take the evidence to Height and come back with the cavalry. The photographs in the box are the keys to the cypher. Higgins, block the door. It will give you more time. And make sure she's safe or God help you.' Impatiently, he motioned toward the window. 'Run!'

The door flew open with a frame-shattering crash. Two men barged into the room. The taller one's nose bore evidence of multiple fractures, whilst his companion sported a scar that ran from his left ear to his jaw.

'Good evening, gentlemen,' Sévère greeted them with a smile, swallowing his fear for Olivia's safety and a failed mission. He wasn't afraid of pain, especially not now that half his body was already on fire.

The scarred man's lips twisted as he looked around in the room. 'And what have we got here, eh?'

'Tom's got quite the bump on his head,' the other said. 'But he's a tough one. You wanted him quiet, you should have finished him off.'

So it wasn't the Midwife who had raised the alarm. Interesting. Sévère filed that detail away for later consideration.

'And how fares our dear Catherine?' Sévère kept his voice steady, measured. "I presume she's hosting another ball in Chiswick?'

'Shut it.' The tall one stepped forward, cracking his knuckles. 'You're not talking your way out of this one.'

'But if he's a friend of Mrs Burnham—' the scarred man said.

'Look around, would you?' the tall man snarled at his companion.

Sévère adjusted his cravat. 'I believe it's in everyone's best interest if we discuss this like civilised men.'

'There's nothing to discuss.' The tall man pulled a blackjack from his coat pocket.

'Oh, but there is. Your mistress will be keen to know who's currently occupying her office and the reasons behind my presence. She'll also want to know what I have discovered.'

'He's bluffing, isn't he?' The scarred one asked.

'Am I? You are aware that the army takes a dim view of its officers supplementing their pay with illegal activities. What would the newspaper print about two soldiers moonlighting as brothel guards?' Sévère raised an eyebrow. 'The outcome would be...unfortunate for you.'

They exchanged glances. The scarred man was about to say something but the tall one shut him up with the shake of his head. Sèvère's suspicion was confirmed. These two were soldiers.

He said, 'Major Cunningham is a dear friend of mine. Although "dear" might be a bit of an...understatement. He and I share certain interests. Perhaps you two aren't personally familiar with him? Perhaps you've been referred to Mrs Burnham by Rear Admiral Farnsworth or Colonel Sinclair? It's of little importance. What matters is that a very influential benefactor of Mrs Burnham was having doubts about his safety and privacy. It seems those doubts were warranted.' Sévère motioned at the mess in the office

Scowling, the tall man began to circle around Sévère.

'I make it my business to know things, gentlemen. Just as Mrs Burnham makes it her business to know things about her clients and associates. What do you suppose might happen if these men should discover their secrets aren't as safe as Mrs Burnham promised?'

The tall man paused in front of Sévère, expression dark. 'Are you threatening Mrs Burnham?'

'Not in the least. I'm merely pointing out that discretion works both ways. You let me walk out of here, and I'll ensure Tom's negligence doesn't make it into my report.'

The tall man spat on the floor. 'You've got nerve, I'll give you that.'

'I prefer to call it common sense. Now, shall we part ways amicably?'

The two men shared a look. The scarred one produced a nod. The tall one smirked and gestured toward the door. 'Off you go, then.'

Sévère knew they planned to knock him unconscious the moment he turned his back on them. Delivering him to their superiors was likely their intention. He knew he'd not make it to the door, let alone leave the house.

He was trapped. With a sigh, he made a final attempt. 'That won't do, gentlemen. As you can see, I'm not quite done assessing the security of this place. It would be appreciated if you left me to it. Good night.'

The tall man erupted in laughter. The scarred one looked perplexed and muttered, 'What the bloody hell is this?'

'He did say good night, didn't he?' the tall man said, still chuckling.

He raised his blackjack and cracked it against Sévère's head.

Twenty-Four

HEIGHT'S DRAWING room reeked of cold pipe tobacco and wet wallpaper. Higgins dropped the stack of ledgers on a table. Olivia slammed the box down next to it, sending a small vase with lavender sprigs wobbling.

'Catherine Burnham operates the White Lilly, an organisation that professes to be a charity. It's entirely rotten. They abduct children and auction off their innocence to wealthy men in Burnham's Chiswick mansion. Afterwards, they process their victims in her clearing house in Kent before shipping them off in caskets, drugged and unconscious, to the continent.'

Height cinched his night robe tighter. 'And this is your evidence?' His mop of black hair stuck up at odd angles.

'Yes. Unfortunately, it's encoded. My husband knows how to decipher it. He said the key is in here.' She tapped on the box. 'He's being held at the White Lilly. You must help us save him.'

'Let me first examine—'

'Examine?' Olivia's laugh held no humour. 'While they're subjecting him to God knows what?'

Higgins, his weathered face grave, said, 'They might kill him if you hesitate, Inspector.'

'Exactly!' Olivia seized Height's wrist. 'We can prove that members of parliament are involved. Policemen, magistrates, industrialists, and high-ranking military men. What do you think they'll do with a witness? Serve tea and biscuits? Please, we need your help!'

Height rubbed his thick eyebrows. 'Damnation. This complicates matters.'

'Complicates? I'll tell you what's going to complicate matters. My husband's corpse if you don't move your arse!'

'I can't raid a house without proper—'

'Then arrest him.' Olivia's voice cracked. 'Arrest him for burglary if that gets you and your men there fastest.'

'The moment we enter the premises under false pretences, any evidence we find becomes inadmissible.'

'Fuck your evidence!' Olivia's fist connected with the table. The vase tipped and vomited its contents across the tablecloth. 'We went there to rescue those girls. While you lot dither over proper procedure, they're being subjected to horror men like you don't even dare speak about!'

Higgins straightened the vase and moved the ledgers away from the small puddle. 'Sir, time's running out.'

Height braced himself against the edge of the table. 'If I organise a raid, we'll need warrants. That takes time. However, if I report a burglary in progress...' He paused, eyes narrowing. 'And once we're inside, anything in plain sight is fair game...'

'Choose fast. Because if you won't help, I'll go back there myself. And I'll shoot my way to my husband.'

Height cleared his throat and nodded toward a window where the horses dozed in the soft glow of a street lamp. 'I'll get dressed and meet you outside.'

Olivia's patience had long evaporated by the time they arrived at Division H Headquarters, and Height disappeared inside.

'If they've hurt him—' she pressed through her teeth.

'We'll get him back.' Higgins' voice drifted through the hatch. 'And forgive me for saying this, but the coarser your language, the less your impact. Height respects you. Your husband adores you. Anyone else... Well, just don't use the word *fuck* with police and judges.'

She grumbled, fully aware that he was correct, a fact that irked her endlessly. 'Twenty minutes to gather his men. Twenty more to reach the White Lilly. We'll be too late, Higgins.' She dug her knuckles into the leader seats, wishing she could fly or turn back time or...become whatever was needed to fix this.

When Height finally reappeared, she was on the verge of losing all hope.

'The police carriage is around back. I've got five good men who will follow us. I give you my word, we'll get your husband out.'

'Your word? Your word won't stop them from killing him while you faff about with procedure.'

Height took off his hat and climbed into the brougham. 'Now, shall we waste time bickering or shall we discuss your case? We have twenty minutes. Ample time for a good overview.'

Olivia groaned but conceded.

They forced the front door and rushed up the stairs, led by Higgins and Olivia.

'What happened here?' Height asked when he saw the mess that was Mrs Burnham's office.

Nausea hit Olivia as she spotted smears of bloody fingerprints on the exposed floorboards. She was oblivious to the servants spilling into the room and enquiring what the police were doing in the house, oblivious to Higgins pulling her aside, murmuring platitudes in his raspy voice.

'The Midwife. They might have brought him to her. And if he isn't there, we go to Chiswick,' she managed to say to Higgins. 'Tell Height to move his men.'

The inspector left an officer behind to collect evidence for a burglary and an abduction, and anything else that might be suspicious should he come across it.

They boarded the brougham and left, the police carriage following close behind. Olivia tried to assure herself that they would reach their destination just as slowly as those who'd taken Sévère. The thought offered little comfort. She didn't know where he was being brought, and she'd already wasted too much time with Height. But she had no choice. She needed help.

Closing her eyes, she took deep, measured breaths and considered what Sévère would do in her place.

He would make sure the mission didn't fail. They'd worked too hard to throw it all away now.

'How much do you trust your men?' she asked Height, motioning toward the police carriage.

'I have complete faith in them.'

'None of them are on Burnham's payroll? Are you sure? Lives depend on it.'

Height nodded.

'Higgins, stop the horses!' she called out.

'Tell your men to raid Catherine Burnham's Chiswick estate. She's keeping abducted children there. She pretends to help them find positions as servants in wealthy households. The children learn the truth once they're sold off. Sévère might have been brought there.'

Height gazed out of the brougham window, his eyes unfocused in the darkness. He turned back to Olivia and said, 'If I do this, I'm jeopardising my career.'

'You could turn a blind eye and let that monster do whatever she desires. Just as so many have before you.'

He sighed and shook his head.

'For heaven's sake, man! We've risked life and limb for this! What has to happen for you to take the small risk of being downgraded by your superior? Is the price you're demanding my husband's life?'

With compressed lips and flaring nostrils, Height pushed open the brougham door and approached the police carriage. A moment later, the carriage made a sharp turn and sped away.

Height returned and climbed back inside. 'Mr Higgins, let's go.'

Unspeaking, they drove to the Midwife's quarters and alighted. When Height saw Olivia and Higgins pull their revolvers as they approached the front door, he followed suit.

As Height was raising his arm to knock, Higgins kicked in the door.

Olivia rushed through and collided with a maid. The girl's squeak of surprise was quickly stifled by Olivia's hand over her mouth.

'Where is your mistress? We're searching for a man who's been brought here against his will. He'll be hurt.' Olivia removed her hand from the maid's face.

The girl gulped a lungful of air and stammered, 'The mistress left. There is no man here.'

'Inspector Height, Scotland Yard. I am here on official

police business and require your full cooperation in this matter. Where is Mr Sévère?'

Taken aback, the girl needed a moment before replying, 'Who is Mr Sévère?'

'My husband. He's been forcibly taken. We suspect he's been brought here or to another property owned by your mistress,' Olivia said.

'I don't think my mistress owns any houses. She only rents this one. And there's no gentleman here, as I said before. May I ask why the police think my mistress took this man?'

Height looked at Olivia, eyebrows raised.

Olivia ignored him. 'You said your mistress is gone. Where did she go and when is she expected to return?'

'She didn't say where she was going. I don't think she will return any time soon. Gave me ten pounds and said I'm no longer in her employ.' The girl didn't seem too perturbed by the prospect.

'May we have a look around?' Height asked.

'The gentleman is already looking.' The maid pointed through the entrance hall and down the corridor at Higgin's vanishing frame.

Height muttered an oath and followed after the coachman. Once he was out of earshot, Olivia addressed the maid, 'Your mistress has been complicit in the rape and abduction of hundreds of young girls. You were aware of what she was doing, weren't you?'

'Of course.' There was no shame in her admission. How strange.

'We need to find my husband. I fear your mistress' cronies are going to kill him. Can you offer any insight as to where they might have taken him?'

The maid's eyes strayed around the room, blinking. Olivia

prepared herself for a deluge of lies. To her surprise, the girl said, 'Have you tried the White Lilly?'

'Yes. They took him from there.'

'Hum. Perhaps one of the brothels, then?'

A surge of hope, as intense as boiling oil, washed over Olivia. 'Where exactly?'

~

After an agonising hour-long drive, they reached Marylebone and Burnham's high-end brothels. Another half hour passed searching them, with no trace of Sévère. Higgins insisted they couldn't take the horses any further without a few hours of rest and good feed and water. Height appeared to have lost all faith in Olivia's promises of sufficient evidence to help throw Burnham and her associates in prison.

Height said, 'Burnham is well known to the police for operating brothels that cater to high society. She promises privacy, opulence, and discretion. Scotland Yard has made numerous attempts to regulate or close down her establishments. All in vain. Her brothels are under constant scrutiny. You know all too well that she has powerful allies, so I can't help wondering how you came by the substantial evidence you claim to have obtained.'

She eyed him warily. 'Do I need to be worried that we left much of that evidence in your home, Inspector?'

His exhausted expression hardened. 'You persistently offend me, then expect my help. I've had too little sleep to endure your foul mood for much longer, Mrs Sévère.'

'How would *you* feel if your wife had been taken by criminals?'

He groaned, ripped off his hat and rubbed his scalp. 'I'll send a telegram to Chiswick, instructing my men to notify us immediately should they discover anything.' With that, he marched off toward the next post office.

She turned to Higgins who was tending to the horses, offering them water and oats. She found herself at a loss for words. Taking a cab to Chiswick before hearing from the officers they'd sent there would be foolish. Yet, remaining idle felt even more foolish.

An idea crossed her mind. 'The guard you knocked out in the White Lilly—'

'I apologise. This was my fault. I should have just...' he gestured helplessly.

'Killed him?' She let out a bitter laugh. 'If we killed everyone who stood in our way, few people would still be breathing. That guard, do you know if he was a policeman?'

'Maybe.' Higgins hesitated, mulling it over. 'Hum. Military, I think. Yes, he might have been a soldier.'

Olivia's mood brightened. 'Hand me your revolver and any bullets you're carrying. I shall pay a visit to an old acquaintance.'

Twenty-Five

'HELLO EVERET,' Olivia murmured in a saccharine tone.

The figure in the bed let out a cough. An eye fluttered open. The man appeared almost comical in his nightcap, greying mutton chops, and rounded belly. Without her intimate knowledge of him, she might have underestimated him. However, beneath his grandfatherly veneer lay a well-toned physique and a ruthless disposition.

His sleepy gaze vanished in an instant. Grunting, he heaved himself upright.

'That's enough,' Olivia snapped. 'I suggest you move slow enough to avoid startling my fingers. They are quite eager, you see.'

It was a phrase he'd often used on her. *I have quite eager fingers, you see.*

His gaze found one revolver, then the other.

She said, 'I'm pointing one at your cock. The other at your belly.'

'What is it you want from me? Money? Haven't I given you enough?'

She scoffed. 'Never enough to tolerate such a pig as you.'

'Aren't you—'

'Shut your mouth. If you value your bollocks and your life, you'll speak only when spoken to and you'll answer each and every one of my questions truthfully.'

'Begging your pardon?'

She sighed. 'You've read about Judge Peregrine?'

He snorted.

A sinister grin spread across her face as she spoke softly as though telling him a bedtime story, 'We, the jury, having duly considered the evidence presented before us, found Colonel Everett Sinclair guilty of the violation of underaged girls, the wilful and malicious aiding and abetting in the systematic abduction, drugging, rape and trading of hundreds of children, many of them orphans without protection, many being shipped to the continent for further exploitation, and the gross abuse of his position, influence, and power, to conceal his nefarious activities and obstruct the course of justice.'

Gradually, Sinclair's expression derailed.

'Having weighed the gravity and multitude of these offences, and in consideration of the irreparable harm inflicted upon countless innocent souls, we, the jury, have decreed that the only fitting punishment is death. We have therefore ruled the execution of Colonel Everett Sinclair. Let it be known that this verdict has been reached with the utmost solemnity and in the interest of true justice, which the accused for so long denied to others.'

'You are jesting.'

'Oh, believe me, I am not. I know about your investments in the Quincy Casket Company, and your involvement in shipping drugged children to the continent. You're protecting those shipments, pretending they aid in maintaining diplomatic relationships with Belgium. You are a supporter of the White Lilly and Catherine Burnham. You help her run London's white slave trade. You finance the abduction of orphans so that they can be sold at a profit.'

'Now, listen, I'm... I'm certain we can come to an agreem—'

'I told you to shut your mouth, Everett. However, it seems you are in luck. I require something from you, and you, in turn, require something from me. This night might turn out beneficial to both of us.'

His eyes bounced between her face and the two revolvers she held in a relaxed grip. She waited for him to make a peep, but he didn't. A wise decision.

'I might be persuaded to overlook certain incriminating evidence against you, evidence discovered at the White Lilly along with cyphers and keys.' She thought of the box and what it contained: photographs of children, prettied up for buyers and marked with a name, month, and a cryptic word. She suspected Sévère had found a pattern there that would unlock the encoded secrets of Burnham's ledgers.

'I'm listening,' Sinclair grumbled.

'The White Lilly was guarded by three men, men loyal to you. They've taken someone I'm rather fond of. I demand to know his whereabouts.'

Sinclair was all puzzlement. 'How would I know? They don't report every detail of their actions.'

She clicked her tongue and shook her head. 'Ah, Everett, dear. You have seen battle, yes?'

A single nod was his response.

'Have you ever faced an adversary who had nothing left to lose?'

For a long moment, he remained silent. 'Can't say with certainty that I have.'

She kept her voice even and cordial. 'I'm sure you haven't. You are, after all, still breathing. Now, let me tell you something crucial for your continued survival: You wouldn't want to give me the slightest inkling that my husband is no more. You want me to find him, alive and well. Because if he's gone, *nothing* on earth will stop me from riddling your body with bullet holes.'

His breathing quickened. A bead of sweat trickled down from his temple.

'You know your men well. You place enough trust in them to act swiftly during a crisis, even without your involvement. All I require from you is the location of my husband. Afterwards, you're free to run to the colonies and do whatever helps you sleep at night. But rest assured, Catherine Burnham is heading for prison, and she might not be keeping your secrets on her way there.'

'You say my men have taken him? I need to know where.'

'The White Lilly, during our raid.'

He huffed. She noticed a flicker in his eyes that dropped lead down to her stomach.

He said, 'Unwanted witnesses are disposed of at sea. He'll be on a steamer bound for Antwerp. If you hurry, you can still save him.'

She glanced toward the windows. A gap in the heavy drapes showed that daybreak was approaching. She forced a smile and turned back to the Colonel. 'You have influence, dear Everett. You are a distinguished military officer. People heed your words, yes?'

The stench of rotting fish and burning coal saturated the docks. Gas lamps cast weak bubbles of light into the murky pre-dawn gloom. Cranes groaned overhead, their chains rattling as dockers loaded cargo onto waiting ships. Seagulls wheeled and screamed, diving for scraps amongst the wooden crates and barrels that littered the wharf.

Olivia wove between stevedores pushing loaded handcarts, carefully avoiding cobblestones slick with fish scales and seawater. Desperately, she searched for a familiar face. Every passing minute was another minute closer to the steamship's departure - another minute closer to Sévère's watery death.

Near the customs house, she caught sight of a woman she knew, leaning against a warehouse wall, flashing gap-toothed smiles at passing sailors.

'Annie, good to see you. I need your help.' Olivia pressed a sovereign into the woman's palm. 'There's a girl being shipped to Belgium. In a casket.'

Shocked, Annie blinked at the gold, the immense wealth she now held in her palm. 'Must be some girl, that.'

'I'm trying to save a friend. She's just a child. They took her, drugged her, and locked her in a casket. She'll be shipped out today. I have to get aboard the steamship to Antwerp before it's too late!'

'Christ.' Annie glanced over Olivia's shoulder. 'You haven't much time. Follow me. Quick and quiet-like.'

They hurried past towering stacks of timber, Annie leading the way to where an elderly docker sorted through manifests by lamplight. His back was stooped from decades of hard labour, his hair more grey than brown.

'Alf.' Annie touched his arm. 'My friend needs help getting aboard the Belgian steamer.'

The old man's rheumy eyes fixed on Olivia. 'That cargo's special-like. Guards everywhere. Can't get near it.'

'I have money.' Olivia pulled out her purse.

Alf's gnarled fingers drummed against his knee. 'Might be something could be arranged. For the right amount.' His voice dropped lower. 'But it'll cost you dear, miss. Very dear.'

The terrible lightness of Olivia's remaining two sovereigns and nine shillings burned in her pocket. 'How much?'

She pounded a fist against the door of the second-hand clothes shop until it rattled on its hinges. 'Open up, blast it! It's an emergency!'

A candle flickered behind a grimy window. The bolt scraped back and a wizened face peered out. 'We're closed!'

'My beau had an accident. I need clothes for him right away. Can't have him wandering about in the buff, now can I?' Olivia proffered nine shillings. 'I pay well.'

The shopkeeper's eyes widened at the sight of the money. The door creaked open.

Inside reeked of mothballs and damp wool. Olivia grabbed the first serviceable items she found — corduroy trousers and jacket, sturdy boots, a knapsack, a necktie, a worn-out shirt, and a cap large enough to conceal part of her face. The shopkeeper attempted to engage her in conversation but she cut him off, tossed him the coins and dashed back onto the streets.

In a secluded back alley, she stripped off her dress behind a row of barrels. The trousers were too large, but she cinched them tight with a length of rope. Her long braid she tucked under her shirt, fastened the necktie around her throat, and pulled the cap low over her head. She folded her blouse and skirts, wiped off her shoes and stuck everything into the knapsack, then smeared dirt across her face and hands.

The sky was lightening and the steamship would soon depart. Her heart bruised her ribs as she sprinted toward a pawnbroker's shop. Just one more thing to do before she could board the steamer.

And so little time left.

. . .

The Calypso's steam whistle startled a flock of seagulls into flight. Olivia adjusted her cap, making sure her hair didn't stray from its confines, before hoisting a wooden crate. Its weight nearly made her buckle. Around her, dockhands scurried across the wharf, their boots thundering against wooden planks.

She fell into step behind a group of stevedores, matching their stride and laughter. Her knapsack was pressed against her spine, the crate cut into the soft flesh of her shoulder. Steam billowed from the ship's funnels, mingling with the Thames' morning mist.

A burly foreman barked orders from the gangplank. 'Clear the way! Half hour till departure!' He winked at Olivia, tipped a finger to his hat and slid his hand into his rear pocket to finger her last sovereign.

She ducked her head and hunched her shoulders, blending in with her surroundings.

Two crew members loitered near the entrance to the hold, sharing a cigarette. Their casual stance suggested they weren't guards, but rather taking an impromptu break. Olivia paused, pretending to adjust her load while studying their positions.

'Oi! You there!'

Her muscles tensed, but the shout wasn't directed at her. A man was berating a young dock worker who'd dropped a crate.

The commotion drew the attention of the smoking crew members. Olivia seized her opportunity, striding past them with the confidence of someone who belonged. The darkness of the hold swallowed her as the air grew heavy with the scents of wet rope and salt.

She descended the narrow steps. Voices seeped up from below — workers stowing the last of the cargo. Between the stacks of crates and barrels, glimpses of movement caught her eye. She kept her head down, spat on the floor and let the dock-workers pass without a second glance. The voices of the loading crew grew fainter as they moved toward the stern. She listened to their footsteps, waiting until they faded to silence before she moved deeper into the belly of the ship.

A gap opened between two towering columns of cargo. Olivia slipped through, lowering the crate to the floor with a grunt, and using it as a stepping stool to get a better view of the hold.

It was a maze with no sign of caskets. Panic clutched at her heart. Every shadow, every creak of the ship's wooden bones made her flinch.

'Get a grip!' she growled and walked on.

Near the stern, she spotted a lone figure perched on a crate and lazily rolling a cigarette. A rifle was propped up nearby. Olivia straightened her spine, lifted her chin, and strode towards him.

'You there!' She thrust Colonel Singclair's signet ring and his Royal Fusiliers badge in the guard's face. 'Colonel Sinclair sent me. There's been a mistake. Someone stuck a man of Mrs Burnham's in one of those coffins.'

The guard picked up his rifle and scrutinized her. 'And you are?'

'None of your concern. All you need to know is the colonel sent me to get the man and escort him to Chiswick. Mrs Burnham will have my head and yours too if he's been harmed.'

He wavered, his glance shifting between the ring, the badge, and her face, then tipped his head toward the space behind the stack of crates he sat on. 'Caskets are over there.'

She stepped onto a crate and peered down. Four caskets lay in a tidy row, their surfaces rough and unpolished. One bore a black X on its lid.

'That him?' she asked, gesturing at the marked coffin.

The guard produced a crowbar. 'I guess.'

As he started prying the nails from the lid, Olivia casually asked, 'The others are the usual cargo, then? Or mishaps?'

The guard grunted as he extracted the first nail. 'Aye. Three more from Mrs B's collection.'

The nails screeched their way out of the wood planks. Olivia's fingers found her revolver and cocked the hammer as the scream of another nail leaving wood masked the click of her weapon. She needed to be certain about the other caskets before she acted.

'How many times have you transported Mrs Burnham's special deliveries?'

'Lost count.'

Another nail popped free and Olivia pulled the trigger.

Part Five

I would rather die of passion
than of boredom.

Vincent van Gogh

Twenty-Six

THE PALL MALL GAZETTE

We, the jury, having duly considered the evidence presented before us, find Colonel Everett Sinclair guilty of the following heinous offences:

1. The rape and violation of underaged girls.

2. The wilful and malicious aiding and abetting in the systematic abduction, drugging, rape and trading of hundreds of children, many of them orphans without protection, many being shipped to the continent for further exploitation.

3. The gross abuse of his position, influence, and power, to conceal his nefarious activities and obstruct the course of justice.

Having weighed the gravity and multitude of these offences, and in consideration of the irreparable harm inflicted upon countless innocent souls, we, the jury, have decreed that the only fitting punishment is death.

We have therefore ruled the execution of Colonel Everett Sinclair by a bullet to his heart in his own bed and home. This reflects the abduction of countless innocent souls from the safety of their parents' embrace.

Let it be known that this verdict was reached with the utmost solemnity and in the interest of true justice, which the accused has for so long denied to others.

Let it be known that we are watching you, men of law, money, and power. You can no longer hide your heinous crimes from us.

Signed
Raphael Thorne Peregrine
Lord Chief Justice of the People's Court, London

Editor's Note. In a shocking turn of events, Colonel Everett Sinclair was found shot to death in his own bed the day before yesterday. An investigation into his shocking death is ongoing, with murder being likely.

We will continue to report on this developing story including the allegations made against Colonel Sinclair, and we urge our readers to stay informed and vigilant, as the actions of those in power can have far-reaching consequences for the most vulnerable members of our society.

The Pall Mall Gazette remains committed to uncovering the truth and holding those responsible accountable, regardless of their position or influence.

Once more we would like to extend our invitation to Justice Peregrine for an interview that fully protects his anonymity.

'I appreciate your time, Mr Sévère. And I'm relieved you've recovered from your ordeal.' Inspector Height settled into a chair across from Sévère. Netty set down refreshments on the desk and left.

'I trust my wife was of assistance in your investigation while

I rested,' Sévère said and lit a cigar. He placed it on the rim of a crystal ashtray, then leaned back in his wheeling chair. 'How fares our dear Catherine Burnham?'

Height exhaled and took a sip from his teacup. 'Can't say she's particularly content with her private quarters at Newgate. The three girls you rescued from the Calypso were a fortunate find. It's only their testimonies and the circumstances of their discovery that keep this woman confined until she faces trial. I still find it hard to believe the sheer number of influential men arguing for Burnham's release.'

'It was to be expected. The ledgers and the box, if you please.' Sévère jerked his chin toward the cardboard box the inspector had placed on the floor when he entered the office.

Height retrieved the evidence they'd found in Mrs Burnham's office, and said, 'It's remarkable how you escaped from that coffin and overcame the guard. How did you manage to break free?' He dropped the box on the desk and lifted the lid.

Sévère offered a measured smile, one that said he knew exactly what Height was doing. 'As I already explained to the harbour police, I had help. A sailor freed me. He was silent throughout — shared no name, nor explanation of how he discovered me. Shall we talk about our case now?'

Height inclined his head and withdrew the first ledger.

'All of them, if you would. And the box. However, I must address the legalities first: The evidence meets court requirements. Our entry into the White Lily was occasioned by urgent circumstances — we believed there were several missing children present and at risk. This intelligence came from the woman known as the Midwife, who presented herself as Edith Sharpe — likely a false name. She was accompanying us and claimed co-tenancy of the premises to which she granted us access.'

'Then why not use the front door?' Height asked, clearly suspicious of Sèverè's convenient explanation.

'She warned of guards.' Sévère slid a document across to Height. 'My wife and I have meticulously documented the circumstances of our entry and of our subsequent findings that fully support the lawfulness of our investigation. Mr Higgins witnessed the document.'

'The man who drives your carriage.'

'Precisely. Now, regarding the contents of the box we found on a bookshelf in Mrs Burnham's office. Open it, if you please.'

Height complied, extracting a collection of photographs.

Sévère continued, 'Each is a photograph of a child. We need to present these to our clients for identification.'

'The evidence must return to the station with me. Your clients will need to view them there.'

Sévère gave a single nod. 'Each photograph bears a first name, likely the child's, and a word followed by a month on the reverse. You'll notice that this word changes with each month.' He extended his hand, waiting for Height to hand over the photographs. 'Here are the ones labelled January, February, and March,' he said and placed six pictures on the desk. 'All with the same word on the back.'

'Ornithology,' Height murmured. 'What does it mean?'

'It's the key to the corresponding records. Burnham is using a Vigenère cypher. Find the ledgers from January to March of this year, please.'

The inspector flipped through the ledgers and placed the ones Sévère requested on the desk.

Sévère picked up one ledger. 'This page begins with "TZIM HYDS OT EW I AM VK SW ZCZ YGHUAZ BJY MKR EIG ZD ZF FZ R CR YHP." If you use the word "ornithology" as the key, the first letter T of the encoded text must be shifted by fourteen positions in the alphabet because the first letter O of the key is the fourteenth letter of the alphabet, counting from zero, and so forth.' Sévère worked through the encoded message letter by letter, then slid the paper to the inspector.

'Five orphan girls to White Lilly on Monday. Transport to Antwert the following morning,' Height read. 'What of other details?'

Sévère snorted. 'You share my wife's impatience. You'll have to decode all the ledgers to find the full details.'

'Hum, that will keep me occupied for a few days. I meant to enquire after Mrs Sévère. She endured quite an ordeal.'

'Yes, thank you. She's well.' Sévère knew Height's concern was perfunctory. The inspector was far too shrewd to fully accept Olivia's and Higgins' tale about her taking a hansom to Chiswick in search of her missing husband, only to discover police already raiding the premises and quietly returning home. Yet Height had not a shred of evidence to dispute their account. His investigation now focused on identifying the young sailor who had rescued Sévère and three girls from the Calypso, and sold Colonel Sinclair's military decorations to a pawn broker.

'Let me know if you need help with deciphering,' Sévère said. 'But I'd have to ask our normal rate, you understand.'

Height huffed.

'I've taken the liberty of preparing a case summary for you,' Sévère continued unperturbed. 'The innocence of abducted children is usually auctioned off right here in London, primarily during monthly events at Burnham's estate in Chiswick. We infiltrated one of these auctions and compiled a list of attendees, the ones we could identify.' He pushed a sheet of paper toward Height. 'The White Lilly is at the core of this network. It's registered as a charitable organisation for orphans. All of the Lilly's six orphanages are harvesting grounds for the white slave trade. Mr William Burroughs was able to corroborate that the Midwife was on their payroll, ostensibly to provide medical assistance. He also confirmed that the number of runaways is three times higher compared to orphanages not connected to the White Lilly.'

'Because they aren't runaways,' Height murmured.

'No, they most certainly are not. The White Lilly has an interesting set of board members and investors: The Duke of Harlington. Lord Percival Mountbatten, Baron Taddeus Winthrop, Sir Edward Blackwood, Lord Reginald Asworth—'

Height swallowed hard. 'Ashworth?'

'The very one. Rear Admiral Farnsworth. Colonel Sinclair and Brigadier Whitacker are also listed as investors in the White Lilly.'

'The same Colonel Sinclair who was shot in his bed?'

'Yes. He, Farnsworth and Whitacker were providing protection for Burnham's shipments to the continent. Conveniently, one can find the Lilly's board members in the financial records of Quincy Casket Company; Blackwood and Winthrop are both investors. Shipping manifests show fortnightly shipments of caskets made by Quincy Casket Company. Our corrupt military men are listed as owners of the shipments, all of which were categorised as diplomatic cargo. Several of the individuals I've just mentioned are also listed as major donors of the Lilly's orphanages: Ashworth, Cunningham, Farnsworth, Sinclair, and Whitacker.'

Height slumped back in his chair, dragging a palm across his face. 'I daresay we shall soon see another missive from this so-called Judge Peregrine.'

'If that's your primary concern, you've got your priorities askew. Now, regarding Mrs Burnham: her name is conspicuously absent from the financial records of the White Lilly, the casket makers, the orphanages, and the Midwife's ledgers. But we have the statements of the three girls rescued from their coffins, alongside the statements of parents whose children went missing at train stations. Half the time, an elderly woman offered to mind the children and luggage whilst the parents went to purchase tickets. The descriptions fit Mrs Burnham, and the parents should be able to identify her. Don't you find it strange that she's doing this herself? It's almost as if she savours the hunt.'

Height nodded slowly. 'It's definitely not to save money on procuresses. That woman makes a fortune with her brothels alone.'

'How much?'

'Nine-thousand pounds annually.'

Sévère whistled. 'A veritable fortune! And still not enough for her, it seems. Interesting. The white slave trade must earn her at least that much, if not double. What the bloody hell is a person doing with such wealth?'

Height shrugged. 'For some, wealth is an endless void. They could bathe in sovereigns and still crave more.'

'What came of the Kent operation? And your associate, the man pressured to abandon the Burnham investigation?'

Silently, Height began to return the photographs to the box with deliberate care, studying each face as though etching them all into his mind. 'He told me prosecution seems unlikely, so I've tempered my hopes. The raid...' He paused, his expression darkening. 'In my years with the police, I've rarely encountered anything so grim. We discovered just one girl, barely thirteen, confined to a cramped chamber. Nothing else — no documentation, no other children, and the household staff remain stubbornly silent.'

After a weighted pause, he continued, 'I'm not the first to notice signs of corruption in our highest ranks. While the evidence against Mrs Burnham is substantial, her connections may render her untouchable. The law wasn't designed for cases like this.' His voice grew quiet. 'And perhaps neither was I.'

With a laugh, Sévère said, 'It's my wife who's insisted I change the law to protect young girls and women. I've been trying to since our wedding day. But not until I found members of the House of Lords among Burnham's clients and allies did I realise how difficult an amendment of the law would be. That's how naive I was.

Height cleared his throat and shifted uncomfortably. 'There's another matter I'd like to discuss with you and your wife, Mr Sévère. I've discovered a connection between Linton Frost and Burnham.'

Twenty-Seven

SÉVÈRE'S BACKSIDE ACHED. He shifted in his wheeling chair. The grand vaulted ceiling of Westminster Hall carried Burrough's resonant voice across the sea of attendees — legal minds, academics, suffragists, social champions, and curious onlookers.

Burrough's measured rhetoric found its target with precision. Expressions of unease flickered across faces in the crowd, though many listeners signalled their accord. Despite addressing such dire matters, he held the assembly spellbound as he methodically exposed the law's shortcomings.

'When we speak of protecting the vulnerable, we must acknowledge our own complicity in their suffering through our silence.' Burrough's thick fingers wrapped around the edge of the podium. 'The law, as it stands, offers more shelter to the predator than the prey. Consider, if you would, the devastating impact of our failure to protect society's most vulnerable members. When a child of twelve can be purchased for the price of a fine dinner, what claim can we make to being a civilised nation?'

Beside Sévère, Olivia sat rigid, her hands clasped tightly in her lap. While Burroughs's speech touched raw nerves, his professional detachment seemed to reach even the most conservative members of the audience, who found themselves nodding along.

'Consider, my learned colleagues, that our laws deem a child of thirteen capable of consenting to her own violation. That the burden of proof lies not with the perpetrator, but with an innocent who has already endured unspeakable pain and humiliation.'

A low growl escaped Olivia when Lord Ashworth reclined in his elevated chair with a dismissive eye-roll. Known to the public as a member of the House of Lords, chairman of the Social Science Association's jurisprudence section, and champion of orphanages. But to Olivia and Sévère, the man up in the chairman's seat was a predator of children and orchestrator of London's flesh trade.

Throughout the hall, papers rustled and pens scratched whilst Burroughs continued his address. 'The suggested amendments present us the opportunity to address these injustices — to raise the age of consent, give teeth to prosecution, and protect our most vulnerable.'

Sévère caught Burroughs' eye and gave a slight nod of approval. The man was passionate and precise in equal measure.

The applause had scarcely died when Winston Fairfax took the podium, vibrating with barely contained anger.

'As we deliberate in this grand chamber, children are being sold right now on London's streets!' Fairfax's voice cracked like a whip. 'Just yesterday evening, I purchased three girls - aged nine, twelve, and fourteen. The entire exchange took less time than ordering tea at a café. I returned these girls safely to their homes, their innocence intact, but hundreds more remain trapped in this abhorrent trade.'

Murmurs of shock rippled across the chamber. Fairfax continued his verbal assault, methodically detailing his transactions with procuresses. His tone grew sharper as he outlined the law's protection of criminals rather than victims. Several of the more seasoned barristers squirmed visibly, their complexions deepening towards crimson.

'These merchants of innocence conduct their trade in plain sight, protected by the very statutes meant to obstruct them. When I attempted to bring charges, I am informed my evidence fails to meet the legal threshold.'

And so he went on. The atmosphere in the hall curdled. Where William had fostered rapport, Fairfax cultivated outrage. A swell of protest began at the rear of the chamber, surging through the rows. Several distinguished members rose to their feet, decrying Fairfax's 'vulgar theatrics!'

'Outrageous!' one cried from the centre seats. 'Such inflammatory rhetoric—'

'Our law exists to shield these men and women,' Fairfax shouted over the growing tumult, 'who sell our children like cattle in our streets!' He brandished a sheaf of papers. 'These are records of transactions: names, dates, locations. The brothel keepers who facilitate these sales. The men who purchase children's innocence. Shall I read these names off for all to hear?'

Pandemonium broke out, and several individuals made a hasty exit. Ashworth pounded his gavel, calling for order. Fairfax shouted over the din, 'Their identities and deeds will be exposed to the public tomorrow!'

In the dimness of the rear row, Olivia's hand found Sévère's. Her grip was iron, her palm cold with sweat. He returned the pressure, knowing of the memories that haunted her, sharing the rage that made her tremble.

Burroughs's seemingly solid foundation of support now disintegrated under Fairfax's hammer blows of truth.

Olivia slipped through the heavy oak doors of St Mary's Chapel, her black mourning dress whispering against the flagstones, a black veil obscuring her face. Winston Fairfax occupied the third pew, absently chewing on a pencil, his notebook splayed across his knees.

She settled behind him and gave a subtle cough. 'Mr Fairfax.'

He jerked around. 'What—'

'If you'd like to hear Judge Peregrine's message, I advise you to keep facing forward. Olivia kept her voice low. 'He has taken notice of your investigations. And he thanks you for publishing his letters in full.'

'Oh.' Fairfax twitched as if to turn but restrained himself. 'Has he indeed? And what does he think of my efforts?'

She remained silent, waiting for his thin patience to crack.

'Surely there's more,' he said. 'After all, the Judge's approach is hardly a secret—'

'I'm just his messenger.' Olivia folded her hands and leaned closer to Fairfax, 'whose task is to assess whether you merit additional confidence.'

'I've spent nearly a decade fighting this battle. A decade of battling laws that abandon those who need protection most. What further proof of my commitment to this cause could he want?'

'Perhaps the Judge wishes to know your true motivations.'

'My motivations?' His exclamation echoed off the vaulted ceilings. 'The answer is simple: Someone must act.'

'And you see yourself as that someone?'

'I believe in justice.' He paused. His shoulders lifted with a measured inhale. 'Which seems to be failing yet again. Burnham's solicitors are negotiating with the Crown. It seems if she pleads guilty and agrees to a fine, she'll walk free within days.'

'That's hardly news to Judge Peregrine.' But that it was happening so fast shocked Olivia.

Fairfax fidgeted in his pew. 'I could be of use. I have connections, influence—'

'Yet in ten years, what have you and your connections and influence achieved?'

He sighed. 'Sometimes the pen is not enough.'

'Indeed. The Judge might consider your request for an interview but requires specifics. Names of the procuresses and brothel keepers who supplied you when you pretended to buy maidens. Do they have ties to the White Lilly and Catherine Burnham? Or do they operate independently? What details have you learned about the white slave trade that you haven't published?'

His head jerked sideways, instinctively seeking her veiled face.

'Ah, ah, Mr Fairfax.' She shoved her gloved fingers against his cheek, forcing his eyes forward.

'My apologies,' he grumbled. 'It is only that...I know what the Judge would do with this information and I can't in good conscience...I mean I can't be involved in murder.'

Olivia laughed. 'Yet you would happily profit from it. I see now what you are made of. Good day, Mr Fairfax.'

Olivia stood by a window in their detective agency office, her back turned to Sévère and Height as she watched the fog creep across the cobbles below. A silence stretched between them, broken only by the occasional creak of Height's chair as he uncomfortably shifted in it. The inspector was asking a lot and

Olivia wouldn't grant his wishes. They were at an impasse. Her second one that day.

'Mrs Sévère, I would gladly share my findings about Chief Magistrate Frost and Mrs Burnham if you would finally be forthcoming with the truth.' Height sounded defensive and perhaps even a little hurt.

Olivia pivoted to face him, eyebrows arched.

'I need your honesty. You've known Linton Frost for years. Why your sudden interest in Mrs Burnham? Surely these missing children cases aren't your sole motivation. What do you know about Frost's association with Mrs Burnham?'

'Inspector, my wife is as surprised by this new information as I am, and I must—' Sévère said.

'I speak for myself,' Olivia interrupted Sévère, then threw at their guest, 'And I warn you, Inspector, that questions about my past rarely yield the answers people expect.'

Height's gaze didn't waver. 'Colonel Sinclair's death. Peculiar timing, wouldn't you say?'

Olivia felt weariness settle in her bones. 'Are you suggesting we had a hand in it?'

'Magistrate Frost's murder. Colonel Sinclair's murder. Both proclaimed in the papers by this mysterious Judge Peregrine. Each linked to Mrs Burnham's establishments.' Height sagged against the backrest of his chair and raked both hands over his face. 'The trial's being sabotaged from within. You wouldn't know anything about that, would you?'

Sévère's cigar smouldered in the ashtray, untouched as usual. 'You overstep, Inspector.'

'Do I? Mrs Sévère, were you acquainted with Mrs Burnham before your marriage?'

A chill descended upon the room.

Olivia sauntered up to Height and looked down on him with

disdain. 'Isn't it peculiar that whatever I have to say, the police never believe me? Am I not a reliable witness of my own life, Inspector Height? Are you among the majority who believe intelligence is to be found exclusively in the male crotch? You fancy yourself clever, don't you? Trying to trap me with implications about my past. But here's what you're missing: Your opinion means nothing to me. You are inconsequential. What matters are the girls being sold right now, while you sit here playing your little games.'

'This isn't a game! The case is falling apart!'

'And what are you doing about it? Seeking the blame *here* of all places?' Olivia spat.

'Perhaps,' Sévère said quietly, 'you'd do better to safeguard your surviving witnesses, Inspector, rather than dwell on the past. Once Burnham walks free, chances are their lives are forfeit.'

Height leapt to his feet. 'That's exactly what I'm trying to do! But I'm powerless to protect anyone without fully understanding what I'm protecting them from. The magistrates are restricting my access to our evidence more each day.' He turned to Olivia. 'Whatever happened between you and Burnham, whatever connection you had to her — I need to know.'

'No.' Olivia met his gaze. 'What you need to put into that head of yours is that Burnham's clientele includes members of the House of Lords, that she owns the loyalty of judges, magistrates and policemen. That she's been selling children to London's elite for years.' She moved closer, her voice dropping. 'But you already know all that, don't you, Inspector? Yet you keep believing these men will happily put Catherine Burnham behind bars, all without the slightest protest. So I have to ask again: what are you going to do about it?'

Height opened his mouth, then shut it with a growl.

'How many more children need to vanish before you

reassess your opinion of me, my husband, and this whole sordid affair?'

'That's not fair—'

'Neither is finding twelve-year-olds locked in a coffin.' Olivia turned back to the window. 'Now, I do have one useful bit of information to share with you. I trust you remember Alexander Easy? Good. The man was still breathing when my madam and her guard took him from my room. What they did to him, they never told me. But we all know he died and was thrown in the river.'

For a long moment, Height only stared at Olivia. Then he said, 'Why are you telling me this now?'

'Because Rose, my ward, is beyond their reach now.'

'You had an obligation to come forward. Instead, you lied to me!'

'Oh come now! When did you or any one of yours ever lift a finger for me and women in my position? Where were the police when I was taken from my parents and turned into a nine-year-old whore and plaything for Magistrate Frost? Why would I have had cause to do you any favours unless it served my own interests?'

'And now it serves your interest.' He shook his head.

'Indeed it does. And it serves yours as well because the madam and her guard know rather more about the Midwife and Mrs Burnham than they've let on.'

'I doubt we'll see him darken our door again,' Sévère remarked drily after Height's departure.

'I don't give a fig if he doesn't.'

Sévère wheeled his chair to where Olivia stood by the

window, watching drizzle run down the panes. He took her hand in his. 'You saved my life. Again.'

For once, she did not feel like retreating from his touch. How strange. She turned to study his face, wondering when this happened. How had she come to see him in such a radically different light?

'Do you want to talk about Sinclair?'

She shook her head.

'About the others? Burnham?'

'Not tonight. I'm tired, angry, and exhausted. A combination that only results in ill-conceived plans.' After a pause, she added softly, 'Do you want to talk about your abduction?'

He shuddered, shut his eyes and shook his head. Then he began to brush his thumb across the back of her hand, drawing small circles. 'Get some rest. We discuss your plans. I won't hold you back but I'd like us to plan together. Two minds are better than one. If you're willing'

Unspeaking, she nodded. 'Have you heard about the protests demanding stricter laws against child exploitation? The House of Lords is continuing to downplay the issue, of course, though public pressure is mounting. I wish it would make a difference.'

'It will, Olivia. Parliament will soon face an avalanche of protests.'

'But not soon enough.'

Twenty-Eight

THE PALL MALL GAZETTE

In a dramatic operation, the Metropolitan Police conducted a raid on a property in Kent, believed to be a hub of the white slave trade operated by the notorious Mrs Catherine Burnham. The raid resulted in the rescue of a thirteen-year-old girl, whose harrowing testimony has shed light on practices most foul.

The poor girl recounted her ordeal thus: 'I was taken from my parents and the madam who purchased me insisted I settle my debt.' She revealed how this cruel individual falsely claimed she was of age and owed over £50, before confining her within a small closet. 'I gave up trying to escape. They always found me.'

Mrs Catherine Burnham, the mastermind behind this trade in human flesh, was arrested before the raid. However, her connections to corrupt officials and members of the House of Lords have raised grave concerns about her prosecution.

The White Lilly, ostensibly a charitable organisation, has been exposed as a front for Mrs Burnham's activities. Under the guise of helping orphans, the organisation has been facilitating the sale of innocent children to wealthy clients. Among Mrs Burnham's patrons are to be found Lord Reginald Ashworth, the Duke of Harlington, Lord Percival Mountbatten, Baron Thaddeus Winthrop, Sir Edward Blackwood, Major Alistair Cunningham, Rear Admiral Horatio Farnsworth, Brigadier Archibald Whitaker, the late Colonel Everett Sinclair, and the Prince of Wales.

The Pall Mall Gazette shall continue to report on this most shocking affair and asks its readers to demand justice for the countless young victims of Mrs Burnham and her associates.

Sévère wheeled his chair to the nearest wall and slammed a fist against it with a sharp crack. A bead of crimson welled on his knuckle. He licked the small laceration. A metallic tang crept over his tongue.

With the taste lingering, his thoughts turned back to Height's letter. He tugged the bell pull and waited. Several long moments later, Netty arrived. With clipped words, he instructed her to summon both Higgins for assistance with the stairs and have Olivia come to the office below.

Sévère sat in front of the fireplace, letting the warmth seep into his battered body. The assault had left his torso and legs a mottled canvas of purple-black marks. The flames sputtered and hissed. He wondered whether Netty had resorted to cheap pine out of misguided thrift. He made a mental note to discuss the firewood stores with her. Ash or birch would see them through winter properly.

When Olivia entered, the letter from Inspector Height lay crumpled in Sévère's angry fist. He smoothed the paper against his knees, though creases remained stubborn.

He waited for his wife to take a seat next to Higgins, then said, 'I received a message from Inspector Height. I regret to say his investigation into the missing girls remains as fruitless as ours. After all this effort, there is still no sign of Alice Green or any of the other girls.'

Olivia's response came with weary understanding. 'And there might never be. Once a girl belongs to a madam, she believes herself an outcast, beyond redemption. So they hide.'

'Surely they yearn for their parents?' Sévère asked.

She sighed. 'Not openly. The madams poison their minds. Make them believe they're ruined, that they're worthless scum. Only clients could want them now. Even should the police raid the right brothel, the girls would likely deny their own names.'

Higgins rotated his hat absently, his careworn features more sombre than before.

Sévère said, 'I need both of your help to find them. Their parents deserve answers. After everything we've done to break this trade, we've yet to find a single child of our clients.'

'What else did Height write?' Olivia nodded toward the letter.

'There seems progress with Burnham, at least. Madam Rosseau and her man have provided testimony. Detailed accounts of Burnham's operations. Height seems confident no judge could dismiss the evidence of the breadth of cruelty committed by Burnham with merely a fine and a plea deal.'

'And the Midwife?' she asked.

'Vanished. Height's men found not a trace.'

Higgins cracked his knuckles. Olivia offered him a conspiratorial smile.

'Should we pursue her?' Sévère looked from his wife and the coachman.

Olivia shook her head. 'She'll have fled to fresh hunting grounds where no one knows her face or trade.' Her eyes held a cold certainty that made Sévère's chest tighten. 'We'd waste resources chasing shadows.'

Part Six

Love me...with all the abandon
of a sudden wild rain.

Sanober Khan

There is a kind of sadness that comes from knowing too much, from seeing the world as it truly is. It is the sadness of understanding that life is not a grand adventure, but a series of small, insignificant moments, that love is not a fairy tale, but a fragile, fleeting emotion, that happiness is not a permanent state, but a rare, fleeting glimpse of something we can never hold onto.

Virginia Woolf

Twenty-Nine

THE EMBERS WERE DYING. The room began to grow chill. Olivia tucked a blanket around Rose's shoulders and smoothed a wayward curl from her temple. The child's eyelids fluttered with a gentle sigh of sleep.

Drawing her night robe tighter around herself, Olivia picked up a candle and slipped from the room. She blamed her restlessness on the noises the wind was making that night, its howling through branches, the rattling of the shutters, the faint creaking of the house.

The thought of warm milk with honey touched her mind. Perhaps it would help to soothe her frayed nerves. A strange fire raged inside her, a fever that made her feel as though she'd run far without ever taking a breath deep enough to fill her lungs.

Careful not to raise the servants, she set off for the stairs.

A whisper of a draft teased the candlelight. She cupped her palm around the small flame and squinted into the darkness ahead.

A wedge of yellow light spilt across the floor from beneath the door to Sévère's quarters.

She took a step toward it and then another, noticing that the door stood open a crack. Had he forgotten to shut it, or was he about to emerge? She shifted the candle to her right hand, mindful of hot wax should the two of them collide. Silent as a shadow, she drew near.

A muffled grunt followed by laboured breathing drifted through the gap. As though he had fallen and was struggling to rise. Was he hurt? Her pulse quickened as she eased the door wider and peered inside.

What she saw stopped the breath in her mouth.

He clung to a metal bar mounted in the doorway between his study and bedchamber. The muscles in his back and shoulders rolled beneath his skin as he hauled himself up, again and again.

Fury seemed to come off him in waves.

Lamplight licked at the perspiration coating his spine. While his right leg bent at the hip and knee when he coiled his body with every pull-up, his left leg did not follow so easily.

Her feet carried her into the room, or perhaps it was something else that pulled her forward. A treacherous floorboard produced a faint squeal as she stepped upon it. She caught her breath.

This was a mistake. She shouldn't have come. Not tonight.

At the sound, he dropped to the floor and balanced on his right leg to catch his crutch from where it rested against the doorframe.

'Good evening, Olivia,' he said, maddeningly casual about finding her in his room, she wearing only a nightgown and a robe, with candlelight and her long black hair spilling over her shoulders and breasts.

'Sévère,' she managed. 'You left your door open.'

He studied her for a moment, perhaps waiting for an explanation for her presence. When she offered nothing, he turned his back on her. 'Then close it.'

His curt dismissal stung her pride. She stumbled a step back, colliding with the door and effectively closing it. From the inside.

Seemingly believing she'd left, Sévère reached toward the pitcher on the washstand. His fingers quivered as he grasped it. Whether from poor balance or weakened grip, the ewer slipped from his grasp, landing with a loud *clonk*. A small flood spilt over the floorboards.

Growling an insult, he aimed a kick at the offending vessel but only managed a glancing blow with his left foot. He staggered. The wall caught his back, preventing a fall.

'Curse this wretched—'

'Allow me to assist,' Olivia interrupted and strode up to him.

'Are you *still* here? I do not require help.' He panted, his expression not that of a wounded animal too weak to strike, but that of a cornered predator ready to kill should a threat dare come closer.

'Step aside.' She gathered the hem of her nightdress.

He answered with a snort and remained where he was, unmoving.

'Very well.' She edged between the puddle and Sévère, unavoidably brushing against him. She aimed a kick, and the ewer sailed across the chamber without so much as a wobble until it crashed into a vase with lilies. The vase exploded, the lilies tumbled to the floor and so did the water.

With a pleased expression, she sat down on the floor and rubbed her foot.

'There goes an heirloom,' he grumbled. After a pause, he added, 'Have you hurt yourself?'

'No,' she lied, inspecting the welt that was beginning to

form, trying to banish the memory of his abdomen pressed against her back.

Sévère sank down beside her and cradled her aching foot in his hands. His thumb traced little circles against her skin.

Her gaze was trapped by the sight of his long fingers encompassing her ankle, his thumb running over her flesh, making it tingle.

'Gavriel...' she whispered. Her thoughts whirled like autumn leaves, none settling long enough to guide her next move.

His gaze met hers, dark eyes bottomless as midnight waters.

Use me, he'd said to her.

Use me. The offer hung between them.

Use me. The meaning remained tantalisingly unclear.

Use me.

'Stay perfectly still,' she whispered and lifted her hand to trace his jaw, his chin, his lower lip. His gaze never left hers as she leaned in. Softly, she brushed her lips across his temple, his eyelid, the side of his nose. Nothing about him reminded her of the countless men who'd used her in her past. His scent was uniquely Gavriel — crisp linen, the saltiness of clean sweat, and a faint whiff of cigar smoke in his unruly hair. And so she continued her exploration and found herself surprised at the tenderness of his mouth and his gentle surrender.

Her sigh ghosted across his skin before he drew back.

'I'm too old for you,' he said in a voice as rough as sandpaper.

'I must confess I forgot your age.'

'Thirty-two. Nearly twice your years.'

A knock cut off her reply.

'Mr Sévère? Is everything all right? I heard a crash,' came from the other side of the door. 'Sir?'

Groaning, Sévère smacked his head back against the wall. 'Go away, Netty! And stopper your bloody ears, goddammit!'

With a squeak, the housekeeper's footsteps pattered away along the corridor and faded up the staircase.

When his gaze met Olivia's again, she couldn't decipher what it held.

'Twenty-one,' she stated firmly.

'Twenty-one?'

'It's the perfect age. I shan't settle for anything else. My ideal match must be twenty-one, with a full head of chestnut hair and eyes like summer skies. Impeccable dental hygiene is essential, and daily bathing non-negotiable.' She tilted her head, studying him. 'Should I put an advertisement in the papers?'

He dropped his face into his palm with an incredulous laugh.

'And he mustn't smoke, for I won't have my kisses tasting of ashtray,' she added.

Sévère's head snapped up.

'Perhaps,' she tapped her chin thoughtfully. 'Perhaps he ought to be rather plump. Round as a pudding.'

He seized her hand and pressed it against his chest, his expression fierce, but before he could speak—

'You have changed since the first time we met,' she said.

'Is this pity? Because I'm well on my way to a cripple, a half-man creature.'

'You are less of an insufferable ass, certainly. Do you think I kissed you from pity because I'm a whore?'

'You are *not* a whore,' he growled and squeezed her fingers so hard that she flinched. His gaze softened as it fell to their joined hands, and he began tracing gentle circles on her skin. 'You are my wife.'

'On paper.'

'And I am your sentimental fool of a husband.'

'Gavriel,' she said. 'It was only a kiss.'

'Do you regret it?'

A wry smile was her only answer.

'What do you want, Olivia?' The gentleness in his voice made her chest tighten.

She held his gaze, her dark eyes revealing nothing.

'I'd like to know what it is that you want. You are so good at telling me what you don't want. But please, I need to know: What do you want from me?'

Shaking her head, she breathed a sigh. Her gaze hardened. 'I wanted my home and was given a locked cupboard in a brothel. I wanted my mother and was given a cruel madam. I wanted my brother and father and was given hundreds of needy clients. I wanted freedom and an apiary to call my own.' Her fingers drifted to the spot where a bee had stung her—it felt like both weeks and lifetimes ago. 'I nearly died. And still, I want more.'

'More of what?' The question hung between them, soft as silk.

A cold smile rushed across her lips. 'I often wonder why men tremble at women seeking fair treatment when they ought to fear us demanding revenge.'

He huffed a laugh. 'Because they are fools.' And then he waited, his gaze lingering on her face, his body a silent query.

'I don't know what I want from you, Gavriel. Perhaps... something beyond this. I still yearn for a home, for freedom and revenge. What do *you* want from me?'

He drew a breath, slow and deep. 'I want your trust.'

'That's all?'

'It is *everything*.'

She lowered her gaze, her voice barely a whisper, 'I'm terrified of heights.'

He stilled. 'I...I don't understand.'

'I'm terrified of heights, Gavriel.' She dipped her fingertips to his lips, stood and left.

Thirty

INSPECTOR HEIGHT MARCHED into their office and collapsed in a leather armchair with a weary sigh. His shirt and waistcoat were rumpled, his cravat askew. Dark circles shadowed his eyes, and his hand trembled as he accepted the cup of tea Olivia offered.

'The whole system is rigged.' Height's voice cracked. 'Burnham strode into that courtroom like she owned it. Perhaps she does.'

The room seemed to tilt beneath Olivia's feet.

Sèvère's words, 'Tell me about the hearing,' sounded to her like he was underwater.

'The judge summoned to chambers when the trail had barely begun. A quarter of an hour later, Burnham was entering a guilty plea with a measly two hundred pound fine.' Height's cup clattered against the saucer. 'She earns that much before breakfast if her accounts are accurate.'

'What of her ledgers?' Sévère leant forward.

'She takes five pounds for each transaction — two for herself, three supposedly for the girl. Hundreds pass through her hands yearly. Then there's nine hundred pounds annually from each of her eleven London brothels. The foreign sales aren't even recorded.' Each of Height's words dropped a physical weight on Olivia's chest. 'The total exceeds ten thousand pounds per annum, and that's just what we — what you — could prove.'

'The judge is in her pocket, clearly,' Sévère said icily.

'There's worse.' Height withdrew his notebook, its pages dog-eared and tea-stained. 'Before the hearing, she was bragging about her continental connections. Paris, Berlin, Brussels. Her driver was equally loose-tongued, prattling about monthly payments from Leopold himself. Eight hundred pounds, so he claimed.'

'And neither showed an ounce of concern.' Olivia wasn't shocked or even surprised. She didn't have the energy for it anymore.

'Treated the trial like a social call.' Height's laugh held no humour. 'Complete with her silk parasol coordinated to her millinery.'

The setting sun peeked briefly through the clouds. Olivia wished she could shut the damn thing off for good. 'The judge's chambers. What exactly happened there?' she asked.

Height shrugged, his gaze dropping to his tea. 'I wasn't invited. But when they returned, his *lordship* wouldn't meet my eyes.'

'One must wonder how many of his colleagues frequent Burnham's establishments,' Sévère murmured.

'Wonder all you like. We'll never prove it. There will be no court records. Witness statements, police records, my own notes — all will be destroyed by...' Height checked his pocket watch, shuddering. 'Already gone. They're ash.'

'How convenient.' Sévère's crestfallen gaze was stuck to a point somewhere above Height's head. 'And she keeps abducting children and shipping them in caskets to the continent.'

'You should have seen her escort. High-ranking military men, Lords, members of parliament — all of them brazen enough to display themselves openly.'

'She's released, I take it.' Olivia said with an empty voice.

'Tomorrow morning, eight o'clock.'

'And what are you going to do about it?' she asked Height, without even looking at him.

He pushed himself up and slammed his empty cup on the nearby desk. 'Nothing. I handed in my resignation, effective next month.'

'So you don't need to worry your little head about abused children? How convenient for you,' Olivia spat and swept from the room.

Sévère had always felt an eery sense of emptiness once a case was concluded, the culprit behind lock and key, brandy poured, fireplace lit.

This, though. This wasn't mere emptiness. This was devastation.

From the corner of his vision, he studied his wife. She stared into the flames with empty eyes, her form rigid yet without any strength left, like an abandoned marionette. Her face bore neither rage nor anguish, only a bottomless void.

He placed his hand, palm up, on her armrest. She gave no sign she noticed his wordless gesture of comfort.

'Tomorrow, we dust ourselves off and begin anew,' he said. His words rang false and empty, even to his ears.

Briefly, she glanced at his offered hand. Then with a sharp intake of breath, she rose and quit the room.

A wave of weakness hit Sévère, forcing him deeper into his chair. He mentally prepared himself for a new battle. Not one for justice. One to keep Olivia from falling further into dark despair.

But what comfort could he possibly offer? Amending a law that seemed to be meaningless in the hands of those tasked to uphold it?

He tipped his brandy down his throat, then emptied Olivia's glass as well.

If his damned body wouldn't pain him so mercilessly, he'd kick in a wall or two to rid himself of all this built-up frustration. Helplessness gnawed at him, and if he felt this way, he could barely fathom Olivia's anguish.

A soft knock announced her return. The sight of her attire struck him. But shouldn't he have known?

'I thought it unfair to leave without saying goodbye.' She perched on an armrest, hands clasped over her knee. She wore one of his ensembles, tailored to her frame. Respectable, yet not too fine for a late-night stroll through questionable parts of the city. Though he couldn't see the revolver, he knew she carried it.

'They've scheduled her release for eight o'clock tomorrow,' he said, slightly puzzled.

'When all of London can witness how deep the corruption runs? Hardly. They'll sneak her out when no one's watching.' Olivia cleared her throat and clapped her palms against her thighs. 'I should be leaving. Don't want to miss her.' She showed her incisors in a wolfish grin.

When she moved to leave, he grasped her wrist. 'Olivia—'

'Don't try to stop me.'

'I wouldn't dream of it. Especially not in this. I wish... Bloody hell!' Desperate, he attempted to stand but his body failed him. He collapsed back into his chair with a wince. 'Won't you wait until I can accompany you?'

'No.'

The finality of that lone word was a slap in the face. He released her and pushed back a few feet. 'You wait for your shot to present itself. Then you take it and flee at once. You don't dawdle. Do not aim at her head. Aim at the chest or belly. It doesn't matter which. And then you run. And by god, woman, if they should catch you, I'll...' He balled his fist and slammed it onto the armrest of his chair. 'I swear on everything sacred, I'll have you out and—'

'They'll send me to the colonies. Australia has nice weather, I hear.'

A laugh burst from his mouth. 'In that case, I'll simply follow you.'

Was that a ghost of a smile he saw crossing her lips?

'Olivia,' he said, 'I am not done trying to figure out what it is that's growing between us.'

'But what if I am done?'

'You have solved the riddle already, then?'

Her body stilled. 'No.'

'Are you afraid to discover the answer?'

The shift in her demeanour was immediate. 'Are you making demands?'

'Where's the fun in that? Besides, you are armed and I rather value my life.'

She turned her gaze to the darkness beyond the window-panes, her voice barely audible. 'The divorce papers are on my bedside table. Should I be caught, you must distance yourself from me publicly and immediately. Besides, I will have broken the law, and with that, our marriage contract is void.'

'I don't give a fig about the contract!' burst from him.

'But I do.' And with that, she was gone.

~

The yellowish fog cloaking Newgate began to thin as drizzle descended. Olivia's feet were numb with cold, the cuffs of her trousers spattered with the vile mixture that pooled in every hollow around the prison: rainwater, piss, and dog shit. With fists deep in her pockets, she made her tenth circuit of the prison, counting the minutes until the doors would open.

Trying to keep an eye on both the front entrance and rear exit left her frustrated. The revolver nestled against the small of her back radiated her body heat back to her. She'd tucked the ammunition, wrapped in a handkerchief, into her rear pocket — too wary of an accidental discharge to carry a loaded gun against her body.

When the clip-clopping of hooves approached, she slipped into the shadow of a doorway. A black hackney coach materialised from the thinning fog, drawing up at the prison's rear entrance. The driver alighted swiftly, deployed the coach's steps, and opened its door. A man in top hat and dark greatcoat stepped out with no acknowledgement of his coachman.

She withdrew the revolver from beneath her shirt, opened the chamber, and methodically loaded all six rounds.

The prison's backdoor creaked open, spilling lamplight through the drizzle. A woman emerged between two constables, crossing the small courtyard toward the iron gate.

Olivia eased the cylinder shut.

The man in the greatcoat acknowledged the approaching party. Pleasantries were exchanged. Soon, the policemen touched their helmets and withdrew.

The woman hooked her hand around the man's offered arm.

Olivia turned up her collar and concealed the revolver beneath her coat, then crossed the cobbles with measured steps, her head bowed against the weather.

The coachman remained oblivious as she melted into the

darkness behind the carriage. Though the man in the greatcoat glanced up, sensing perhaps some subtle disturbance. He dismissed it and returned his attention to his companion, extending his arm to assist her ascent.

As the woman placed her foot on the steps, her lips curved at some pleasantry he'd murmured.

The first shot took her in the chest.

Olivia had the feeling someone twisted her right wrist. She steadied herself and squeezed off a second round, then swung the revolver towards the dark-clad figure of the man. Despite the darkness, she knew he was a stranger to her. No one she'd ever met, neither in her brothel rooms nor through her detective work. But she knew the split-second of hesitation had cost her dearly. She should have eliminated him first before he managed to wrench the weapon from her grip.

A fist hurtling at her face was the last thing she saw before darkness claimed her.

She woke with her cheek pressed to the wet cobbles and manacles biting her wrists. She blinked. Without raising her throbbing head, she surveyed her surroundings. A pair of constables stood nearby. The woman lay motionless on the street. No sign of the four-wheeler or the man in the greatcoat.

'We'll catch hell for this, mark my words!'

'Quiet! He's coming to.'

'It's a woman, you dolt. Look at her hair!'

'You mean the mutton chops?' A nervous braying followed the remark.

'Shut your mouth. Inspector's coming.'

She heard the slamming of Newgate's rear door. Footsteps drew closer. A pair of polished boots paused beside her before continuing towards the prone figure. Lord, she prayed the woman was dead.

As the third figure crouched by the body, she recognised Height's bushy eyebrows and moustache. He glanced her way then, looking rather unhappy.

'What happened here?' he demanded.

"She shot Mrs Burnham!' one blurted while his companion added, 'Came at us and fired a shot before we could react!'

'Indeed. Just the one shot, then?' Height asked.

'Struck her in the face, I did. Clapped her in irons straight after. Damned mess!'

Olivia snorted. 'Well, what actually happened, was—' Pain exploded in her ribs as a boot connected.

Height rounded on the constable instantly, sending him sprawling into a muddy puddle, then demanded the constables' badge numbers and the name of their supervising officer. Dismissing their protests, he ordered them to fetch a police wagon for himself and the prisoner.

Once they'd gone, he crouched beside Olivia. 'You've landed yourself in quite a bit of a pickle. Though that's hardly unprecedented, is it?'

It wasn't exactly what she'd expected him to say. Neither were his fingers working on her manacles, clearly picking the locks as he murmured, 'I suggest you share what you know because this is the last time we'll be seeing each other, Mrs Sévère.'

'A gleaming black hackney coach. Rather posh. The driver wore a black coat and top hat. The constables seemed familiar with him. Exchanged pleasantries before handing Mrs Burnham over.'

'Did you recognise him?'

'No.'

He sighed. The shackles clattered to the ground.

'I'm telling you the truth. I wish I knew that man because he'd be next on my list.'

'Your list? Never mind that now. I need you to give me a black eye. I suppose you know how—'

Her fist connected with his nose. 'I do apologise! But why set me free?'

'I can't seem to find a good reason for locking you up.' Gingerly, he probed his face.

'Shall I give you another?' Olivia offered.

'Perhaps that would be more convinc—'

She didn't let him finish before landing a blow to his eye.

He groaned. 'They saw your face. We'll search your residence within the hour. Best make yourself scarce.'

She stood. 'You should sit in that puddle over there. And those lockpicks - I'll take them. Wouldn't do to have them found on you. Oh, and...'

He landed hard on the wet pavement as her fist connected once more.

'My deepest apologies. But any suspicion from your fellow officers about your loyalty would be far worse than these bruises. Incidentally, those two dolts never learned to properly search a lady's hair. Two simple pins and nimble fingers are all one needs to pick a lock.' She stepped away, then hesitated. 'If you're having sleepless nights wondering who killed the Chief Magistrate, rest easy, Inspector, I did it. And Sinclair. Oh, and her, too, of course.' She motioned to the lifeless form nearby. 'And I promise to do it again every time I cross paths with a monster of such calibre.'

'What?!'"

The rear door creaked open, and Olivia made sure the two constables emerging from the doorway witnessed her shoving a boot into Inspector Height's face.

She was very gentle this time.

Sévère was in his nightclothes when the door to the hall gave a great shudder. The hollering of the police demanding entry could be heard all the way to his bedroom.

Which meant half the neighbourhood was awake now.

He knew without consulting the clock that it was half-four. He'd been restlessly moving about and fearing the worst since Olivia left. It seemed the worst had just come to pass.

He'd get her out of prison, whatever the cost.

His housekeeper's anxious voice drifted up the stairs as he extinguished his bedside candle and reclined. Time to play the role of the weakling.

'What's happening?' he whined as Netty hammered at his chamber door.

Several people entered, flooding the room with noise and harsh light.

Feigning drowsiness, he shielded his eyes. 'What is the meaning of this?'

Inspector Height peeled away from the cluster of constables, sporting a fresh bruise around his eye. 'Mr Sévère. We're here to take your wife into custody. The charges are three counts of murder, plus assault upon an officer of the law.'

A laugh burst from Sévère. 'Excuse me?'

'Where is she?'

'In her chambers, of course! She's been there all evening. Netty, kindly escort these gentlemen to my wife's quarters. Though do ensure they maintain proper decorum. My wife shall receive them when she sees fit.'

Height gestured for his men to proceed. Then, he approached Sévère's bed and said with a lowered voice, 'For her sake, I trust she isn't here.'

Height was turning to leave when Sévère indicated the inspector's face. 'My wife's handiwork?'

A quick glance at the door, then Height replied in a whisper, 'She required some persuasion, but then took to it with ease.' Then, raising his voice, 'Seeing that you are of poor health, I shall return tomorrow for your account. Remain at home. Now, if you'll permit me to speak with Mrs Sévère—'

'Sir! Her chambers are empty! The bed hasn't been touched. Her maid claims no knowledge of her whereabouts or departure. But we discovered this.' The constable presented an envelope marked 'Divorce Papers.'

'Blast it all!' Height snarled. 'Those incompetent fools! They'll answer for this!'

'You spoke of multiple murders,' Sévère said. 'What exactly are the charges against my wife?'

Height fixed his gaze on Sévère. 'She was caught after fatally shooting Mrs Burnham. While in custody, she broke free of her restraints, struck me when I believed her secure and confessed to the murders of Chief Magistrate Frost and Colonel Sinclair before rendering me unconscious.'

Thirty-One

THE PALL MALL GAZETTE

We, the jury, having duly considered the evidence presented before us, find Mrs Catherine Burnham, Sir Edward Blackwood, Lord Reginald Ashworth, the Duke of Harlington, Lord Percival Mountbatten, and Baron Thaddeus Winthrop guilty of the following heinous offences:

1. The systematic abduction, rape and violation of underaged girls and boys.

2. The trade of hundreds of children, many of them orphans without protection, many being shipped to the continent for further exploitation.

3. The gross abuse of their position, influence, and power, to conceal their nefarious activities and obstruct the course of justice.

Having weighed the gravity and multitude of these offences, and in consideration of the irreparable harm inflicted upon countless innocent souls, we, the jury, decree that the only fitting punishment is death.

We have therefore rule that the executions of Mrs Catherine Burnham, Sir Edward Blackwood, Lord Reginals Ashworth, the

Duke of Harlington, Lord Percival Mountbatten, and Baron Thaddeus Winthrop are justified. We will come for you when you least expect it.

Let it be known that this verdict has been reached with the utmost solemnity and in the interest of true justice, which the accused have for so long denied to others.

Let it be known that we are watching you, men of law, money, and power. You can no longer hide your heinous crimes from us.

Signed
Raphael Thorne Peregrine
Lord Chief Justice of the People's Court, London

Editor's Note. The notorious Madam Catherine Burnham, trafficker of innocents and proprietress of ill-repute, met her end mere moments after her release from Newgate Prison. Our children may rest easier tonight, though they owe no gratitude to the magistrates and constables who failed them.

We have confirmed that as of this morning, the other named individuals remain unharmed. Further reporting on the accusations against Sir Edward Blackwood, Lord Reginald Ashworth, the Duke of Harlington, Lord Percival Mountbatten, and Baron Thaddeus Winthrop will follow. Again, we extend our offer to anyone of the People's Court for a completely confidential and anonymous interview.

Thirty-Two

THREE MONTHS later

For the first time in his life — or perhaps for the third or fourth time, and he'd simply forgotten those other times — Sévère was rendered utterly and completely speechless.

It wasn't so much the grandeur of the chamber itself, let alone the splendour of Westminster Palace. It also wasn't the dozens of nobles, bishops, and perversely wealthy men assembled there.

It was that he'd never imagined they would assemble because of him.

He'd never imagined his many annoying letters to the House of Lords would have any effect other than, well, to *annoy*. Most of this was William Burroughs' doing. The man had bribed, sweet-talked, and blackmailed his way into the offices and even homes of influential men until Sévère's suggestions for an amendment of the Criminal Law Act were considered and gradually gained favour among a first few members of parliament.

The public outrage Olivia had caused pushed it all along nicely.

That day's session of the House of Lords was restricted from the public, owing to the sensitive nature of the topic. Sévére had little interest in listening to these men anyway.

He had more important things to attend to.

Limping away from the gallery before the doors were shut, he made his way to St. John's Chapel. He enjoyed the short walk despite the sharp bite of wind and tapioca snow. Higgins followed a few steps behind him, ready to step in should Sévère require assistance.

He motioned for his coachman to wait outside the chapel as he entered. The creaking of the wooden door echoed through the empty building. Up in the galleries, he spotted a lone, veiled woman in black. She lifted a black handkerchief as he stepped into the pews and sat down.

He hadn't seen her in months. His chest constricted when he heard her footfall on the flagstones behind him. She sat down at his side, a gentle touch of her leg against his her only greeting.

'You are safe?' he asked.

'I am. How does it feel?'

Frowning, he looked at her sideways.

'To walk again. To be freed from a marriage of convenience. To have a session of the House of Lords dedicated to you,' she clarified.

Lonely, he wanted to say, but didn't. 'It's good to be rid of that damned chair. It's good to finally be heard. How does it feel for you?'

'I reserve any judgement until that damned law has been changed.'

'The process has just begun. Legal reform is slow and challenging. And this, especially, is going to be a long battle.'

She nodded. 'I probably have to make more noise to hurry them along.'

'Mr Burroughs and I will see it through. And I'd much rather see you safe.' *And happy.*

'I'd much rather get more of these monsters off the streets. They continue their heinous acts with impunity. Even with amended laws, corrupt officials will likely find ways around them. How's Rose?'

'Pestering Alf and shadowing Higgins whenever she's not in school.' He hesitated before adding, 'She's not telling me anything. Not that I'd expect otherwise. But from what I can see, she's improving. Her conversations with Higgins have grown beyond monosyllables.'

Olivia nodded. 'Good. I'm glad.'

He wished he could see her face. 'She's asking for you.'

A pause stretched between them before she asked, 'Could you find any of the children Burnham shipped to the continent?'

His stomach churned. Had she not read the papers? 'Not a single one. Burroughs and Height are working with Antwerp's harbour police but the trail goes cold after the caskets left the city.'

'Perhaps they need my assistance,' she said, her voice taking on a dangerous edge.

He bit his tongue, afraid he'd beg her to stop what she was doing. It would not end well for their first conversation in months. 'I've sold the house,' he said instead.

'Have you? What are your plans now?'

'I...' He exhaled the tension that had been sitting between his shoulder blades for months. 'I had thought to find you and...' What did he want to say? *Follow you? Take you to France? Ask for your hand?*

She remained silent.

'When I received your message last night, I...' His voice faltered at her touch.

'One last time?' she asked, setting an ink bottle and delicate brush upon the pew between them.

His mind went utterly blank as she drew back her sleeves and gloves to expose her wrists.

He swallowed. *One last time.*

What farewell could he offer the keeper of his heart? A woman who had endured countless hollow declarations of 'love' until the word itself brought only pain. A woman who never needed the wings he gave her because she'd found her own long before. Asking her to stay, asking anything of her, felt like shoving her into a cage. Everything inside of him warred against the very idea of it. And yet, he could not imagine a life without her in it.

What kind of man are you? he asked himself silently. With careful movements, he removed the stopper, dampened the brush tip and cradled her wrist in his palm.

'Don't look,' he whispered.

— END —

Afterword

THIS BOOK IS INSPIRED by events leading up to the Criminal Law Amendment Act 1885, specifically on W.T. Stead's reports on child prostitution and sex slavery in Victorian London, the resulting public uproar, changes in legislation, and the unsettling case of Mary Jeffries, a prominent figure in Victorian London's underground world.

Mary Jeffries ran a network of upscale brothels catering to elite clients with highly secretive and disturbing tastes. Despite her notoriety, police refused to prosecute her. Only a private initiative by the London Committee in April 1885 brought her to trial. Even then, the case was highly controlled. The judge discouraged witnesses from naming any clients, and the trial featured careful oversight from Home Office observer Mr Batchelor and Treasury-appointed legal counsel.

At a pivotal moment in the trial, Jeffries and her legal team held a private discussion with the judge, who returned with a strikingly lenient deal: Jeffries was to plead guilty and pay a

£200 fine—a hefty amount for many but affordable for her, as she reportedly earned over £9,900 a year from her eleven high-end brothels. Her client list was rumoured to include aristocrats, MPs, and even the Prince of Wales. She openly bragged about sending young girls abroad, allegedly supplying prominent figures like the King of Belgium for a steep monthly fee.

Victorian London was a hub of child trafficking, and the Criminal Law Amendment Act aimed to address this by making sex with girls under thirteen punishable by life imprisonment and criminalizing the abduction of girls under eighteen. However, actual enforcement was shockingly low. Records from London's Old Bailey reveal that from 1880 to 1890, only 1,051 cases of sexual assault reached court out of a population of 4.8 million, with very few resulting in guilty verdicts. For example, just 112 out of 321 rape cases led to convictions, none with life sentences.

In 2021, approximately 6.3 million victims of sex trafficking globally were reported by the International Labour Organization (ILO). Women and girls comprise the vast majority of these victims, accounting for about **99%** of those trafficked for sexual exploitation. Less than 1% of the millions of sex trafficking victims — approximately 50,000 — were "detected and reported" to the UN in 2020, with no numbers provided on actual rescues.

The UN stated that trafficking victims must rely on "self-rescue" as anti-trafficking responses are falling short.

ARLINGTON & MCCURLEY MYSTERIES

Only two people in this world know my name. I am one. The other is believed dead.

Dr Elizabeth Arlington keeps her past buried. But when a woman is killed in a train accident, she falls into old habits and examines the body. All evidence points to murder.

Soon, a second victim is found, and a photograph left at the scene incriminates Elizabeth. Now the prime suspect, she must hurry to catch the killer before the police arrest her.

But when he strikes again, Elizabeth discovers a terrifying truth.

The Arlington & McCurley Mysteries are a continuation of the Anna Kronberg series.

Get the series at **www.anneliewendeberg.com**

THE 1/2986 SERIES

I've reached my expiration date. Not that it matters. We're all going to die.

To sixteen-year-old Micka, all words have flavours. Her emotions come with such force that she can't help but carve them into her skin. The night she decides to kill herself, she meets Runner — a mysterious stranger who makes her question everything she's learned about the end of the world.

His message is terrifying: It wasn't some mysterious disease that killed ten billion people. We did this. Humanity sleepwalked into climate disaster and ecocide, just to butcher and rape until blood stained the seas.

Micka is sure Runner is lying. Her instincts urge her to stay far away from him. But he makes her an offer she finds hard to resist.

There are only two rules she must follow:

Kill.

Survive.

Because the final wars were never meant to end.

Get the series at **www.anneliewendeberg.com**

community.anneliewendeberg.com

Acknowledgements

NONE of this would have happened if not for my fans and Patreon supporters. Thank you so much, lovely people!

Loads of thanks to Tom, trusted friend and proofreader.

And to you, who have read this story all the way to the end.

Made in the USA
Monee, IL
13 August 2025